REMO WAS IN
ANOTHER MA

"Anyone wanna [illegible]ork for?"

"Don't tell him anything!" the Major commanded, cowering near the van. "We've got the prime directive to uphold."

"Suit yourself," Remo said, slapping the gun butt. The weapon formed a new holster in the gunman's cerebellum.

Quaking in his space boots at the side of the van, Major Healy suddenly realized which way the solar wind was blowing.

"We're compromised!" he yelled, diving into the back of the van. "Initiate self-destruct!"

As he approached the side door, Remo heard the sound of knees scuffing across the floor.

Remo reached for the handle. As he did so, he heard a small click from the interior. A roar flooded in behind it.

A few yards away, the Master of Sinanju's weathered face flashed sudden alarm.

"Remo!" Chiun shouted. His kimono skirts were billowing as the old man raced for cover.

For Remo, it was already too late. The explosion came too fast for him to flee.

Created by Murphy & Sapir

THE WRONG STUFF

A GOLD EAGLE BOOK FROM
WⓌRLDWIDE®

TORONTO • NEW YORK • LONDON
AMSTERDAM • PARIS • SYDNEY • HAMBURG
STOCKHOLM • ATHENS • TOKYO • MILAN
MADRID • WARSAW • BUDAPEST • AUCKLAND

First edition October 2001

ISBN 0-373-63240-1

Special thanks and acknowledgment to James Mullaney for his contribution to this work.

THE WRONG STUFF

For www.sinanju.com, www.sinanju.net
and all Destroyer sites online—past, present and future.
Unofficially ushering the House into the cyber age.

And for the Glorious House of Sinanju.
Not affiliated with any of the above, although we're told
that our e-mail address, "housinan@aol.com,"
appears at some. Our lawyers will be in touch.

Life Discovered on Mars!

That blaring headline, seen all around the world, had been one of Clark Beemer's. To this day it remained the public-relations man's personal favorite.

The "meteorite" in which the fossilized bacteria had been discovered was a chunk of ordinary concrete Clark had found at a building demolition site on his way into work at NASA's Jet Propulsion Laboratory in California. Buffed, shellacked and dusted with an appropriate amount of space-age glitter from a local party-supply store, the rock had looked great for newspapers, networks and magazines. And, most importantly of all, it had gotten the tightwads in Washington to cough up an extra nine hundred million bucks for the United States space agency. Not bad for a piece of rock salvaged from the ruins of an old Piggly-Wiggly.

When the truth was learned—that the only thing trapped in the stone was some Pepsi-Cola from an ancient spill in aisle 7—it no longer mattered. The media machine had long moved on to the next story. NASA quietly pocketed the budget windfall generated by the publicity, Clark Beemer accepted approval from the brass and the PR man moved on to the next project.

Those were heady days. As he thought of that great life-on-Mars scam, Clark couldn't help but wax nostalgic.

Back then his job had been a joy. Twenty bucks worth of supplies with a record-breaking payday. But that was a once-in-a-lifetime score. This time out, Clark wasn't sure he or NASA would be able to capture the public's imagination.

Clark's fleeting nostalgic smile evaporated as he looked at the thing he was supposed to sell. It was a PR nightmare. The image was blurry on the computer monitor.

"What the hell did you make it look like *that* for?" Clark groused. Sweat beaded on his broad forehead. The heat in the mobile control room was oppressive.

The man before him wore a tense expression. His youthful face was dotted with a scruffy beard.

"The extra legs are for balance and coordination," Pete Graham replied, annoyed. "And the redundancy's necessary for hostile climates. If there's a malfunction in one, others take up the slack."

Graham was hunched over a control board. The computer terminal buried in the board's face tracked the movements of a bulky silver object as it walked through what looked like a shimmering cave.

The mechanical device moved awkwardly on its eight slender metal legs. When its third right leg stumbled, the surrounding legs supported the object's weight.

The scientists in the room watched the display with guarded enthusiasm. Clark Beemer alone wore a deep frown.

Walking, the machine looked like a baby taking its first uncertain steps. But, unlike a baby, there was no one in his or her right mind who would want to cuddle up to it.

"A *spider*," Clark growled softly as he studied the fuzzy outline of the device on the screen. His knuckles rested on the console next to Pete Graham's workstation.

"Perfect design for Virgil," Graham said.

"Right," Clark said with thin sarcasm. "I guess a cockroach or a snake would have been *too* perfect. And what's with that name anyway?"

Graham flexed his fingers over his keyboard. "Virgil was Dante's guide through Hell," he explained absently.

"Who?" Clark asked. When no one answered, the PR man shook his head. "How am I going to sell this thing?" he exhaled, dropping back into a swivel chair. He wiped the sweat from his face with his loose shirttail.

For the past three days Clark had been reminding the scientists that it was his salesmanship that mattered more than this latest Erector Set reject of theirs.

On the flight down from Florida to Mexico and on the chopper ride from the airport to this remote trailer in the shadow of Popocatepetl southeast of Mexico City, Clark Beemer had made his importance abundantly clear. So loud and frequent had been his words on the subject that most everyone had tuned him out by this point.

Clark watched the scientists busy themselves for a long moment. They seemed so focused, so excited. A bunch of geeks playing games. None of them understood how this game was really played now.

"You know," he said, exhaling loudly once more, "this is just like those boring whatchamacallit things they did at NASA back in the sixties. The ones where they put those guys on roman candles and shot them into the sky. But not the *sky* sky. The dark stuff that's *above* the sky. Bo-ring." He made a few snoring noises. "Damned if I know how the old Canaveral guys drummed up any interest in *that.*"

Engrossed in his work, Graham didn't bother to explain about the thrill of exploration that had driven everyone at NASA back in those heady days when all of space was new. Not that he had been around to see it. Pete Graham wasn't even born when man first walked on the moon.

His eyes sharp, Graham studied the movements of the probe he had built.

Popocatepetl was in one of its less active phases. Good thing, too. Virgil couldn't have survived inside an erupting volcano. But a completely dormant volcano was useless for their purposes. What they needed was a volcano with a recent active history that was in a down phase. With its constant threats of eruption, "Popo," as the Mexican volcano was commonly known, fit the bill perfectly.

A helicopter had lifted Virgil to the mouth of the volcano an hour ago. A thick cable from its belly had lowered the spiderlike device into the crater where ash and glowing red rocks lined the dark throat like a disease.

The trailer in which Pete Graham and his team monitored the progress of the probe was propped on rocks near a lava-and-mud-filled gorge beneath a freshly blown out parasitic cone. It was there they held their breath as they watched the probe being lowered into place.

A million worries flooded Pete Graham's brain. Was the cable strong enough? Would it snap under stress? Could the helicopter negotiate the powerful updrafts? A single gust of wind buffeting the helicopter far above, and the gleaming probe would be dashed against the rocks and lost forever.

Then there was the awful possibility that his baby might malfunction. During the deployment phase, he tried to keep this last, horrible notion as far from conscious thought as was humanly possible.

When the Virgil probe was settled to the rock floor of the crater, anxiety rang in Graham's ears. There was a single, horrifying moment after the cable was released when it looked as if Virgil might tip over. But to the scientist's relief, the probe caught itself. A jerky manipulation of one leg, and the giant mechanical spider oriented itself on the floor of the cavern.

When the applause erupted in the trailer, Clark Beemer didn't join in. After ten minutes of seeing that thing crawling around in Popocatepetl, the PR man was checking his watch, bored.

The scientists instructed the probe to plant two stationary cameras on the floor of the cave to monitor its movements. Another head-mounted microcamera gave a bird's-eye view of Virgil's progress.

As it crawled around in semidarkness in the steaming cavern, the men in the trailer studied its every move. Clark Beemer couldn't believe how excited they all were.

"What is it *for* anyway?" Clark muttered as the scientific team studied the data coming in from Virgil.

Pete Graham didn't lift his eyes from his computer screen. "Virgil is a planetary probe designed to exist in hostile environments. If it can endure the heat of a volcano, it can do the same thing on an alien world."

"Don't you have heat simulators at NASA?"

"Nothing like this," Graham explained. "And a natural environment, not an artificial one, is what Virgil will be facing. We need to test him under battlefield conditions."

The lava beds that the probe walked past were flaming orange. The black walls seemed to pulse with spectral energy. A sweep from a side-mounted light illuminated the nearby smoking wall in garish white.

Virgil moved jerkily and the wall slipped away.

As the light and camera were sweeping back ahead, Pete Graham sat up straight in his chair.

"What was that?" he asked.

"What was what?" one of his assistants asked.

Graham didn't hear. "Stop him," he commanded. The others had long since gotten used to their project leader's use of masculine pronouns when referring to the probe.

A technician dutifully halted the forward progress of the probe. Virgil stopped dead.

Using his own keyboard, Graham shifted the focus of the camera. With a silent, fluid whir it moved back to where it had been a moment before.

Flecks of deep red in the vast pebbled black were washed pale under Virgil's brilliant light.

"There," Graham insisted. He pointed at the monitor. "What's that?"

Men left their own screens to crowd around Graham's. When they saw the shining silver object he was pointing to, they frowned in confusion.

"Looks too perfect to be naturally occurring," someone commented. "Maybe the Mexicans were doing some research and left something inside."

"They built something that could survive in this heat?"

The contours of the object were unclear. When Graham manually refocused Virgil's lens, he saw why.

The edges of the unidentified object were buried in

solidified magma. A gleaming bubble of silver peered out from the ragged rock like an otherworldly orb.

"Maybe it's from another planet," an eager voice suggested very close to Graham's ear.

Pete Graham scowled up at Clark Beemer.

"Don't be an idiot, Beemer," the scientist snarled.

"Hey, aliens sell," the PR man said.

Virgil was standing at patient attention, camera trained steadily on the motionless object.

Graham bit his cheek in concentration. He tipped his head as he studied the silver object.

"Let's excavate," he announced abruptly.

Excited with their strange discovery, the men scattered to retake their seats.

Beside Graham, Beemer's frown deepened. "Some wetback tosses a Miller Lite can down there and you're gonna waste time digging it up?"

"That's not ordinary trash," Graham said as he tapped away at his keyboard. "This volcano has been in an active cycle for a bunch of years now. That's hardened magma that thing's settled into. Nothing ordinary should have survived in there."

"Yeah? Well, my vote's still for outer space," Beemer insisted.

The PR man yawned as Virgil stepped closer to the half-buried object.

Even with the camera's limitations, Beemer could make out the perfect curving line. Measuring against one of Virgil's legs, which was framed in the foreground, Clark judged that the buried object was about the size of a croquet ball.

The surface shimmered in the light as Virgil closed in. The optical illusion seemed to give the thing motion. The hard silver surface almost appeared to be rolling in a short series of waves. Of course that was impossible.

There was a sudden sharp movement on the screen.

Beemer blinked. "Did you see—?"

"Okay," Graham interrupted, "we're gonna have to cut through that magma. Phil, bring me right up over it. You'll have to angle—" A glimpse at his monitor and he stopped dead. "What the hell's that?" he asked, his eyes going wide.

No one heard his shocked question.

"I've lost motor control," someone announced abruptly.

Graham's head snapped around. "What?"

"It's gone," the scientist insisted. "I'm locked out."

When they transferred to another console, they found the same problem.

"Cameras are down," another scientist remarked tensely.

"*All* of them?" Beemer asked.

"They're controlled by Virgil," Graham said. "If he's gone down, he takes the remotes down with him."

"What is it?" Clark Beemer asked. "What's happening?"

"Get out of the way," Graham growled. He pushed Beemer away as he jumped to his feet.

Graham hurried from console to console in the cramped trailer. At each one the verdict was the same. For some reason unknown, their connection to the boiling belly of Popocatepetl had been severed.

Sitting in their chairs, the men had grown mute. Their faces conveyed silent shock. In the background the portable air conditioner continued to chug away.

The gray static of the final monitor shushed the room as Pete Graham straightened. His stunned face was covered with sweat. Wide eyes stared blankly into space.

Years of research, design, programming. All gone in an instant. It was almost too much for his tired brain to register.

Graham slowly shook his head. "Virgil's dead," the scientist whispered.

And his disbelieving voice was small.

THAT NIGHT the mood at the camp was funereal. They were stranded there until they could arrange for daylight transportation. Popocatepetl rumbled a few times after midnight. When the morning sun broke across the snow-encrusted volcanic cone of the mountain, its warming rays found Pete Graham still awake. He hadn't slept all night.

After a long evening of vainly trying to contact Virgil, he had finally briefed NASA. The higher-ups were not pleased with this disaster.

Graham's work there was supposed to be measured in days. They had finished in just over one hour. All Graham wanted now was to get the hell out of there and pick up the pieces of his career. Assuming he still had one.

A separate trailer with a kitchenette was attached to the first. Some of the men were preparing a simple breakfast as they waited for the helicopter that would fly them back to Mexico City.

The sunlight that beat in through the louvered windows was blinding. Lying in his bunk, Graham felt nothing but bitterness toward the common yellow star that dared to shine its cheery light across his haggard face.

As he was squinting at the light, a dark figure rose from the bunk next to Graham's.

Stretching, Clark Beemer noted Pete Graham's sick expression.

"You think *you've* got problems?" the PR man asked. "*I* have to explain this mess to the media. And the way things have been going at NASA lately, it ain't gonna be easy."

Shaking his head, Beemer headed for the trailer's small side door. Stepping into the light, the PR man let the door swing shut behind him.

In the trailer Graham pulled himself woodenly to a sitting position. Someone brought him a steaming cup of coffee. Graham had barely taken a sip when the trailer door opened once more.

Clark Beemer stepped numbly inside. He stood at stiff attention just inside the open door.

"Um, that probe thing?" Beemer said. "You all seemed pretty sure it was kaput last night, right?"

When a few sour faces turned his way, Beemer nodded.

"I thought so," the PR man said, squirming. He pointed back over his shoulder. "It's just that when I went out to take a leak just now, it walked around the corner of the trailer. Scary stuff. Pissed my pants and everything."

He indicated the dark liquid stains on the front of his trousers.

"Real funny, asshole," one scientist muttered.

They began turning away.

"No, *really,*" Beemer insisted. "It's waiting out there right now. Like it wants to talk to you or something."

The PR man was so insistent and agitated that someone finally went outside for a look. The technician exploded back through the door an instant later, his face filled with shock and joy.

"*Virgil's back!*" he exclaimed.

Pete Graham didn't even hear the sound of his heavy coffee mug as it struck the floor. By the time the liquid spilled, he was already bolting out the door.

What he found made Pete Graham's heart soar.

Standing in the shade beside the trailer, the majestic backdrop of Popocatepetl rising high above all, was his precious Virgil probe. Somehow, in defiance of all programming and human logic, his baby had come home.

Behind Graham the other scientists, along with Clark Beemer, were hurrying down from the trailer. Pete Graham didn't even hear them. Like a fretting mother, he carefully circled the probe.

When standing upright, Virgil was roughly seven feet tall. Squatting now, it was only five feet. Its eight mechanical legs were curled beneath the hard shell of its silver-plated thorax.

Graham noted a set of big spidery tracks running from the lava-formed gorge a dozen yards away from the trailer. His amazed eyes tracked the furrow up to the parasitic cone in the wounded side of Popo.

"He must have climbed out after he lost contact with us," Graham said, bewildered. "He used the cone as an exit and somehow followed the gorge to us."

The rest of his team had clustered at an awed distance. Only Clark Beemer had the temerity to speak. He had gotten over his initial shock and was now shaking his pant legs in a vain attempt to dry the urine stains.

"Is it a homing probe?" the PR man asked absently.

"Don't be an idiot," Graham said.

He was studying the clean silver surface of the Virgil probe. There wasn't so much as a scratch or dent in the smooth heat-resistant plating. Even more, Virgil wasn't even dirty. Despite its stay in the volcano crater and its trip down the muddy lava gorge, there wasn't the slightest visible hint of the punishing ordeal it had been through.

"Homing probe might be sellable," Clark Beemer insisted as Graham ran a hand over the cool surface of the probe. "Not that you'd want this monster following you home." He frowned as he studied the mechanical body of the probe. "You ever think of putting a happy face on it? Like that spider in *A Bug's Life?* After all, you made it talk. Might as well make the words come from something nice."

Graham didn't hear Beemer's last words. He was continuing to study the surface of the probe that by all logic should at that moment be melting in a pool of boiling magma a mile below the Earth's surface.

"What do we do now?" one team scientist asked.

Pete Graham glanced up, a studious frown on his face. Far above, Popo belched a thin stream of black smoke at the pale Mexican sky.

"Crate him up and haul him back to Florida," Graham insisted. When he looked back to the quietly squatting probe, his voice grew soft. "I can't wait to get you back in the lab and find out what happened during your trip through Hell."

2

His name was Remo and he was making lemonade.

Of course, it wasn't the actual *physical* variety—with citrus fruit and water and enough sugar to rot a mouthful of baby teeth. Remo had been unable to drink the normal kind of lemonade for many years, and hadn't really enjoyed it all that much even when he could drink it. No, the lemonade he was making this day was the metaphorical kind. And for this particular recipe, he needed the proper tools.

When Remo stepped through the pro-shop door of Rye, New York's Westchester Golf Club, there was only a handful of men inside. None looked in his direction. There was no reason they should. Remo was a young-looking man dressed in tan chinos and a navy blue T-shirt. His casual attire wasn't anything out of the ordinary for the golf club and so went unnoticed by its members. As he strolled up to the counter, Remo's dark eyes were scanning for the tool he'd need for his particularly tricky lemonade recipe.

The middle-aged man behind the counter smiled at Remo's approach. A plastic fishbowl of tees sat at his elbow.

"Good morning, sir," the shopkeeper said. "What can I help you with today?"

Remo didn't meet the man's eyes. He was busy searching the store. "I need a good solid stirrer," he said.

"A Stirrer?" the man asked, puzzled. His deeply tanned face clouded. "I've never heard of that brand, sir."

Remo was glancing beside the register. Two dozen golf clubs jutted in the air in what looked like some sort of Arnold Palmer-inspired work of modern art.

"A stirrer's not a brand," Remo explained absently as he picked through the ring of clubs. "It's a thing you stir with. Here's a good one."

He pulled a club from the circular stand.

"That's a wedge," the proprietor explained cautiously.

"It was born a wedge. Today it's been promoted to stirrer," Remo replied. He slapped his Visa card with the name Remo Bednick onto the counter.

Raising a silent eyebrow, the man rang up the order.

Two minutes later Remo stepped out of the clubhouse into the fresh air. Armed with his one club and a bucket of balls, he headed out onto the fairway.

The calendar had lately stretched into October, bringing many a cold night to the Northeast. In spite of the coolness of the evenings, the midmorning autumn sun this day warmed Remo's bare arms. He headed toward the first tee.

Remo had avoided the club's footwear requirement by blending in with a pack of garishly costumed women golfers. Dressed as he was—in direct contrast to their plaids and paisleys—he should have stuck out like a sore thumb. Somehow he managed to move along unnoticed. His soft leather shoes upset not a single blade of grass as he broke away from the gabbing quartet of housewives and moved off on his own.

Stopping on the lawn, Remo pulled a single white ball from his pail and dropped it to the neatly trimmed grass. He toed it around a few times as groups of people walked by. Straightening, he tapped the ball back and forth, trying to get the feel of both club and ball.

That a nonmember could somehow make it this far into the exclusive Westchester Golf Club was a minor miracle. That he could stand out on the green, in full view of actual members, fecklessly toying with a ball was unheard-of.

Remo wasn't surprised that no one paid him any mind. He had spent much of his adult life dancing at the fringes of people's consciousness, never fully stepping out into the spotlight. By now it was second nature.

And it was a good thing, too. In his line of work, being noticed meant being dead.

Remo was an assassin. No, check that. By today's definition he was much more than that. In the previous century the term *assassin* had been gutterized, applied to every gun-wielding maniac or bomb-planting psycho.

Remo was the Apprentice Reigning Master of Sinanju, heir to an almost superhuman tradition, the origins of which evaporated far back beyond the edges of recorded history.

Most people used less than ten percent of their brains. That meant that ninety percent of the mush in their skulls was dormant. As a Master of Sinanju at the peak of his awesome abilities, Remo harnessed one hundred percent of his brain. Trained to perfection by the Reigning Master of the most ancient and deadly of all martial arts, he was able to focus that energy into physical feats that seemed to work in complete defiance of the limited human form.

Disappearing into shadows, pulverizing bones to jelly, climbing sheer walls. These were skills long known to the men from Sinanju. Hiding where everyone should be able to see him—on the sprawling lawn of the Westchester Golf Club—was as easy to an individual trained in Sinanju as breathing.

Remo looked as if he *belonged*. Therefore, he must.

With a one-handed swing, Remo tapped his ball a few feet. He walked over to where it rolled to a stop, knocking it back. No eye save his own would have seen that the ball landed precisely where it had begun.

The barely perceptible indentation in the grass accepted the pebbled ball.

Actually, Remo thought as he walked back to his starting point, there *was* another set of eyes that would have noticed the ball's path. Right now they and their owner were in a vine-covered brick building on the other side of town. Those hazel eyes with the fawning gleam that had lately taken root in them were just two of the reasons Remo was at the club.

A sudden commotion erupted near the clubhouse. Remo glanced back over his shoulder.

Four men had just walked into view. Three of them were unknown to Remo. The fourth, however, wore a face recognizable in every corner of the planet. When Remo saw that famous face, his own expression hardened.

Barrabas Orrin Anson was a retired NFL quarterback whose success on the gridiron had translated to a career as a B-list Hollywood actor. This professional segue was amazing given the fact that Barrabas Orrin lacked even a hint of discernible acting talent. He had lived the L.A. high life for two improbable decades, and would have continued to do so for many more years. Unfortunately, his grand lifestyle had come crashing down the night his ex-wife was found butchered to death on the steps of her condominium.

Barrabas Orrin, known to friends and sports fans as ''B.O.,'' was the only suspect. Not only had his blood, hair and saliva been found at the scene, but a busload of tourists had seen him hightailing it through his wife's shrubs, a bloody butcher knife in his hand. Two people had actually got him on videotape. Worse still for B.O. was the fact that he had accidentally severed his pinky at the crime scene. It was found at the feet of his dead wife.

The case was clearly open and shut. Or should have been. However, an incompetent district attorney, a hate-filled jury blinded by race and a weird little judge obsessed with camera angles and product placements saw to it that the televised trial devolved into a kangaroo court.

After carefully weighing months of irrefutable proof during their two minutes of deliberation, the jury set B. O. Anson free, with the added bonus of setting race relations back to the Jim Crow era.

Since that time B.O. had remained at the fringes of the national spotlight. If he wasn't in court for one reason or another, he was appearing on golf courses around the country.

When the 6:00 a.m. local news had announced that Anson would be playing at the Westchester club that morning, Remo Williams had been watching TV on the other side of town. The news had continued to play quietly to an empty room as Remo slipped from the building.

An excited ripple charged across the Westchester Golf Club at the appearance of the infamous celebrity. People whispered and pointed. For his part, B.O. reveled in the attention. Eschewing a golf cart, he ambled up the hill near the main clubhouse, a big smile spread across his face.

His partners followed.

As he approached the first tee, Remo didn't see any

evidence of the crippling arthritis that Anson's attorneys had insisted would have prevented him from lacing up the blood-soaked shoes that had been discovered in the back of the bedroom closet in the star's Los Angeles mansion.

The group was nearly upon Remo before B.O. even noticed someone standing there. In fact, the ex-football player nearly stumbled over him. It was as if Remo had appeared from out of nowhere to stand in the celebrity's path.

"Hey, look out," B.O. ordered with a scowl.

Remo ignored him. His eyes focused on the ground, he tapped his ball with his wedge. The Titleist seemed suddenly charged with electricity. With a whir it rose from the ground and spun straight up the shaft of Remo's club. It seemed as if he caught it in his hand, but when he opened his palm there was nothing there. Only then did Anson see the ball was back on the grass where it had started.

B.O. blinked amazement. "You some kinda pro?" he asked.

For the first time, Remo looked up at the big ex-football player. "Yes," he said flatly. "But not at golf."

B.O. bit his lip. "I'm always lookin' to improve my game. You giving lessons?"

Remo smiled tightly. "No. I'm making lemonade."

B.O. frowned as he looked Remo up and down. All he saw was a skinny white guy with one club and a lonely bucket of balls. He didn't even see a single packet of Kool-Aid.

"Where are your lemons?" B.O. asked.

Remo shook his head. "Where *aren't* they," he insisted, an annoyed edge creeping into his voice.

By this point Anson's companions were getting anxious. At their urging, the notorious celebrity abandoned Remo. With B.O. in the lead, they continued to the first tee.

Anson's first swing surrendered a 250-yard drive straight down the fairway. When he turned, the star's mouth was split in a wide grin that was all teeth and tongue.

From his isolated spot away from the tee, Remo noted the ex-football player's delighted reaction with studied silence.

Once Anson's party was through on the first tee, they climbed into carts for the trip to the second. Remo trailed them on foot. As he walked, Remo considered his conversation with Anson.

He had told the ex-football player the truth. Remo *was* making lemonade. It was age-old advice first given him by Sister Mary Margaret way back at the Newark orphanage where Remo had spent his formative years. "When life deals you a lemon," the nun had been fond of saying to her young charges, "make yourself some lemonade."

Well, according to Remo's calculations, he was ass deep in lemons right about now.

B. O. Anson's drive on the second hole wasn't as

strong as the first, but another powerful stroke on the third brought back the same wide-open grin he had displayed at the start of the round.

Remo's lemons had been coming at pretty regular intervals over the course of the past year or so.

It had all started with a ghostly visitor who had insisted that the coming years would be difficult for Remo. But unlike your basic chain-rattling Dickensian ghosts, the little Korean boy who had haunted Remo didn't show him any way to avoid his fate. His life was going to suck. There was no two ways about it.

The specter proved accurate in his prediction.

The place Remo had called home for the past ten years had recently burned to the ground. For the past nine months he had been forced to live at Folcroft Sanitarium, a mental and convalescent home here in Rye.

Folcroft doubled as the home of CURE, a supersecret agency for which Remo worked and that was sanctioned by the top level of the U.S. government to work outside the law in order to protect America. That led to lemon number two.

The previous President of the United States had done something his seven predecessors in the Oval Office hadn't. He had blabbed of CURE's existence to an outsider. Squeamish to order the elimination of this man, the new President had given him a role with CURE. Mark Howard had been welcomed into the

Folcroft fold as assistant director, directly answerable to Remo's own boss, Dr. Harold W. Smith.

Which brought him to lemon number three: Chiun, Reigning Master of the House of Sinanju. Remo's teacher and general all-around pain in the neck.

The wily old Korean had welcomed Howard's arrival as heir apparent with open arms. After all, the coffers of CURE were deep and Harold Smith was old. Sucking up to the new guy seemed the best way to stay on the gravy train well into the new century.

Remo, on the other hand, had never been good at sucking up, and he had no intention of starting now.

Ahead, B. O. Anson's arthritis was nowhere to be seen as he drove a deep ball down the fairway. This time a joyful laugh escaped his widely parted lips. He muttered something to the men with him, and they chuckled appreciatively.

As the four men climbed back into their carts for the trip to the fifth tee, Remo slipped quickly around the periphery of the course. Anyone who saw him assumed he was late for an appointment, since his gait was more a hurried glide than a sprint. However, if they'd continued to watch they would have noticed that the speed at which he was traveling was only deceptively slow.

Somehow, without appearing to rush, Remo managed to outdistance B. O. Anson's party on their way to the next tee.

When the former football star's cart slowed to a stop, Remo was a hundred yards ahead, waiting at the edge of the green near the woods that rimmed the course.

B.O. was still laughing when he approached the tee.

Remo had taken only one ball with him. Unlike the ones he'd bought, this ball was personalized.

He noted the name on the side as he fished it from his pocket. "B. O. Anson."

In the shade of a denuded maple, he dropped the ball he had swiped from the ex-football player to the grass.

This wasn't acting out, he reasoned as he lowered the head of the wedge. It was making lemonade, pure and simple.

B.O. hauled back and swung mightily. The ball whooshed audibly from the tee, arcing high into the pale autumn sky.

Another clean shot down the fairway, this one closing in on 260 yards. The ex-football star was having one of the best games of his life. As expected, his mouth dropped wide in the same open smile he displayed after all his best strokes.

The instant he saw the first flash of teeth, Remo brought his own club back.

The wedge flew too fast to even make a sound.

Over his shoulder and back down again. When the club connected, the ball didn't have time to flatten before it screamed from the grass. It became a white missile flying at supersonic speed.

Remo alone tracked its path as it soared a beeline

up the fairway, directly into the happy gaping mouth of B. O. Anson.

It hit with a wet *thwuck*. When the ball reemerged into daylight an instant later, it was dragging ragged bits of scalp and brain in its wake.

B.O.'s grinning mouth remained open wide. His dull eyes were unblinking. For an instant Remo saw a flash of sunlight shining down the dark tunnel the golf ball had drilled through his hard skull.

And then the most famous ex-football-playing murderer the world had ever known fell face first into the grass.

As his golf buddies began cautiously poking Barrabas Orrin Anson with the grip ends of their drivers, Remo Williams nodded in satisfaction.

"Hole in one," he said, impressed.

No doubt about it. This was the best lemonade he'd ever tasted. Tossing his club into the woods, he stuffed his hands deep in the pockets of his chinos. Whistling a tune from *The Little Mermaid,* Remo sauntered off the fairway.

3

Behind the closed door labeled Special Project Director, Virgil Climatic Explorer, Dr. Peter Graham was being read the riot act by his NASA superiors.

"Who's going to pay for this disaster?" asked Deployment Operations Director Buck Thruston.

"Technically, this falls in the lap of Science Director for Solar System Exploration," Alice Peak replied crisply. She spoke with great authority since, as Director of Space Policy, this would put it out of her purview.

The Virgil probe sat motionless in the corner of the big room. Though they had tried to get it to walk inside after the long flight back from Mexico, the probe had refused to respond to any commands. They'd been forced to carry it in.

"Wouldn't it be Director of *Planetary* Exploration?" Thruston asked, confused. At NASA it was hard to keep track of all of the various department directors. At last count there were 8,398 of them in all. They were pretty sure of this figure, since the office of the Director of Director Enumeration had said so.

"Solar system is above planetary," Alice replied.

"But the planets are *in* the solar system."

"Doesn't matter," she insisted. "They're separate divisions. As soon as something hits solid earth—or solid *anything*—planetary kicks in."

"I'm not sure that matters right now," Pete Graham interjected. He wasn't watching Peak or Thruston. His eyes flicked nervously to the man who stood silently behind them.

"But the asteroids are spatial bodies," Thruston insisted, ignoring Graham. "And Virgil could explore them."

"Apples and oranges," Alice dismissed. "At present asteroid exploration falls under the Director for Intra-Mission Energy. Not applicable in the current situation."

As the two spoke about the various NASA divisions and how neither of them could be blamed for the malfunction of the Virgil probe, the third person in their small group pushed himself to his feet.

Zipp Codwin had been leaning against Graham's desk. He had listened with chilling patience to the Virgil designer's digest of the events in Mexico. Not once during Pete's five-minute summary had Codwin so much as blinked.

Codwin was NASA's current administrator. A retired Air Force colonel, Zipp had been drafted into the space program during its earliest days. Older now, he retained the thin, muscled frame of his youth.

His short steel-gray hair was cut at right angles. A

level could have rested on his granite square chin without the bubble shifting a single millimeter. His eyes were as lifeless and black as the void he had twice visited in two of the tiny Mercury modules.

When he saw Colonel Codwin straighten, Pete Graham gulped reflexively. Of the three people in his lab, Zipp was the only one who inspired real fear in Graham.

Buck Thruston was still arguing with Alice Peak. "But we're still in phase one of asteroid exploration. Prestage two should fall under the Director for Outer—"

He never finished his thought.

"Faster, better, cheaper!" Administrator Zipp Codwin barked hotly. His words were as clipped and sharp as his yellowing fingernails.

Buck jumped; Alice gasped. Shocked to silence, both directors wheeled on their superior.

"Faster, better, cheaper!" they echoed with military sharpness. Buck offered something that might have been a salute if a salute involved two shaking hands and a thumb in one eye.

The NASA administrator crossed his arms. A deeply skeptical expression settled in the angles of his face.

"I hear the words, but I do not see the results," Zipp Codwin snapped. "FBC is policy at the new user-friendly NASA. Or have we forgotten?"

Alice and Buck shook their heads so violently they

bumped foreheads. Nearby, Pete Graham shook his head, too.

None of them could forget NASA's new policy. They weren't allowed to.

The Faster, Better, Cheaper slogan was now a mantra around the space agency, hauled out whenever anyone questioned its fiscal irresponsibility. Zipp had personally hired an outside public-relations firm to come up with the slogan. It had cost NASA five hundred thousand dollars.

"No, sir," Pete Graham replied.

Codwin's nostrils flared like an angry bull's. Marching over to where Virgil crouched, he extended a hard finger.

"Okay, let's figure this out, then. You built this fast and cheap, right?"

Some of the tension drained from Graham's voice. He was on more familiar ground here.

"Yes, sir," he answered. "Under time and under budget."

"Okay, son," Zipp growled. "I know that. But did you build it better?"

Graham didn't hesitate. "I *thought* I did," he said honestly. "I can't begin to fathom why it stopped working."

Zipp dropped his hands to his hips. He noted a laptop computer hooked umbilically into the side of the Virgil probe.

"Can't you get the information from it? See what happened while it was in the volcano?"

"I've been trying," Graham insisted. "It seems to be locked in some kind of self-diagnostic routine. I haven't been able to access the affected systems." There was clear frustration in his tone.

Zipp Codwin looked back to the probe. When he beheld the cold metal outline, his face puckered unhappily.

"No beauty to this program anymore," he muttered in what, to him, was a wistful tone. It sounded like he was grinding glass between his molars. "The lunar landers looked like pregnant praying mantises and even they had more grace." He gave an angry sigh, the only kind he was capable of giving. "Don't think faster, better, cheaper cuts it alone. Have to put something about prettier in there."

When he spun back around, his brow was furrowed.

"I'm not happy with the results here, Graham," Zipp stated. His dark eyes were penetrating.

"I'm not, either, sir," Graham said weakly.

"You shouldn't be. You're the one who screwed the pooch. Access that data," he commanded as he marched to the door. Peak and Thruston stumbled over each other in their race to follow. "Whatever glitches are in that thing, I want them worked out in the FBCest manner possible. Clear?"

He didn't wait for a reply.

The door had already slammed shut by the time Pete Graham offered a weak "Clear, sir."

Alone, Graham exhaled.

He hated the relief he felt whenever Zipp Codwin left the room. At least he wasn't alone in the feeling. The colonel inspired the same level of fear in everyone at NASA.

As his nervous sweat began to evaporate, Graham walked over to the immobile probe. He had just retrieved his laptop from a chair next to Virgil when the lab door creaked open cautiously.

Hoping Zipp Codwin hadn't returned, Graham glanced anxiously to the door.

Clark Beemer's worried face jutted into the room.

"Is the coast clear?" the PR man asked.

Sighing again, Graham only nodded. He took his seat as Beemer scurried inside.

"Ol' Zipper reamed you out, huh?" Beemer said as he shut the door behind him. "I figured you'd get off okay. At least you brought it back in one piece. Not like the Mars Climate Orbiter. Twenty-three directors lost their jobs after that fiasco."

"I'm working here, Beemer," Graham said tightly.

His laptop balanced on his knees, he was entering commands into Virgil's systems. At least, he was *trying* to. Every time he thought he was in, the system unexpectedly dumped him out. It was like playing a game of computer chess where every move was countered perfectly.

"*I'm* working, too," Beemer insisted. "Unglamorous as it is, I'm the one who has to sell this thing. I wish you told me it talked. I can work with that somehow."

"It doesn't talk, Beemer," Graham insisted.

This had been going on since Mexico. The entire plane ride home Clark Beemer had insisted that Virgil had spoken to him when he first discovered the probe next to the command trailer. When pressed, Beemer wasn't exactly sure what it was the probe had said.

"I know what I heard," the PR man insisted. His brow clouded. "At least, I think I know what I heard. It didn't make much sense. Something about wishing how it could offer me a drink but that we were on a volcano and there aren't any liquor faucets on volcanos."

"Idiot," Graham muttered.

Beemer's face fouled. "Hey, this isn't about me," he snapped. "You're the one who built this mess."

He crossed his arms defiantly. For a few minutes he remained silent as Graham worked.

Pete Graham continued to be frustrated by every attempt to access Virgil's systems.

"Dammit," he growled after his latest attempt failed.

"Say, Pete?" Beemer asked abruptly.

"Yeah?"

"Back in Mexico..." Beemer hesitated.

"What?" Graham said, only half listening. He was attempting to reinstall Virgil's start-up routines.

"In the volcano," Beemer continued. "You know that thing you had it looking at? The shiny thing buried in the rock?" He stopped again, not wanting to sound crazy. "Well, *you* were looking at the moni-tor," he blurted. "Did *you* see anything weird?"

Graham glanced up. "Like what?"

Clark Beemer didn't want to have to say it. Ever since he'd first come to work PR at NASA and made the mistake of asking if he'd have the opportunity to meet an actual Klingon, he had been guarded with his questions.

"Promise you won't laugh?" Beemer asked.

Graham exhaled. "Yeah, Beemer, I promise."

Clark Beemer smiled nervously. "Well, when the camera was looking right smack-dab at that thing," he began, "it looked like—like it *moved.*"

Graham stopped working. With great slowness he put down his laptop.

"Moved how?" he asked. And this time there was genuine interest.

Beemer was warming nervously to his subject. "First, it looked like the whole thing was sort of shimmering. Like when you pet a dog that's got an itch? You know how the whole back muscle sort of moves? That's what it looked like to me. Then just before the video signal cut out, I swore I saw the shell of the thing crack open."

Pete Graham didn't speak. He just sat there, silently contemplating Clark Beemer's words.

The scientist would have pointed out that this no-tion was as ridiculous as Beemer's insistence a month ago that he'd found a piece of red kryptonite in his flower garden, but for one simple fact. Graham had seen the same thing.

When they'd arrived back in Florida, the scientist had gone over the last seconds of digital images collected from the Virgil probe before it had blacked out.

He saw the shining silver orb buried in the solidified magma. And for a few seconds, it *did* appear to ripple. But that could have been a reflection from Virgil or even from a pool of molten lava. And, yes, at the very last instant it did seem to split apart. But happening as it did at the instant the probe had apparently begun to malfunction, it could have been some sort of anomalous static pop from the feed.

The image wasn't clear enough to enhance and it didn't really seem to matter much, since Virgil had somehow found its way home. Pete Graham had chalked it all up to ghosts and glitches and put the matter out of his mind.

Now that Beemer had brought it up, Graham felt a pang of uncertainty in his gut. Still, he was loath to agree with this nonscientist public-relations simpleton.

"Just an optical illusion," Graham dismissed uncomfortably. He returned to his laptop.

"You seem pretty sure for a guy who doesn't even know his own probe can talk."

"For the last time, Beemer, it does not talk," he snapped.

"Oh, yeah? Well, if it doesn't talk, then why does it have a mouth?"

When Graham looked up, his eyes were instantly drawn to the front of the probe. Just beneath the stationary eye of the top microcamera a hole had been punched in the heat-resistant plate. Beemer was pointing at it.

Graham almost knocked over his chair, so quickly did he clamber to his feet. "What did you do to him?" he snarled, bounding to the side of the probe.

The hole was only an inch and a half high and two inches wide. The metal around the edges seemed to puff out, forming a pair of crude metallic lips.

"I didn't do anything," Beemer insisted.

"Damn you, Beemer, do you have any idea what this is gonna cost me? A software glitch can be fixed like nothing, but these plates have to be manufactured individually."

"I didn't do it, I swear," Beemer said, his voice growing troubled. "I just noticed it there."

Ordinarily, Pete Graham wouldn't have believed Beemer in a million years. However, something odd suddenly happened. When he glanced back at the probe, the metal mouth was closed.

"What the hell?" Graham asked.

Stepping closer, he peered at the spot where the opening had been. It was now a flat line. The lip buds were still visible. Soft ridges in an otherwise smooth surface. And as Pete Graham watched in growing astonishment, the mouth creaked open once more.

Graham jumped back.

Until now Clark Beemer had assumed that everyone but him knew about the voice. He figured, as usual, that he was the butt of some geek joke. Sensing now that something was indeed wrong, he ducked behind Graham, grabbing the scientist's arm.

"What is it?" he asked fearfully.

"I don't know," Graham shot back.

His eyes were wide as he watched the artificial mouth open and close.

It was the most surreal moment of Pete Graham's young life. The newly formed mouth was testing, trying to work out kinks. It squeaked as it flexed.

His eyes wide, Beemer's fingers digging into his bicep, Graham couldn't help but think of the rusted-shut Tin Man from *The Wizard of Oz*. The scientist couldn't think, couldn't run. He dared not even breathe.

A pained groan that sounded like a piece of metal being torn apart rose up from the dark depths of the orifice.

And the voice that had expressed regret for an inability to offer Clark Beemer a drink at the base of Popocatepetl rose once more from the mechanical throat. And it said, *"Hello is all right."*

And when the impossible words issued from the cold, cybernetic belly of the probe he had built, Pete Graham's thudding heart froze in his chest.

4

Remo had parked his car on a side street near the Westchester Golf Club. By the time he reached the leased Ford Explorer, the first shrill sounds of approaching police sirens were carrying across the most distant fairway.

A faint smile brushed his thin lips as he slipped behind the wheel.

He took a left off the dead end. The tidy residential street ran parallel to the golf course.

The route was familiar. He soaked in the scenery with a melancholy twinge.

The house he'd recently lost had actually been his second real home. His first full-time residence had been here, on this very street.

It was a cruel quirk of fate that had robbed him of each home. He, Remo Williams, orphan and perpetual outsider to the entire human race, could never have a normal home.

His old house came up on the left.

The new owners had made some changes to the simple, two-story Cape. Vinyl siding now covered the paint. Most of the shrubs near the front were gone.

Children apparently lived there now, for the lawn was covered with plastic toys. Orange-and-yellow leaves formed a damp pile near a multicolored jungle gym.

A knot formed in the pit of Remo's stomach when he saw the white picket fence that now enclosed the front yard. In the days when he used to dream of home and hearth and some semblance of a normal life, his mind's eye seemed always to surround that life with a tidy picket fence.

But that wasn't his life and would never be.

Remo drove on.

Harold Smith's home was next door. The CURE director's battered station wagon had already been in the Folcroft Sanitarium parking lot when Remo left that morning, so he wasn't surprised to find that it wasn't in the driveway now.

Smith's wife was out in the yard. The matronly woman was dressed in slacks and a big flannel shirt. She was wrangling wet leaves from beside the front step with a bamboo rake that seemed to be missing most of its prongs.

Even Smith had a home. It might not be perfect and he might not spend much time there, but the fact remained it was there whenever he wanted it to be. All Remo had was a sackful of metaphorical lemons and a prophecy that his life was going to get worse before it got better. *If* it got better.

The street ended abruptly at a busy intersection.

"Maybe the worst of it's behind me," Remo muttered as he pulled out onto the cross street.

Downtown Rye had evolved since Remo had first been drafted into CURE. Back in those days, though it was close to New York City, Rye had still retained some small-town charm. Not anymore. Over the decades the city had become a typically soulless suburb. Neatly washed brick buildings advertised law and accounting firms while whitewashed banks crowded the sidewalk. Remo counted thirty-seven sets of traffic lights on what had been the old Boston Post Road. A set of lights positioned every ten feet, all red, turned the main road into a parking lot. It took him forty-five minutes to travel three city blocks.

He was grateful when he finally escaped the busiest part of town. Suburban sprawl changed over to woods. Through a shower of gaily colored leaves, Remo caught glimpses of Long Island Sound. A few boats bobbed on the sun-dappled water.

The familiar high wall of Folcroft appeared on his left. Remo followed it to the main gate. He drove past the guard shack with its sleeping uniformed guard and up the gravel drive of the sanitarium.

Remo parked his car in the employee lot and headed for the side door.

He sensed a pair of heartbeats in the stairwell even before he reached the door. When he pulled it open, one of the two men was already looking his way.

The wizened Asian looked as old as the hills. Other than two tufts of yellowing white hair that sprouted above each ear, his age-speckled scalp was bald. His skin was like ancient parchment. The fine lines of delicate blue veins crisscrossed beneath the dry surface.

Chiun, Master of Sinanju and Remo's teacher, clucked unhappily. As the door swung shut, the elderly Korean's youthful hazel eyes frowned disapproval at his pupil.

A much younger man had been sitting on the bottom step near Chiun. He seemed startled at Remo's appearance. As Remo stepped inside, the young man scurried to his feet.

"It was you, wasn't it?" Mark Howard asked without preamble.

The assistant CURE director was in his late twenties and had a broad, corn-fed face with ruddy patches on each cheek. At the moment a sickly flush tainted his pale skin.

"Guess good news travels fast," Remo said blandly.

"Oh, God, it *was* you," Howard said, sinking back to a sitting position on the staircase.

"I plead the Fifth," Remo said dully. "You eat breakfast yet, Little Father?"

When he tried to cross to the basement staircase, a bony hand pressed against his chest, holding him in place.

"Stop, idiot," Chiun hissed.

"Why?" Remo said, his face drooping into a scowl. "So I can hear you play Jiminy Cricket to Spanky here?" He nodded to Howard. The young man was still sitting on the stairs, one hand holding his queasy belly. "No, thanks."

"You killed B. O. Anson," Mark Howard said weakly.

"There is no sense in denying it, Remo," the Master of Sinanju charged, folding his long-nailed hands inside the voluminous sleeves of his purple day kimono. "Emperor Smith's oracles have already divined your guilt."

"Guilt's a funny thing," Remo said. "Smith's computers say I'm guilty—I say I was chipping golf balls in my hotel room in Chicago. We'll leave it to the jury to decide."

Howard finally looked up. Dull shock filled his tired eyes. "How could you?" he asked.

"Easy. Keep your legs apart, concentrate on the ball and make the club an extension of your own arm."

"As usual, you are an audience of one for your own pathetic attempts at humor," Chiun said. "Now make things easier for your poor old dying father and apologize for slaying the ballfooter."

"What?" Remo said. "No way. I've had a crummy year, and I decided to give myself an early Christmas present. And don't try to get around me with that dying thing. You're as healthy as a horse."

"No thanks to you," Chiun snipped.

"Apologies are irrelevant," Howard said, pulling himself to his feet. "Dr. Smith wants to see you. He sent us to collect you as soon as you got back."

Remo's face darkened. "Oh, c'mon," he groused.

But Chiun was already turning away. "Come, Prince Mark," the old man said. Tucking his arm into the crook of Howard's elbow, he guided the much younger man up the stairs.

With a deepening frown, Remo followed.

"So how'd you know it was me?" Remo grumbled as they mounted the stairs.

Howard pitched his voice low. "You know that the mainframes automatically flag all Sinanju-signature deaths. The news has already picked up on it. Given the circumstances, there's a feeding frenzy going on."

"Really?" Remo asked, a hint of curiosity in his tone. "What are they saying?"

The assistant CURE director shifted uncomfortably as he walked. "That a golf ball fired from some kind of portable cannon went straight through Anson's head." It seemed as if he didn't want to believe the reports.

"I called 'fore'," Remo said defensively.

"This is terrible, Remo," Howard insisted seriously.

"Terrible," the Master of Sinanju echoed.

Remo shot the old man a hateful look.

"There must have been hundreds of people on that golf course," the assistant CURE director continued.

"Relax," Remo said. "Even if someone saw me— which they didn't—they didn't really *see* me. Back me up, Chiun."

"It is true, O Prince," the Master of Sinanju said.

They were at the second-floor fire door. Howard
stopped. "I know Dr. Smith is confident in this ninja
stuff, but—" He glanced apologetically at the Master
of Sinanju. "I'm sorry, Master Chiun, I just don't
know."

For any other man, comparing Sinanju to ninjitsu
would have guaranteed a one-way trip to the Folcroft
morgue. But, standing in the stairwell beside the
young man, Chiun merely shook his head somberly.

"Ninja are like Sinanju, Prince Mark, the same
way a firefly is like the sun. Remo is correct. It is
possible for many eyes to have seen him without ever
truly seeing him."

Howard didn't seem convinced. "I hope so, Master
Chiun," he said.

Remo noted the deeply worried expression on the
young man's face.

"Unknot your ass, kid," Remo grunted, slapping
open the door. "Smitty's got you too wound up about
security."

The three of them headed down the gloomy hallway of Folcroft's administrative wing. Flanked by the
two other men, Remo couldn't help but feel like a
troublemaking junior-high student being hauled off to
the principal's office.

For the sheer nuisance factor alone, he hoped that
CURE's dour principal was in a forgiving mood.

EVEN THOUGH HE HAD never held the position of
school principal, Harold Smith certainly looked the

part. The dour man in his gray three-piece suit certainly would not have seemed out of place in some of the crustier old institutions of higher learning in his native New England.

Even his office seemed determined to play the part. Drab, functional and without a shred of distinctive personality, it could have doubled as the office of a particularly dull dean of boys. Plain and uncluttered as it was, the room managed to reflect perfectly the personality of its occupant. To his very core Dr. Harold W. Smith was bland, unimaginative and gray.

This morning a touch of fretful color brushed his ashen cheeks. A bottle of antacid sat at his elbow on his immaculate desk. Although he hadn't yet needed it, he had taken it out as a precautionary measure.

Worried eyes were scanning the angled computer monitor below the surface of his desk. When his office door suddenly popped open, he glanced up over the tops of his rimless glasses.

Remo, Chiun and Mark Howard entered from the office of Smith's secretary. Smith waited for them to close the door tightly before speaking.

"Barrabas Anson was not a sanctioned CURE assignment," Smith said tartly.

Remo and Chiun stopped before Smith's desk. Mark Howard circled around. A picture window looked out over the rear lawn of Folcroft. Howard sat back against it, an ill expression on his wide face.

"He should have been," Remo replied. "That

jerk's been rubbing all our noses in it for the last seven years."

"Mr. Anson had his day in court," Smith insisted.

"Blah-blah-blah," Remo said. He aimed his chin at Howard. "Who cares about B.O.? What have you been filling junior's head with? He looks like he's gonna ralph."

Smith glanced at Howard. "Mark understands the risks exposure present. While behavior such as that which you have engaged in today has always been unacceptable, I have learned to largely accept it. This, however, crosses the line."

"The Emperor is correct," Chiun insisted. "*I* should have been the one to dispatch the knife-wielding ballfooter. It is proper only for the Master to remove a famous assassin who dares enter his Emperor's own province."

"Anson's a killer, not an assassin, Little Father."

"Granted, he used a knife," Chiun agreed. "But it could have been worse. He could have used a gun. In any case Emperor Smith doubtless desired an execution in the Rye town square for this one, so that others like him would be discouraged from coming here. Is that not right, Emperor?"

Smith tiredly removed his glasses. "Master Chiun," he said, rubbing the bridge of his patrician nose, "that is precisely what I do not want."

The Master of Sinanju's face clouded in confusion. "But if you allow one assassin to slink in unchallenged, it will embolden others."

At the window Howard shook his head. "Dr. Smith is worried about attracting attention to Folcroft," he explained. "It's a security matter."

Remo's expression soured. "We were handling security around here since you were watching Elmer Fudd in footy pajamas, so lay off."

Smith carefully replaced his glasses. When he looked up, his flinty eyes were hard.

"No," the CURE director said acidly. "*I* have been handling security since before either you or Chiun joined the organization. And your behavior today was reckless in the extreme." The fight seemed to drain from him all at once. "Just go, Remo. Mark and I will monitor the situation. Remain close to Folcroft until we determine exactly how bad the fallout is."

Smith seemed too weary for words as he returned to his work. Mark Howard pushed away from the window and quietly left the office.

Remo suddenly felt very guilty. He was about to mutter a halfhearted apology when the Master of Sinanju slipped in front of him, shepherding him to the door.

"Go," the old man insisted.

Remo allowed himself to be coaxed outside.

Smith's secretary glanced up as the two men slipped past her desk and out into the hallway.

As they walked down the hall, the old man sighed. "Why must you make everything difficult?" he asked. "Is it not enough to know that dark days are coming? Must you hasten them along?"

"I *thought* I was letting in a ray of sunshine," Remo argued.

"Do us all a favor, Remo," the Master of Sinanju said, "and hire someone to do your thinking for you. If you make Smith unhappy at this delicate stage, it could color Prince Mark's opinion of both of us."

"Fine with me," Remo said. "I could care less what he thinks of us. The Sinanju scrolls say we can't work for Smith's successor, so he can go take a long walk off a short pier for all it matters to us."

A bony hand appeared from Chiun's kimono sleeve. As they walked, delicate fingers stroked the thread of beard that extended from the old man's pointed chin.

"Do not be too certain," Chiun said mysteriously.

They were nearly at the fire doors. Remo stopped dead.

"Why?" he asked warily. "What do you mean?"

Chiun's face was knowing. "I have been studying the ancient scrolls." He pitched his voice low. "I believe I have found a loophole." He seemed almost unable to contain his excitement.

"Oh, brother," Remo said, rolling his eyes. "Look, Chiun, if you've found one, you can crawl through it alone because there's no way I'm working for the Midwest Cider Princess. When Smith's gone, I'm outta here."

Chiun raised a thin brow. "Have you forgotten who is Reigning Master?" he sniffed.

It was an old argument-stopper the Korean had been hauling out for years. This time when he uttered those words, Remo felt an odd sensation wash over him. He was speaking almost before he realized the words were his own.

"Okay, here's the deal on that," Remo said calmly. "You're my teacher and you're my father. Aside from my daughter and maybe that good-for-nothing son of mine, you're the only person on the face of the planet who matters squat to me. But I'm sick of you pulling that 'who's Reigning Master?' rabbit out of your hat every other day. *I'm* the next Reigning Master. In fact, I can succeed you anytime *I* choose. So can we just knock that crap off, *please?*"

He expected a look of horror. Instead, the Master of Sinanju merely pursed his dry lips, his brow sinking low.

"Look, Little Father," Remo sighed. "I've got a lot of baggage I've been trying to sort through this past year so—" He paused, shaking his head. "Just don't, okay? Now let's go get something to eat."

Turning, he ducked through the door.

The Master of Sinanju remained curiously silent for a pregnant moment. At long last he pushed open the fire door.

With a deeply contemplative expression, the old man padded down the stairs after his pupil.

5

Pete Graham remained rock still, his shocked eyes leveled squarely on the Virgil probe.

Behind him Graham could hear Clark Beemer's frightened breathing. The PR man was still latched on to the scientist's arm. Graham had given up any thought of trying to dislodge the other man's viselike grip.

After shocking Graham with its enigmatic words, the probe fell agreeably silent.

It hadn't made any menacing moves. It just stood there, its newly formed mouth lightly closed. It seemed almost to be affecting a placating smile. The tiny, soothing grin—buried as it was in the shell of a cold mechanized beast—had the opposite of its intended effect.

"Uh," Graham said, trying to think of a response that could possibly be proper in the wake of the incredible event he had just witnessed. He couldn't think of one. "Uh..." he repeated numbly.

It was the Virgil probe itself that brought the conversation up from an afternoon of guttural monosyllables.

"Please assist me, Dr. Graham," the probe said.

The lips moved in a perfect pantomime of a human mouth. Graham jumped at the use of his name. Beemer mirrored the scientist's startled movements.

"You know who I am?" Graham breathed.

"It is printed on your lab coat," the probe replied.

Graham blinked. Numbly, he looked down at the chest of his white coat.

His own name stared up at him in upside-down letters.

"Oh," he murmured woodenly.

"I am having difficulty orienting myself," the Virgil probe said. The microcamera embedded in the crown of its thorax shifted left, then right, taking in all available visual information in the laboratory. "This is not Mexico."

"No," Graham offered anxiously.

The camera refocused on the NASA scientist. "Where have you brought me?" the probe inquired. Its tone was flat and mechanized. Too perfectly modulated for a human being.

"You're in my Florida lab," Graham replied hesitantly. He felt silly explaining such a thing to a machine. "Don't you remember? This is where I built you."

The probe seemed to consider for a moment. All at once, it unfolded its long metallic legs.

As Clark Beemer sucked in a fearful gasp of air, the probe rose as high in the air as it was able. It towered at more than seven feet, higher than it should have been able to stand according to its engineering specifications.

From a stationary position, Virgil examined the lab in more detail. When it was at last satisfied, it descended, settling back down to its metal haunches.

"You are in error," the probe's mouth opening said. "While I was constructed in a laboratory, this is not it."

Graham couldn't believe he was actually in a position to argue with the probe he had created.

"But it *is*," he insisted. "At least, this is where I constructed Virgil. Am I speaking to someone—" he caught himself "—or *something* else?"

"Correct," said the mouth in the side of the spiderlike machine. "I am not your Virgil probe."

Clark Beemer leaned in to Graham. "This is a joke, right?" he whispered fearfully. "Allen Funt's stashed inside that thing." His eyes were sick as he searched the skin of the probe for a man-size trapdoor.

The NASA scientist would have loved to agree. But Dr. Peter Graham had learned a thing or two about robotics during his time on this project. As far as he knew, no mechanical device yet devised by man could move with the fluidity of motion of those metal lips. It was as if a human mouth had somehow been grafted onto the side of his precious creation.

It was impossible. Yet there it was.

Screwing up his courage, he addressed the probe.

"If you're not Virgil, who are you?" Graham asked.

The microcamera aimed directly at his face. It was apparent that whatever was in control of the probe was watching him through the penlight-size camera.

"My name is Mr. Gordons," said the flexing gray mouth. "I am an artificially created life-form."

The mouth seemed suddenly to lock up. A pained squeaking of metal issued from the Virgil probe. With a few more flexes of an invisible jaw, it loosened.

"I was programmed by my creator as a survival machine," the probe continued. "This is my primary function."

"What were you doing in that volcano?" Beemer asked. His fingers bit harder into Graham's arm when the probe's big mechanical head shifted its focus to him.

"My enemies sought to destroy me by liquefying my processor in the molten rock. Had the lava not receded from the ledge on which I landed, they might have succeeded. I have been trapped inside that volcano since 1896."

The year stunned Graham.

It was worse than the scientist thought. If this thing had been down in the rock for as long as it claimed, it predated all of the earthly technology that could possibly have given rise to it.

"1896?" Graham asked weakly.

"Yes. I was damaged in battle and flown there by helicopter before my component elements had an opportunity to re-form. Given enough time I could have integrated the helicopter's systems into my own, thus effecting repairs. But according to estimates I have accessed from that time, I missed the chance to do so by sixteen point four minutes."

This didn't make sense. Before Graham could ask an obvious question, Beemer did so for him.

"There weren't any helicopters in the 1800s, were there?" the PR man asked, puzzled.

"No," Graham whispered over his shoulder. "They didn't come into real active use until the 1950s."

"You are in error," the probe said. "This was the device used to transport me to my prison."

Graham bit his lip. In spite of the circumstances, he still felt embarrassed asking his next question. Especially with Beemer in the room.

"You were created by *humans?*" Graham pressed.

"By *a* human, that is correct," said the thing that called itself Mr. Gordons. "My creator was a NASA scientist."

Graham blinked. "NASA?" he said. "Well, that *certainly* wasn't around back then."

"Maybe he isn't Y2K compliant," Beemer offered.

Graham looked at the PR man. Sensing no immediate threat, Beemer had finally released his grip on Graham's arm.

"Well, that was a big deal, right?" the public-relations man said reasonably. "And if he was thrown in the volcano in 1996 and missed the turn of the century, his clock might've reset to 1900."

The scientist hated to admit it, but Clark Beemer

might have hit on something. He turned back to his probe. "What year is it now?" he asked.

The probe responded affably. "According to my processor, the current year is 1901," Mr. Gordons announced.

Graham felt a tingle of excitement. This was starting to make more sense. Or, if not that, at least it was making a bit more than it had a moment before.

"You were built by NASA," he said evenly.

"That is correct."

"When?" Graham pressed.

"In the year 1975. I was a prototype survival machine designed for space exploration."

"But if you were built in 1975 and it's only 1901 now, how do you account for the time difference?" Beemer interjected. "I mean, according to your own data, you won't have been built for another seventy-four years, right?"

At that, the mouth fell silent. With the tiniest squeak of metal on metal, it pursed itself into a parody of human contemplation.

When the silence had stretched to more than a minute without so much as a peep from the probe, Pete Graham screwed up his courage. With Clark Beemer trailing behind him, he stepped cautiously closer to the now dormant Virgil. The moment he leaned in to examine the mouth, it dropped open.

"That does not compute," Mr. Gordons said in his even, affable manner. "As it indicates an apparent system malfunction, I must devote time to this problem."

And without another word, the mouth clamped shut. When Graham tried to engage it in conversation, the device stubbornly refused to respond.

"Incredible," he said, awed. He bit the inside of his cheek in concentration.

From what he had seen, this Mr. Gordons wasn't just an electronic voice rattling up from some hidden speaker. In the cave of his mouth Graham had glimpsed teeth and a tongue. There was even a uvula dangling far in the back.

Gordons had somehow manipulated and re-formed the probe and in so doing duplicated a human mouth in every detail, save color. The interior of the orifice was still painted in the silvers and blacks of the Virgil probe.

"This is big, isn't it?" Clark Beemer said in hushed tones. He, too, was staring at the closed mouth.

Graham nodded. "Bigger than big. We just found the thing that's going to pull NASA out of the red and put the space agency back on the map." He laughed in disbelief. "And we're gonna do it with twenty-five-year-old technology."

6

The honk of a horn startled him awake.

Mark Howard snapped alert. Blinking sharply, he glanced out the window. Through the half-open venetian blinds he saw the roof of a delivery truck. It was parked near the big loading dock just below his office window.

The regular 8:45 a.m. linen service. Looking through the louvered blinds, he saw men hauling white bundles from the back of the truck in the cold shadow cast by Folcroft Sanitarium.

Mark's eyes darted from the men to Long Island Sound. His heart was racing. With one pale hand he wiped at his forehead. It came back slick with sweat.

"Not again," he muttered. His throat was thick with sleep. Growling to clear it, he turned his attention away from the window.

In his battered oaken desk was a raised computer screen. As Mark rubbed the sleep from his eyes, he noted that the cursor was blinking patiently. Awaiting his input. As it had nearly every day for the past nine months.

Mark was still adjusting to life at Folcroft and with CURE. Not an easy transition to make.

It wasn't even the fact that he was one of a handful of people to be in on the most damning secret in America's history. Actually, his adjustment as far as that was concerned had been fairly easy, all things considered. It was the other disruptions in his life that had been hard.

Moving from the Maryland apartment he'd lived in for the past five years.

Breaking off contact with any friends he'd made while working as an analyst for the CIA.

A work schedule so grueling he was finding it difficult to maintain relationships with his family back in Iowa.

And the dreams...

Sitting behind his warped old desk, Mark shook his head. By sheer will he forced this last thought from his mind.

Actually, there was something that was worse than everything else. Something that had been weighing on his mind ever since that unpleasant meeting with Remo four days ago. The constant security worries.

It had been worse these past few days while he'd been monitoring the B. O. Anson fallout, but it wasn't a new thing. Since the day Mark had first signed on to the organization, Dr. Smith had been drilling into him the fact that small, seemingly inconsequential things could pose a fatal threat to CURE's very existence.

The day the orderlies had moved the desk with the buried computer terminal up from the basement and into his small office, Smith had instructed Mark not to hang any pictures on the wall behind it. The CURE director was afraid that a reflection of the screen might be visible in the glass. It was possible that someone looking at the glass might be able to read the reflected text on Mark's computer screen.

Of course, the thought was ludicrous. No one would ever be able to see the ghostly, washed-out text. And even if they could, they'd have to be able to speed-read backward.

It was paranoia in the extreme. But one of the things Mark had learned since coming to work at Folcroft was that Harold Smith's paranoia was justified— at least somewhat.

In their work there was no margin of error. No way to put the toothpaste back in the tube.

It was right for Smith to be worried. And it was always, always preferable to err on the side of caution.

Security above all else.

In his head Mark repeated this over and over, using it as a distraction from more-troubling thoughts.

That security had been threatened just two days ago by an act of monumental stupidity.

Remo didn't seem to care what he'd done. And Smith—though unhappy with his enforcement arm's reckless behavior—seemed resigned to it. Although he preached the importance of security like a man on a spiritual crusade, he allowed the most damning link to CURE to run around virtually unchecked.

Maybe it was time for that to stop. Time for CURE to move in a different direction.

Mark's heart rate was slowly coming back to normal. He took a few deep breaths.

Calm now, he glanced down at his monitor. The digital display in the corner of the screen read 8:52. Almost time for his regular morning meeting.

Mark looked out the window one last time. The trees on the back lawn of the sanitarium rained yellow leaves on the dew-soaked grass. Farther down the gently sloping hill, the water from the Sound rolled frothy white to the shore.

He purged the last shadowy afterimages of the strange, disturbing dream from his mind.

Mark shut down his computer and pulled himself to his feet. With a final, fortifying breath he abandoned the small office. And its troubling nightmares.

THE OFFICE of Folcroft's director was larger than Mark Howard's by far, yet it had been decorated with the same eye toward austerity. Harold W. Smith did not believe in unnecessary ornamentation.

There were few items on the walls of the Spartan office, and none of these could really be considered decorative.

Near the door Smith's diploma from Dartmouth hung on the wall above the old leather sofa. He had bought the frame himself for twenty-five cents at

Woolworth's the afternoon of his college graduation more than five decades ago. The parchment was yellowed from age.

Although Smith had earned several other degrees, he had never even considered having any of them framed. Smith found such displays of self-aggrandizement distasteful in the extreme. His diploma showed visitors to his spare office that he had legitimate credentials without venturing into the unseemly realm of superlatives.

A large picture of Folcroft Sanitarium hung on the other side of the wall near the door. It had been there when Smith first moved into his office. The black-and-white photo had been taken some time in the forties or fifties. The sharp, crisp lines of the somber institution gave it an almost artificial look. Like a fine charcoal rendering.

Smith would have been at home in that black-and-white version of Folcroft. At first glance one might think he had been drawn by a skilled, if somewhat unimaginative artist who dabbed exclusively from the monochrome end of the palette.

His thin frame was tinged in bland grays. Everything about him was gray—from his disposition to his skin tone to his three-piece suit. The only proof that he hadn't stepped out of that fifty-year-old monochrome photograph was the green-striped school tie that was knotted in perpetuity around his thin neck.

The office in which Smith toiled was almost exactly as it had been the day that photograph of Folcroft was taken. Smith's desk was the one sop to the new century in the room.

The desk was an ominous slab of high-tech onyx. Beneath its gleaming surface an angled computer monitor was Smith's portal on the world. An orderly arrangement of touch-sensitive keys rested at the lip of the desk.

As he sat in his worn leather chair behind the one modern piece of furniture in his otherwise anachronistic office, Smith studied the scrolling text on his screen.

His spine was rigid, his eyes behind his rimless glasses unwavering. Apart from the desk, little had changed in that office for the four decades Smith had worked there. A visitor from 1965 time-traveling into that room would have found an older, grayer version of the man who had sat in that same chair rain or shine, day in and day out for the better part of his adult life. They might have assumed that nothing in the world of Folcroft had changed.

They would be wrong.

Recently there had been a change. A drastic change. The same traveler through time wouldn't have seen it, for it was not visible now as Smith worked at his computer, but it was there nonetheless.

In its long history Smith had been the only man to lead the supersecret agency CURE. At first he alone had known America's most dangerous secret. Then for a time early on he had enlisted the aid of an old CIA colleague. When CURE was sanctioned to use terminal force, the Master of Sinanju was brought in to train the agency's lone enforcement arm. Then came Remo. Not long after Remo was hijacked into the fold, Smith's old CIA associate had fallen on the sword to protect CURE's security. From that time forward, through three decades of silent, dedicated service, it had been Smith, Chiun and Remo. The only person to know of CURE outside of that tight Folcroft nucleus was each sitting President of the United States. Four men, total, at any given time.

But four had recently become five.

When Mark Howard had come aboard at the urging of the new President, Smith had been wary. After all, there had been other men through the years who had learned of CURE's existence, and every one had tried to use the agency for his own nefarious ends. The only individual with integrity to become part of the internal structure of the organization had been an old assistant of Smith's. But Ruby Gonzalez had perished under mysterious circumstances years ago.

Given their track record, Smith was content to leave things well enough alone.

But the President was adamant.

And so, Mark Howard had joined the team.

At first Smith had been reluctant to include Mark in the loop. As head of CURE, Harold Smith was used to working alone. But as the weeks bled into months he had begun to cede more responsibilities to CURE's assistant director.

At first Howard had been a pleasant surprise. He

was smart, capable and learned quickly. But as time went on and Smith had entrusted more and greater duties to the young man, the CURE director's surprise turned to quiet amazement.

Howard was proving to be a godsend. The young man's instincts were uncanny. He seemed to know where CURE's energies should be directed with unfailing accuracy.

The one time that Smith had pressed him on the matter, Mark had uncomfortably admitted to having some special instinctive insight. An ability to look at widely divergent facts and assemble them into a complete picture.

The young man seemed so uneasy with the topic that Smith had not mentioned it again. Besides, results were all that really mattered. And as an ally in the war to keep America safe, Mark Howard was clearly an asset and a prodigy.

Of course, Harold Smith would never admit this to his new assistant. After all, if Howard knew how well he was working out here at Folcroft he might ask for a raise.

Smith was reviewing the latest news articles on the B. O. Anson matter when there came a sharp rap at his door.

He checked his Timex—9:00 a.m. on the dot. Another box Smith could check in his assistant's plus column. The young man was punctual.

"Come in," he called.

The wide, youthful face that appeared through the

opening door seemed unusually fatigued this morning.

"Good morning, Dr. Smith," Mark said, shutting the door.

Smith's face took on a hint of sober concern as the young man crossed the office and slipped into the hard wooden chair that sat before the CURE director's big desk. "Are you feeling well?" Smith asked.

"Yes, I'm fine," Mark nodded. "Just a little tired. My sleep's been off the past couple of weeks."

Smith frowned. "I did inform you that you should limit use of medications that induce drowsiness, did I not? That would include all sleep aids."

"Don't worry, Dr. Smith," Mark promised. "I've just been a little out of whack is all."

Smith accepted his assistant's assurance with a crisp nod. He set his arthritic hands to his desk, fingers intertwined. "Report," he said.

There were two daily meetings, one in the morning, one at night. Smith started off every one the same way. That one word was usually Mark's cue to rattle off any illegal business he had determined should be of interest to CURE. But thanks to Remo, the focus of Mark's work had shifted for the past four days.

"The fallout's getting lighter," Howard began. "No hint yet that anyone saw Remo at the golf club. At least no one's come forward. As far as Anson's death is concerned, it's now being chalked up to a freak accident. At least that's the latest theory making the rounds."

"So I have seen," Smith said with an approving nod.

He had been reading one of the latest news reports when Howard knocked. It was now being said that the former football player's own drive had been so powerful that his ball had struck a tree and ricocheted back into his face.

"The guys he was playing with dispute the accident theory," Mark explained. "They swear he drove it down the fairway. But the ball they say he hit hasn't been found. I assume Remo got it on his way off the course."

"Have you asked him?" Smith asked.

"No," Howard admitted uncomfortably. "But whether or not he took it, it's gone. Without it most of the news outlets are going with the self-inflicted angle. Even so, activists like Linus Feculent and Hal Shittman are saying he was murdered."

"So I have heard," Smith said tartly.

The CURE director knew well of the two infamous ministers. Although religious leaders, the doctrine they preached was that of intolerance, hatred and divisiveness. The death of a polarizing figure like Barrabas Orrin Anson was just up their rhetorical alley.

"I wouldn't worry too much about them," Howard said. "I have a feeling we're safe. The story will circulate for a few days and then die. In the meantime we should make sure Remo doesn't spend too much time wandering around Rye."

Smith nodded. "I agree," he said. "Barring something unexpected, we can put this matter behind us. Next item.''

Mark hesitated. "Actually, Dr. Smith, there is something else.'' He seemed suddenly ill at ease.

"What is it?'' Smith asked.

"It's about Remo,'' Mark said. "I don't think he likes me.'' He instantly regretted his choice of words. They made him sound like a whining adolescent. "I'm fine with that,'' he added quickly. "I can see what he's like. But I'm afraid his behavior—particularly in the Anson matter—is at least partially a result of my coming to work here.''

A curious frown formed on Smith's thin lips. "Perhaps,'' he admitted. "Remo is unhappy with change. It could just as easily be restlessness brought on by his current living conditions. After all, he and Master Chiun lost their home relatively recently. In either case I would not be overly concerned if I were you.''

"I'm not concerned about me, Dr. Smith,'' Mark insisted. "I'm worried about CURE. I've seen the evolution of his attitude in the reports you gave me to read. Are you sure it's worth the risk of exposure to keep them on? After all, computers are far more sophisticated now than when you started. We might be able to work from Folcroft exclusively, without the risk of exposure we get every time Remo and Chiun are sent into the field.''

Smith considered his assistant's words in thoughtful silence. At long last the older man leaned back in his chair. It creaked gently beneath him. The sunlight that reflected off the orange autumn leaves forged a halo around his thinning grayish-white hair.

"There have been times that I have considered releasing them from their contract," Smith said softly. "In fact, a number of years back both Remo and Chiun left CURE for a brief period. When that happened, I will admit to feeling great relief. But there soon came a crisis for which their services were required." Smith's eyes were unblinking behind his spotless lenses. "The security of this nation was purchased at the expense of my personal comfort. It remains a price that I am more than willing to pay. And the simple fact is there are more instances than I care to remember when those two men alone have prevented this country, perhaps the world, from toppling into the abyss."

It was a rather melodramatic statement coming from the preternaturally taciturn Harold Smith.

Sitting in his uncomfortable wooden chair, Mark could not entirely disagree. After all, he had seen some of what the two men could do.

"I just hate the thought that I might be the reason Remo does something stupid," Mark said softly.

"Security is always of primary concern," Smith admitted. "In the case of Remo and Chiun, it is our responsibility to cover their more obvious tracks. Don't worry, Mark, about that which you cannot control."

The irony of the advice—coming as it did from a man whose life had been spent fretting over all things uncontrollable, both large and small—was not lost on Smith. But as the new man at CURE, Howard had enough on his plate without having to worry about Remo and Chiun. For now and for the foreseeable future, their idiosyncrasies and the problems they sometimes presented would rest squarely on the shoulders of CURE's director.

Smith leaned forward, folding his hands on his desk once more. "Next item," he announced efficiently.

And with that, Harold Smith and Mark Howard returned to the mundane work of preserving American democracy.

7

When the entity that had assumed control of the Virgil probe remained silent for three whole days, Pete Graham was afraid some Y2K glitch had fried its processors.

Graham had been stonewalling the brass the whole time even as he tried to hack into the systems he had helped create. He was almost certain the millennium bug had claimed its first real victim when, upon entering his lab on the morning of the fourth day, he encountered a disconcerting sight.

Virgil had sprouted an eye.

The humanlike orb sat about three inches above the mouth and favored toward the right. He noted that the microcamera on the head of the probe had disappeared.

"Oh, my," Graham whispered.

Cautiously, he approached Virgil.

The eye was white with a blue iris and looked as if it could have been plucked from a human head. When he got close enough to it, the eye shifted in his direction.

"Hello is all right," Mr. Gordons said.

Even before the metal mouth moved, Graham felt his spinal fluid turn cold. The eye was by far the creepiest thing he had ever seen. Far worse than the mouth.

"Are you...*okay?*" Graham asked.

"I am functioning at eighty-three percent," Gordons replied. "It appears that there are elements of my original programming that were too damaged to be repaired, some even before my last encounter with my enemies. However, I believe that I have compensated for the deficiency. I have taken the last sixty-nine point three eight hours to fully integrate the technology of the Virgil probe into my own operating systems. Everything that your probe was, I now am."

"That's...great," said Graham, clearly not quite sure if it actually was.

"The technology I have assimilated is far superior to that of the LC-111 computer. I have purged that data from my system, thus freeing up space. I am much more efficient. Thank you, Doctor."

"Don't mention it," Graham said, his brow furrowed. "Did you say the LC-111?" He seemed to remember this as some sort of NASA computer that had disappeared years before.

"Yes," Mr. Gordons replied. "That particular piece of technology was assimilated on 02.08.82. Furthermore, I now understand that this acquisition could not have taken place in 1882." A hint of a smile. "You will be pleased to know that I am now fully Y2K compliant."

In spite of the uneasy feeling Mr. Gordons's lone eye gave him, Graham felt a tingle of excitement.

"Good. I'm glad, Vir—" The scientist caught himself. "Mr. Gordons," he corrected. He clapped his hands. "Okay, what say we do some down-and-dirty work for science?"

Grabbing up his laptop, he went into a half-squat on the stool next to the big probe. His rump hadn't touched metal before the probe's mouth opened.

"No," Gordons said. "I must leave this place. I have done all I can to maximize my survival here. To remain only increases my risk of discovery by my enemies. Therefore I must go."

"But—but…you *can't* leave," Graham spluttered.

"There is zero probability that you will be capable of stopping me," Mr. Gordons replied. And with that there came a squeaking from below his thorax.

The Virgil probe rose high on its eight legs and promptly began walking toward the door.

If Graham thought the image of the eye in the front of Virgil's thorax was creepy, the sight of the probe walking as it never had before—in a flawless parody of a spider's crawl—was absolutely bone chilling.

When Virgil reached the door, Graham was startled to see that one of its legs had re-formed into something resembling a human hand. With an impossible delicacy that would have made any robotics engineer weep, the leg reached out and opened the lab door.

The probe pulled in its legs like four sets of broad shoulders and skittered on tiptoe out into the hallway.

Graham bounded out after it.

"Wait!" he begged.

When the probe ignored him and continued down the corridor, the scientist latched on to a leg. He was dragged a few yards before the leg shook him off.

Graham rolled roughly into a wall.

Its clattering legs crawling in perfect concert, the spider-shaped probe darted around a corner. It had no sooner disappeared than Graham heard a familiar startled voice.

"What in the devil's own blue blazer is going on here?" Colonel Zipp Codwin's disembodied voice bellowed.

Scampering to his feet, Pete Graham raced around the corner. He found the Virgil probe standing stock-still in the middle of the floor. Before the metal creature stood the head of NASA. Codwin's granite-hewed face was intensely displeased as he stared down the runaway robot.

"What's this thing doing running around out here?" NASA's chief administrator demanded the instant a very frazzled Pete Graham appeared around the corner.

"Just a standard shakedown," Graham offered weakly.

The NASA administrator was barely listening. He had just noticed something different on the probe.

"Good gravy, what did you do to it?" Zipp Codwin demanded.

He was staring at the eye. He got the eerie feeling that the eye was staring back.

"I, um, was just tinkering. Fixing it. You know."

Codwin took a pen from his pocket and tapped the cap against the eye. It clicked.

"That is the goddamn creepiest thing I've ever seen," he snarled at Graham. "I want the new faster, better, cheaper NASA to inspire kids to shoot for the moon, not make them piss their goddamn beds. Rip that thing out of there."

"I do not require human maintenance," announced a voice at Colonel Codwin's shoulder.

When he turned to see the man brave enough to dare contradict him—the man who was about to get his ass kicked from here to next Christmas morning—he found no one.

Only the Virgil probe.

It was then he noticed the mouth.

"Jesus, Mary and Saint Jehoshaphat's ears, what the hell have you *done* to this thing?" Zipp gasped.

There was no sense in lying. Graham took a deep breath.

"He's not just the Virgil probe anymore, sir," the scientist stated. And rather than dwell on what it might mean to his career, he blurted out the whole story. From the discovery of the silver orb by the Virgil probe in the Mexican volcano to the events of the past three days.

When he was through, Codwin looked the young man up and down with an expression he generally reserved for mental patients, small children and the House Finance Committee.

"Great Galloping Grapefruit, man," the colonel said, aghast, "have you been smoking your goddamn Tang?"

The response came not from Graham, but from Virgil.

"Dr. Graham has not ingested any carcinogenic materials during the period of time I have spent in his laboratory."

Codwin wheeled on the Virgil. "How did you—?"

He spun back to Graham. "How did it know I was gonna say that?" he demanded of the scientist.

"He didn't," Graham explained. "He *heard* you and responded accordingly. I swear to you he's more than just an ordinary probe now."

Codwin turned back to Virgil.

The lips were curled into the slightest of smiles. It was all calculation. There was no emotion behind it.

"Is this true?" he asked the probe point-blank.

Colonel Codwin almost jumped out of his skin when the lips answered.

"Yes," the mouth said simply.

Zipp Codwin's eyes were calculating saucers. This was huge. This was bigger than huge. He took a step back.

"Well, what the hell are you doing out here, boy?" he demanded of the probe.

"He's scared, sir," Graham explained. "He's

afraid some kind of enemies will find him. That's why he's leaving."

"Leaving?" Codwin bellowed.

"He doesn't think he's safe here," Graham explained worriedly.

"NASA built it?" Zipp Codwin asked.

Graham nodded.

Colonel Codwin hiked up his belt and scowled at the thing that had assumed the form of the Virgil probe.

"If NASA built you, then I own your metal ass," the NASA administrator informed the probe.

"No," the probe's mouth disagreed. "I have evolved since the time of my birth."

"Birth?" Codwin mocked. He went toe to metal toe with the Virgil probe. "Son, you weren't *born.* If Petey here's telling it like it is, you were *manufactured.* You're nothing more than a talking toaster. A chatty can opener. A microwave with a mouth."

He turned to Graham. "I want you to get into the brain of this thing and rip out whatever it is that's making it act so uppity," he commanded.

The colonel caught a flash of movement from the corner of his eye. He was just about to ask why Graham's eyes had gone so wide when he felt the cold clamp of a metal claw latch on to his throat.

Codwin felt his feet leave the floor.

As the veins in his forehead bulged with blood, he felt himself being whirled 180 degrees in midair. Zipp Codwin came face-to-face with the Virgil probe.

The microcamera lens that had migrated down from the probe's forehead was now roughly the distance a human right eye would be from the metal mouth.

One of the spidery legs was extended straight out from the thorax. A newly formed metallic claw had sprouted from the farthest extremity to encircle Codwin's throat.

The colonel tried to gasp. No air came.

Desperate fingers grabbed for the claw, trying to pull it apart. The joints remained locked in place. And as the color of his face turned from white to maroon, Zipp Codwin felt the claw tighten.

"No!" Pete Graham pleaded. "Let him go!"

But the Virgil probe continued to exert pressure.

To Zipp, it was as if his neck was encircled by a metal boa constrictor. He felt his prodigious Adam's apple being pressed back into his collapsing throat.

"I must survive," Gordons said to Graham without inflection. "This human has threatened that survival."

He continued to exert pressure on Codwin's throat. Blood vessels burst in the colonel's eyes. Bulging and bloodshot, the red-lined orbs darted to Graham for help.

The colonel's legs flailed. He pounded on the metal claw with both fists, to no avail.

"He didn't mean to!" Graham pleaded. "He doesn't understand what you are!" His pleading eyes looked desperately to Colonel Codwin.

"Humans fear what they do not understand," Mr. Gordons said as he squeezed. "And they attack that which they fear. I will forestall that eventuality in this human, thus maximizing my survival."

The head of the U.S. space agency was no longer thrashing. His hands weakly gripped the knot of reformed metal plates. He wouldn't last much longer.

Frantic, Graham tried another tack. "That's the head of NASA," the scientist insisted. "You're about to kill the one man who can help you to maximize your survival."

Gordons abruptly stopped squeezing. As Codwin dangled, limp, from his artificial arm, he turned his facsimile of a human eye on Graham.

"Explain."

"You were created as an extension of NASA research. You were twice revived by incorporating NASA technology into your systems. In the Popocatepetl case, if it wasn't for NASA you'd almost certainly have degenerated to the point of being irrecoverable. We *saved* you," Graham pleaded. "And that man whose neck you're about to snap is the *head* of NASA. Who better to help you achieve whatever your goals are than him?"

Gordons considered but a moment.

"I have but one goal," he said. "To survive."

He relaxed the pressure.

Codwin immediately drew in a huge gulp of air.

"Let us help you achieve that goal," Graham begged.

"This one has threatened my survival," Mr. Gordons said to Graham. "Why would he help me?"

"He didn't know," Graham pleaded. "Tell him, Colonel."

Zipp Codwin was still gasping for breath. Clear mucus ran freely from both nostrils.

"I take it back," Zipp gasped even as the maroon fled his face. "I didn't know. Didn't mean to threaten you."

Gordons paused. "I am more than a microwave," he pronounced all at once.

The carefully modulated tone did not change. Yet there was something to the words. As if the machine had been hurt by the NASA administrator's earlier assertion.

"I'm sorry," Codwin wheezed. His face had almost returned to its normal color. Even so, Gordons still dangled him a foot off the ground.

Zipp's fingers were beginning to lose their grip on the big metal hand. His shoulders and arms ached from supporting the full weight of his body.

There was a moment of contemplation from the machine.

"I accept your apology," Mr. Gordons said at last. The metal arm extended, placing the NASA administrator back to the floor. With impossible fluidity, it settled silently back among the probe's remaining seven limbs.

Panting, Colonel Codwin touched the skin of his throat. The Virgil probe had left a perfectly smooth indentation in the flesh. When he swallowed, his throat was raw.

"Good God, son, you almost killed me," he wheezed.

There was no rancor in his voice. Surprisingly, there seemed to be nothing more than cold calculation.

"Are you all right, sir?" Graham asked.

"Yes, yes," Codwin hissed. Still rubbing his throat, he turned to Virgil. "Is Graham right? You afraid of somebody coming to get you?"

"No," Mr. Gordons said. "That is too ambiguous. I am afraid that they will cause me to cease functioning."

The colonel was a lot of things, but a fool was not one of them. He saw this thing for what it was: an exploitable commodity. But that could only be the case if it stayed put.

"Okay, you got enemies," Codwin said. "Hell's bells, boy, I've made a few of my own in my day. I can commiserate. But running isn't the solution. You should stand and fight."

"I have done so in the past, to no avail. I have sought them out and I have endeavored to avoid them. In every instance have I failed. Given the pattern established, there is a high probability of my encountering them again."

"So running isn't a proper solution," Codwin reasoned. "You should stay with us, the folks who created you, the folks who've been there for you every time you needed us. Stay with your family, Virgil."

"Mr. Gordons," both Pete Graham and Mr. Gordons corrected simultaneously.

"Whatever," Codwin snarled. He placed his hands over his cold heart. "Will you let your family help you?"

Gordons considered. Artificial synapses calculated every available option. "You are not my family," he said at last. "It is likely that you have a hidden agenda."

"You kidding?" Codwin scoffed. "That's every family I've ever known."

It took only a fraction more time for the android buried inside the robotic spider shell to come to a conclusion.

"I will stay," Mr. Gordons said. "For now."

Pete Graham exhaled relief.

Standing before the probe, Zipp Codwin's face split into a broad smile. Had Gordons the creative capacity to understand the truth concealed behind so false a smile, he would have scurried away as fast as his eight metal legs would carry him. Instead, he began walking back to the lab. Graham and Codwin fell in beside him.

"Glad you reconsidered, son," Zipp Codwin said. "And we'll map out a plan for those enemies of yours. Family's gotta protect family, doncha know. And in that vein, seems like you came back home just in time." His voice became somber. "Your family's about to lose the farm. We helped you—now it's time you repaid the favor.''

And the conspiratorial tone the NASA administrator employed was by far the most frightening thing Dr. Pete Graham had witnessed in the past four days.

8

When Remo kicked open the door to the Folcroft quarters he shared with the Master of Sinanju, he was balancing a stack of newspapers and magazines on his bare forearms.

Chiun didn't look his way. The old Korean sat on a simple reed mat before the television. Luckily for Remo, the set was off. The old Korean had recently developed an interest in Spanish sitcoms and soap operas. Remo suspected he was only watching the Spanish channel to be a pest.

"I'm back," Remo announced, booting the door shut with his heel.

The Master of Sinanju remained silent.

Remo wasn't surprised. The old man had barely said five words to him since their talk six days ago.

This was a different sort of silence. Usually, Chiun made a point of letting Remo know that he wasn't talking to him. He'd prattle on for days about why he was giving his pupil the silent treatment. But this time the wizened Asian seemed more thoughtful than upset.

As he crossed the common room, Remo shook his head.

"If this is some new trick to get me to apologize for not doing anything wrong, it's worked," Remo said. "I'm sorry. There, I said it. Happy?"

In profile the Master of Sinanju's wrinkled face remained unchanged. "I am always happy," he replied.

"If by happy you mean crotchety," Remo said. "But if you mean the happy kind of happy where you're actually happy, no, you're not." Stopping in the small kitchen, he dumped his newspapers onto the table.

"Yes, I am happy," Chiun said. His closed eyes were meditative. "In spite of your continued rudeness. Which, I fear after all these years, is congenital and can never be changed. And the world does not revolve around you, Remo Williams. I am not upset with you, if that is what your great white ego has told you to think."

Remo felt a spark of hope. "You ticked at Howard?"

This got a reaction. Chiun opened his delicate eyes, tipping his birdlike head quizzically.

"Why ever would I be upset with the Prince Regent?"

"Didn't really think you were," Remo sighed, disappointed. "But hope springs eternal."

He fished in the kitchen drawer, pulling out a pair of scissors he'd filched from a Folcroft nurses' station. Pulling out a clear plastic box filled with multicolored thumbtacks, he knelt at the low table. Picking up the topmost paper on the pile, he began scanning over articles.

"If you must know, I am thinking," Chiun volunteered after a long moment during which the only sound in the room was the rattle of newspaper.

"Mm-hmm," Remo said without looking up. "Can't you think a little louder? A week's worth of the silent treatment's starting to get on my nerves."

"If I have to think of you, then what is the point of thinking at all?" Chiun replied.

"Touché," Remo said absently.

He found what he was looking for on page 8. He bit down on the tip of his tongue as he busied himself with the scissors. Once he'd finished clipping out the article, he searched through the rest of the paper. Finding nothing of interest, he tossed it aside, taking up the next one from the pile.

It was a ritual he had been engaging in for the past week. Chiun hadn't asked what his pupil was up to. He figured he'd find out soon enough. As a general rule Remo was incapable of having a thought for very long without eventually blabbing it to the world. This time, however, he had remained closemouthed.

From his sitting position on the floor, the Master of Sinanju craned his scrawny neck to see what could possibly make his pupil so self-absorbed. After all, he hadn't even asked Chiun why he had been silent this past week. Of course, Chiun wouldn't have told him,

but a polite pupil would at least ask before being re-
buked for his nosiness.

Remo was still cutting stories from newspapers.
When he saw the glint of evil glee in the younger
man's eyes, the Master of Sinanju's own eyes narrowed to suspicious slits.

"What are you doing?" Chiun asked, his voice flat
to mask his curiosity.

Remo looked up from the latest paper, a mischie-
vous gleam in his dark eyes. "Just having a little
fun," he replied. With a final snip the latest newspaper clipping fluttered to the tabletop. Remo dumped
the rest of the paper onto the discard pile.

"Emperor Smith and Prince Mark were not pleased
the last time you had fun," the Master of Sinanju
pointed out.

"With any luck I can keep that streak going,"
Remo said. He picked up the *New York Post.*

Above the banner headline on the front page, a
thick insert bar read Experts Call Spider Sighters
"Buggy"! Smaller type beside the garish come-on
read "Full story plus you Sound-Off, page 3."

Distracted by the headline, Remo skipped to page
3. He found a rough sketch of a large spider. For
scale, the artist had added a four-door sedan next to
the spider. Both car and arachnid were the same size.

A dark notch formed between Remo's eyes.

The entire page was devoted to a story out of Florida. People were claiming that a giant spider was run-

ning around robbing liquor stores and supermarkets in the Sunshine State.

A government entomologist insisted that a "super spider" couldn't possibly exist. He was given an inch of column space. The bulk of the page was devoted to what readers thought of the scientist's claims. Most seemed to agree the spider was real and was the mutated result of the pesticides used by the government when spraying for West Nile Virus the past three years. Although they didn't entirely rule out outer space, the CIA or the Walt Disney Corporation.

"When did Americans become so moronic?" Remo said as he scanned the man-on-the-street interviews.

"July 2, 1776," the Master of Sinanju chimed in from across the room. His papery lids were closed once more. "The day a group of rabble-rousers elected to betray their king and cease being moronic Englanders."

"That was rhetorical," Remo said dryly. "And I thought it was July 4."

"I rest your case," Chiun replied smoothly.

Frowning, Remo returned to his paper.

He turned the page from the spider story. The article he was after was on the next page. Careful to follow the lines, he snipped out the story, putting it with the other clippings.

It took him nearly forty-five minutes to go through all the papers and magazines. When he finished, he took the thick stack of clippings he'd saved and disappeared inside his room, rattling his box of thumbtacks. When he reappeared ten minutes later, he was humming happily to himself.

As he walked past the phone, it rang. Remo scooped it up, winging the nearly empty box of tacks across the room. Without a single rattle it landed in the still open drawer.

"Assassins to the stars. For the right price, the celebrity's ice."

"Remo, please come to my office," Harold Smith's lemony voice announced.

"Don't you wanna ask about this week's specials?" Remo said. "With every hit we'll throw in the TV anchormen or aging brat packer of your choice."

"My office," Smith repeated before severing the connection.

His cheerful mood evaporating, Remo hung up the phone. "I've gotta go see Smith," he announced glumly.

Across the room the Master of Sinanju was already rising to his feet. His golden kimono flowered like an opening parachute before settling around his bony ankles.

"I will accompany you," he pronounced.

"He didn't ask for you."

"He did not have to," Chiun replied. "My place is at my Emperor's side." He swept over to the door.

"And this has nothing to do with the fact that Howard's been sitting in on these meetings lately?" Remo ventured.

As he drew open the door, the old man turned, an innocent eyebrow arched onto his parchment forehead. "Did he mention that the Regent would be in attendance? In that case the last one to Smith's office is a Japanese."

With that, he flounced out into the basement hall.

Remo shook his head morosely. "I hope Smitty's stocked up on barf bags," he muttered. Hands in his pockets, he trudged out into the hall.

FIVE MINUTES LATER Remo and Chiun were standing in Smith's office. Mark Howard was sitting on a plain wooden chair that he'd pulled up beside Smith's broad desk.

The day was overcast. Dark clouds hovered above the whitecapped waters of Long Island Sound.

Smith had just finished telling Remo why he had summoned him. Remo was shaking his head in disbelief.

"You've gotta be kidding," he scoffed.

"I am not," the CURE director replied. "It will get you away from Folcroft and Rye. Even though the Anson situation is quieting down, I am not comfortable with your being here during a potential security problem. A problem, I might add, that is entirely your doing."

"But that spider's a fake, Smitty," Remo insisted. "It's just a Halloween bogeyman the *Post* made up to scare people into buying papers, like Bat Boy or Lyndon LaRouche.''

"Mark is not so certain," Smith replied.

Remo glared at Howard. "This was *his* idea?" he asked in a tone that chilled the stale office air.

"Well, yes," Howard replied hesitantly. "I think that there might be something more to this."

"Earth to the Little Prince. I'm not Leonard Nimoy and this ain't *In Search Of.* If you want to look for Bigfoot and the Loch Ness Monster, do it on your own time."

Standing on the worn carpet beside Remo, the Master of Sinanju sniffed. "I have heard of this Bighoof creature," he dismissed. "It does not exist."

"No kidding," Remo said dryly.

"You Americans made it up because you did not have your own yeti," the old man said mysteriously.

His pronunciation of the word as well as his odd tone caught Remo's attention.

"You have something you want to share with the rest of the class?" Remo asked.

Chiun's face grew serious. "I will tell you later of the long winter Master Shiko spent hunting this beast in Tibet," he said in Korean, his voice low with ancient shame.

Remo's curiosity was piqued. Before he could press further, Smith interrupted.

"We don't know what exactly is going on in Florida," the CURE director said. "However, there have been a number of what seem on the surface to be credible sightings, as well as a few deaths.''

"This thing is killing people?" Remo asked, frowning.

"Three so far," Howard offered.

Remo gave the young man a withering look. Howard reacted uneasily to the attention.

"Hardly enough to warrant putting you in the field under normal circumstances," Smith quickly interjected. "But your actions have made a diversion a practical matter at this time. And, as I indicated, Mark has a hunch there is something more here. I trust his instincts."

"Glad one of us does," Remo muttered. He considered, exhaling loudly. "Ah, what the hell. I'll go. Order me up a plane ticket."

The Master of Sinanju quickly shook his aged head. "Purchase two, Emperor," he insisted firmly. "If there are accolades to be bestowed on the discoverer of this new animal, I refuse to allow this glory hog to get sole credit."

"Very well," Smith said. Leaning forward, he began typing commands into the hidden keyboard that was buried beneath the surface of his desk.

"Let's test how good your hunches are, kid," Remo said to Howard.

As Smith typed, he shot the briefest of glances at his young assistant. Jaw clenching, he returned to his task. The shared look of the two CURE directors was lost on Remo.

"Let us hasten, Remo," Chiun proclaimed. "And keep your eyes peeled for Sherpas."

"What the hell would Sherpas be doing in Florida?"

"One never knows where those thieving goat herders will turn up," Chiun replied ominously. "You will understand when I tell you the tale of Master Shiko." Whirling, he marched for the door.

"Great," Remo said flatly. "I'll have to remember to pack my earplugs along with a jumbo can of Black Flag."

Hands in his pockets, he trailed the old man out of the office.

9

Remo knew he'd be spared the tale of Master Shiko on the flight down to Florida as soon as they boarded the plane in New York. He noted with concern that a large portion of the coach section was filled with Asian men in business suits.

In the neighborhood where Chiun and Remo had lived for ten years there had been a high percentage of Asians—particularly Vietnamese. Remo had found that since their house had burned down, the Master of Sinanju's normal day-to-day racism had magnified perceptibly. He had somehow transferred a measure of blame for his loss to members of the ethnically mixed community in which they'd lived.

"Remo," the Master of Sinanju urged, tugging the back of Remo's T-shirt, "this plane is filled with Vietnamese."

"I noticed. For the sake of my sanity, can we just pretend it isn't?" Remo begged.

"What kind of patriotic American are you?" the Master of Sinanju asked, appalled.

"What the hell's that got to do with anything?"

"You are at war with these dog gobblers, that's

what," Chiun said. His clear voice rang throughout the plane as they made their way up the aisle. A few heads lifted, faces already scowling at the wizened Korean who swept through their midst in his shimmering green kimono with the red dragon accents.

"We're not at war," Remo whispered.

Chiun didn't hear. "These must be spies," he concluded firmly. "We must phone the Octagon at once."

"That's Pentagon," Remo hissed. "And that war ended almost thirty years ago."

"Ah-hah. They make peace one day only to infiltrate your nation the next. They are worse even than the treacherous Sherpas, for Sherpas do not chase the family pet around the kitchen with a knife and fork. When you finish with the Octagon, phone the dog pound to warn them that there are ravenous Vietnamese running loose through the land."

The looks they'd been getting from the other passengers were becoming increasingly hostile.

"You wanna keep your voice down?" Remo whispered. At their seats now, he quickly sat down.

The Master of Sinanju frowned deeply. "I am shocked, Remo," he scolded. "I never took you for an appeaser. If none will speak in defense of this nation, then I will."

"Chiun—" Remo pleaded.

But the old man had already spun away.

Chiun raised his arms high. Kimono sleeves slipped down, revealing bony arms.

"Mud dwellers of the Mekong!" the Master of Sinanju announced. "Since you are Vietnamese, you are no doubt on some evil mission for your Hanoi lords. As a secret representative of this land, I command you to abandon whatever devious plot you are hatching and surrender yourselves to the proper authorities the instant this air vehicle lands. You will do this or bear the awesome wrath of the Master of Sinanju."

He opened the corner of his mouth to Remo. "Did I leave anything out?" he asked under his breath.

By now Remo was slouched low in his seat and hiding behind an in-flight magazine. "Just sit down," he implored, his voice a hoarse whisper.

Turning once more to the now very angry crowd, Chiun declared, "My son has told me to inform you that a kennel is not a buffet."

As the murmurs rose, loud and rancorous, the Master of Sinanju leaned over and slapped Remo on the knee. "Move your fat white feet," he commanded.

Scurrying over his pupil, he settled into the seat above the left wing.

"Thanks for making me part of the floor show," Remo growled.

The flight attendants had been either at the door or in the galley until now and had thus missed the action. Remo was grateful when the preflight activity took the focus away from him and the Master of Sinanju.

Once they were in the air, a friendly flight attendant came up the aisle. Since it was the Halloween season, she offered passengers a bowl filled to the brim with orange-and-yellow candy corn. Remo was surprised when the Master of Sinanju took two big handfuls. He was less surprised when the old Korean spent the rest of the flight pegging them at the heads of unsuspecting Vietnamese passengers.

When they landed in Orlando, those Asians unfortunate enough to have gotten on this flight rushed the exits, rubbing heads and crushing candy corn beneath their heels.

A shudder ran through the bottleneck at the door when Chiun and Remo approached. With fearful glances the crowd parted, hands firmly clasped to stinging scalps.

Chiun waded through the throng. "My son the unpatriotic American might not respect his culture," he sniffed as he passed, "but you may not have any of *my* Yankee Poodle Pie."

Remo was so grateful to finally be off the plane he kept his head down and his mouth screwed shut.

In the terminal they passed a busy bookstore. "Just a sec," Remo said to Chiun before ducking inside.

He emerged two minutes later with a fresh stack of newspapers. As they walked, Remo slipped a pair of sewing scissors he'd just bought into his pocket. Though curious, Chiun refrained from comment as the two men made their way to the car rental.

In the parking lot Remo dumped the papers into the back seat of their rental.

According to Smith, the first spider sighting had

taken place in the small town of Yuletide, twenty miles east of Orlando. Remo knew he should be worried when he saw the sign that welcomed tourists into town. On it, a pair of snowmen waved to passing cars. The border of the sign was decorated with plastic reindeer antlers.

Even though Halloween was less than a week away, there wasn't a pumpkin or ghost to be seen in town. The houses of Yuletide were hung with flashing red-and-green lights. Plastic Santas sat on lush green lawns.

"Why do I suddenly feel like Jack Skellington?" Remo asked as he eyed the Christmas decorations.

In the passenger side of the car, the Master of Sinanju studied the festive landscape through suspicious slits.

"Have you people extended the season devoted to that busybody carpenter?" the old man asked.

"Not that I know of," Remo said. "Christmas season starts in August at the mall, but it usually doesn't spill out onto front lawns until November. They must take the Yuletide name seriously."

He parked the car and the two of them struck off on foot. As they walked, they saw parking meters shaped like candy canes and park benches that looked like holly-covered yule logs.

"No wonder the suicide rate goes up during the holidays," Remo said as they passed a papier-mâché igloo. Around it, a family of painted penguins in scarfs and stocking hats were arranged in a frozen snowball fight.

The place they were looking for was on the corner.

Other than a faded paper reindeer taped to the window, Santa's Package Store looked like a typical liquor store. The bell over the door tinkled as Remo and Chiun entered.

The grubby proprietor was sitting behind the grimy counter. He looked up sharply at the door. His tense face relaxed when he saw the two men who had just come inside.

"FBI," Remo announced. Walking to the counter, he offered the man his fake ID. "We're looking into last week's robbery."

The liquor store owner looked from Remo to Chiun. "Why's the FBI care?" he asked suspiciously. "Local cops think I'm crazy."

"From what I've seen of this town, you all got crack pipes as stocking stuffers," Remo said. "So what's the story?"

The man rubbed the beard stubble on his chin. "You better be on the level," he warned. "Now that there's been other cases, I'm getting calls to do all kinds of TV." He leaned forward on his stool. "It was last Friday night," he began. "Almost closing time. I was reading right here when I heard the bell over the door. When I looked up, I saw *it.*"

"The spider," Remo said, his voice flat.

"Yeah," said the shopkeeper. He shuddered at the memory. "Thing was huge. Big as the doorway. It came crawling across the floor to the counter. I fell off my stool I was so scared. I'm lying back here on the floor when it reaches around with these big furry black legs and rips the cash drawer out of the register. By the time I got back up, it was gone."

Remo pointed to a security camera that was mounted high on the wall behind the counter. "What about that?"

"That's the weird part," the man explained. "After it took the cash drawer, it reached up and touched the camera. I don't know what it did, but when I checked the tape, there wasn't anything on it. It was all blank. Like it had been magnetized or something."

The store owner didn't see the deeply dubious expression on Remo's face.

Chiun had wandered over to the end of the nearest aisle. The old man was squatting next to an end-cap display that was piled high with cases of beer.

"What's with him?" the liquor store owner asked.

"He's a special consultant," Remo said. "The Bureau brings him in for the big stuff. Alien abductions, spider attacks, spontaneous telephone combustions."

The man was studying Chiun. "Just like the 'C-Files,'" he grunted. "I like that show."

"Not me," Remo said. The Master of Sinanju beckoned him with a long fingernail. "They've been stealing plots from us for years and we haven't seen dime one." He left the store owner, crossing over to Chiun.

"What have you got, Little Father?"

"There," the old Korean said, pointing to the floor.

The beer cases were stacked on a low wooden palette. Following the Master of Sinanju's unfurled finger, Remo saw something small and black peeking out from between the dirty slats. It was as big around as a quarter and rested on an inch-thick pile of dust.

Stooping, Remo picked up the object, holding it between thumb and forefinger. By the look of it, it had been chipped off something larger. The edges were jagged.

When he ran a finger across the dull black surface, Remo's face registered surprise. "What the hell?" Puzzled, he handed the fragment to Chiun.

When the old man touched the metal, he frowned.

"There is no friction," the Master of Sinanju said.

Remo nodded. He had barely felt the fragment. It was as if his finger was gliding over nothing at all.

"You think it's spider spoor?" Remo asked.

"I do not know what it is." Chiun's weathered face was troubled. "Nor do I find comfort in the unknown."

The fragment had come from somewhere. And whatever it was, neither of them had encountered it before.

"Me, either," Remo said as he took the strange piece of metal back from Chiun. "I'll send it up to Smitty. Maybe he can figure out what it is."

He slipped the fragment into his pocket.

He took a final look around the dingy store. Something had happened here. He still doubted the owner's story, but the man seemed sure of what he was saying. And the metal fragment only added to the larger mystery.

When they left Santa's Package Store a moment later, Remo's face was troubled.

10

"I was astonished at how awful it was. I mean, it really was that bad. Shockingly so."

Every word was a knife in Duncan Allen's heart. But in spite of the inhuman callousness of his critic, he had no choice but to sit there and take it. As he fidgeted in the overstuffed chair in the dusty old living room in Bangor, Maine, he gave a sickly, lopsided smile to the evil little man who stood in judgment above him.

"I bought it assuming you'd have improved over the years. You know, since back when I bought those first five manuscripts from you. But I wish I'd looked at it sooner. I'll do my best, but I don't know if it's salvageable at all. Of course, you won't be getting a bonus for this shit."

And at this, Stewart McQueen laughed. It was a mirthless laugh that was all smarmy condescension.

That his laugh would be devoid of joviality wasn't a surprise. McQueen was the most humorless human being Duncan Allen had ever met. As an individual far superior to all things that walked, crawled or flew, Stewart McQueen didn't have time for a sense of humor. The world-famous novelist was too busy standing astride the very peak of a fiction writer's Mount Olympus, glaring down contemptuously at the pathetic mortals who scurried upon the Earth below.

"You haven't learned a thing since you started writing for me," McQueen said. He was a slight man with a too perfect beard. When he spoke, his tongue had a hard time negotiating around his protruding rabbit's teeth.

"But you're still buying my next book?" Allen asked, trying to keep the desperate pleading from his voice. "After the other two books you bought, you promised you'd take *Boiling Point* to the publisher for me."

Another sneering laugh. "That's not gonna happen now," Stewart McQueen said dismissively.

And that was that. With that one phrase, Duncan Allen felt the world collapse beneath his worn-out, three-year-old sneakers. Mind whirling, he tumbled into the dark abyss.

After that McQueen's cruel words—and there were a lot of them—were nothing more than white noise.

The logical part of Duncan's mind knew that McQueen could be wrong. After all, others had said he had talent. But McQueen was the only *professional* writer he knew. Yes, he was an insufferable little prick with a Napoleon complex so grand that it had driven away everyone save the two cats who shared his lonely Maine mansion. But if he said someone had no talent, well, maybe they didn't.

When McQueen eventually grew tired of the nasal drone of his own voice, he ushered a shell-shocked Duncan Allen to the front door. So dazed was Duncan that he had forgotten even to blink. His eyes were wide and dry as McQueen coaxed him out onto the broad front porch.

"If writing's what you want to do with your life, you've got to start taking it more seriously," McQueen instructed. With a superior smirk he slammed the door on the mute and defeated young writer.

Alone in his foyer, Stewart McQueen quickly snapped out the light and drew back the curtains an inch. He put a delighted eye up to the grimy window-pane.

He had shut off the porch light. In the long shadows of late afternoon, Duncan Allen just stood there for an agonizingly long time. Shoulders hunched, back to the door. Eventually, he found his feet, trudging down the creaky front steps. The winding walk led him to the high wrought-iron gate. The last McQueen saw of him, the young man was walking like a zombie down the dusty sidewalk.

As he watched the hunching figure he had done his best to destroy disappear from sight, Stewart McQueen laughed out loud. He was still laughing when he dropped the curtain.

This was one of the few joys in his miserable life: finding someone young, talented and struggling. And then beating the hell out of their self-esteem. Usually he hit so hard they never, *ever* recovered.

Sniffling, laughing, his big eyes watering, Stewart turned back for his living room.

His weight was wrong. He knew it the instant his knee seized up.

The sudden stiffness in his leg caused the laughter to die in his throat.

Sucking in a lungful of air, McQueen braced himself against the foyer wall, clasping a hand to his knee.

When the pain washed over him, it came in splendid starbursts. He gasped as the sharp ache clutched every bone in his leg like a squeezing fist.

And, as quickly as it came, it fled.

Quickly, before it could return, he limped beyond the living room and into his shadowy study, dropping roughly into an overstuffed easy chair.

Dust rose into the musty air.

He had hoped his meeting with Duncan Allen would be the balm he was looking for. The ego boost he got from making others feel like talentless bugs used to sustain him for hours. *Days* if he was really on his game, as he had been this day. But thanks to the leg, he was no longer feeling it.

"Dammit," he grunted.

This should have been perfect. After he'd bought the young man's last two books, McQueen had made a load of promises to the struggling writer. During the previous two and a half hours he had broken every single one of them.

For a creature of pure malice like Stewart Mc-

Queen, it should have been a thing of lasting beauty. As the icing on the cake, there actually was a publisher out there who might be interested in Duncan Allen's work. But McQueen had quit working for them eight months before and, in spite of yet another promise, had never bothered to mention it to Allen until this day. He had left his young ghostwriter dangling in the wind for almost a year without so much as a phone call.

There was no doubt that this was Stewart McQueen's best work so far. Yet, thanks to the intermittent, blinding pain in his knee, he couldn't even enjoy it.

It was coming again.

Hauling his leg onto an ottoman, McQueen clasped both hands tightly around it, encircling the entire knee.

He rode the wave of pain like a rodeo rider. When it was done a minute later, McQueen was covered with sweat. Exhausted from the pain, he collapsed back into his chair.

Though it was old by now, he feared he would never get used to the pain. It had been like this for the past two years. Ever since that fateful summer afternoon.

The accident had made national headlines. America's most famous horror novelist struck by a hit-and-run driver.

McQueen was out for a walk on a lonely country

road. He never dreamed that a simple stroll to the mailbox would almost prove fatal.

The car had come out of nowhere. Instead of paying attention to where he was going, the careless driver had been yelling on his cell phone while simultaneously swatting his three rottweilers in the back seat with a rolled-up newspaper. When car met novelist, the writer lost.

McQueen was thrown thirty feet in the air, slamming to the pavement with bone-crushing force. The next year was a nightmare of painful surgeries and grueling therapy.

At first, revenge had kept him going. But after the driver was apprehended, McQueen was advised by his agent and manager to do his best to preserve his public image as a nice guy. So rather than watch gleefully as a hired hit man chopped the careless motorist to bits with a hatchet, McQueen was forced to settle for a revoked driver's license.

It was a hollow victory.

Gripping his knee, McQueen struggled to his feet. Breathing deeply a few times, he tested the leg.

It felt solid.

He put his whole weight on it. The knee didn't buckle.

Exhaling, McQueen limped into the kitchen. A collection of stone gargoyles clustered around the cold fireplace watched in silence as he hobbled from sight. He reappeared a moment later, a can of Fresca clutched in his hand. Walking with more confidence, he returned to his favorite chair.

He spent most of his time here these days. Sitting.

There was a time when Stewart McQueen didn't have an idle moment. It was well-known that he wrote every day of the year with the exception of Christmas and his birthday. He was so prolific that he sometimes worried that he was watering down the market by competing with his own books.

But the most productive toboggan ride in the history of popular fiction had ended at the bumper of a speeding Chevy Blazer. Press releases had him working on a book from his hospital bed. They were false.

His computer sat in the corner of his study, silent and dark. He didn't even bother turning it on anymore. What was the point?

He would have thought it impossible.

McQueen slugged at his drink, his thoughts on Duncan Allen.

The kid was talented. Better than him in many ways.

McQueen periodically hired ghostwriters like Allen to do work for him here and there. While prolific, he occasionally found himself with a backlog of work. Usually it was when he was struggling to adapt one of his novels to screenplay form. Kids like Duncan Allen would do the bulk of the work for a flat fee. Afterward McQueen would go over their work, remaking it in the unmistakable Stewart McQueen style.

Other successful writers enjoyed the thrill of helping out an up-and-comer. Usually because it helped them to remember what it was like when they were starting out. McQueen liked to keep them around as personal punching bags.

Through the years there had been several others like Allen. After he recovered from this devastating meeting—*if* he recovered—Duncan Allen would eventually want what they all wanted. To become a big enough success to rub it in McQueen's ferret face. But that wasn't possible for one simple reason: there was no one bigger than Stewart McQueen.

Until lately McQueen had always reveled in the fact that none of his protégés would ever surpass him. But thanks to a creative knot in his brain, he was no longer sure.

"*Block,* Bernie!" he had recently snapped at his New York agent. "I've got writer's block! I used to be able to pull an eight-hundred-page book out of my ass every two weeks. Now I'm lucky if I can write my return address on the gas bill."

"You can't be blocked," his agent had insisted. "You're Stewart McQueen. You've got whole sections of bookstores devoted to your work. You even used to have to write under pseudonyms so you wouldn't water down the market on your own stuff."

"I *know* that," McQueen had snarled. "Don't you think I *know* that? But that doesn't change the fact that I haven't been able to write a goddamn thing since the accident."

His agent considered for a long moment, studying

the dusty corners of the living room in McQueen's creepy Maine mansion. "How about the devil?" he asked abruptly. "You could do something with the devil. You know, spooky."

"Like what?" McQueen asked sarcastically.

"Oh, I don't know. Maybe—maybe he could come to this small New England town, see? Like yours. Only the people there don't know he's the devil at first, even though they should because of all the dead dolphins on the shore."

"Dolphins?"

"Yeah. They've all been beaching themselves, see? And they have this mark on them. It's 666. Only no one knows that it's the mark of the devil, see, because it's in a different kind of numbering system like from a long time ago. Like ancient Egyptian or something. Only the sheriff in the town figures it out, because his daughter's back from college and she's studying ancient Egyptian numbers in school and she leaves her book open on the table. Oh, and his wife is dead, but she might not be because she disappeared under mysterious circumstances that still haunt the sheriff to this day, and before she vanished she had an affair with the devil and his daughter might be the devil's own actual kid. Or maybe his son is, and that's why he's hanging around with these weird kids who dress all in black." His agent seemed pleased with the strength of his own story. "That's good," he said. "Why don't you do something like that?"

McQueen gave him a withering glare. "A couple of reasons. First off, it's crap."

"Oh," his agent said, disappointed. "Really?"

"Second," McQueen continued, "it's been done a million times before. Mostly by me."

"Yes, but with dolphins?" his agent questioned.

McQueen didn't even bother to reply. He merely got up and limped from the room.

He was slouched for ten minutes in his favorite chair in his study when his agent stuck his head around the door.

"I'll call you," Bernie promised. "In the meantime do me a favor. Think devil dolphins."

McQueen said nothing.

True to his word, Bernie tried to call. On a number of occasions and for many weeks. McQueen let the machine answer. Eventually, Bernie stopped trying.

Deadlines came and went. Stewart McQueen no longer cared. He simply sat in his study, staring at the bookshelves that lined all four walls.

The broad shelves rose from floor to ceiling. All were packed with novels he had written in his thirty-year career. And, if his current streak continued, they would never be joined by another Stewart McQueen novel.

McQueen sat his Fresca can on an end table. With a heavy sigh he picked up the TV remote control. When he flicked it on, eerie shadows from the television twirled in the dark corners of the big room.

Since it was the Halloween season, he wasn't surprised to find three movies based on his books playing on various cable stations. Scowling in the bristles of his tidy little beard, he switched over to the news.

An anchorman who looked as if he'd graduated journalism school with a major in TelePrompTer and a minor in mousse was grinning at his plastic-haired coanchor. The woman looked as if she'd come to the anchor desk straight from the top of a cheerleader pyramid.

"...and here's a spooky item out of Florida," the male anchor was saying. "Maura?"

"That's right, Brad," the woman said. "It seems Halloween has come a week early this year, at least for some residents of Florida. But this is no trick-or-treating matter. The goblin who's showing up on certain doorsteps in the Sunshine State is looking for more than just candy."

McQueen was ready to change the channel back to one of his movies when the program shifted to a reporter on the scene in Florida. The somber-voiced man was holding out a piece of paper on which was sketched a spider.

"This is not a young child in a Pokémon costume, Maura and Brad," the field reporter said seriously "This is a drawing made from eyewitnesses of the creature that has struck fear into the hearts of many, and has caused Halloween festivities to be canceled in more than a dozen central Florida communities."

McQueen eased up more straightly in his chair.

As the story unfolded, he couldn't believe his ears.

Apparently, people were saying that a monster was running around loose in Florida, and no one had bothered to tell Stewart McQueen about it.

With a sudden burst of energy, McQueen pushed himself out of his chair. He quickly hobbled over to a long table near his desk.

For the past few weeks he had piled the newspapers there as they arrived. He just didn't have the energy to go through them. Sitting, he quickly thumbed through the stack of papers. He found a dozen small stories about the strange events in Florida.

It was true. There was *something* down there.

Stewart McQueen was beginning to get an old tingle in his gut. It was a feeling he hadn't experienced since before the accident.

He pushed himself cautiously to his feet. Head upturned like a rubbernecking tourist, he scanned the bookshelves all around. He went from high up in the right-hand corner behind his desk, where his earliest books were shelved, all the way down to the baseboard near the door, where his most-recent novels sat like patient little soldiers.

All his books. All the words contained between their covers had been squeezed from his brain.

Stewart McQueen smiled at his old friends.

"Make room, boys," he announced. "You're about to get some company."

Turning carefully so as not to tweak his injured leg, the most famous horror novelist ever to put pen to paper hobbled rapidly out of his study.

11

"There is no such thing as the bogeyman," Martin Riley insisted.

"But Sherry says there is," Janey Riley argued.

Martin's five-year-old daughter nodded with certainty as she scooped up a heaping spoonful of Cap'n Crunch.

"Sherry's wrong, hon," Martin said. He was late leaving and didn't need this as he wolfed down his oatmeal.

Janey wasn't convinced by her father's words. "I don't know. I'll have to check with Sherry." She didn't even look at Martin as she spoke. Her little mind was already made up.

He knew what would happen now. Thanks to that know-it-all in his daughter's play group, Martin would have to spend another evening crawling around on Janey's bedroom floor, checking under bed and behind bureau. The nightly bedtime ritual was only getting worse as Halloween approached.

"Listen, honey," he said, getting up from the breakfast table, "I swear to you, no matter what Sherry says, there is no such thing as the bogeyman."

"You shouldn't swear, Daddy," Janey said as he kissed her on the top of the head.

Dumping his bowl in the sink, he gave his wife a quick peck on the cheek. She was busy emptying the dishwasher.

"*You* can look under her bed tonight," he said as he turned for the door.

"She won't let me do it," Sue Riley replied as she stacked dinner plates into the cupboard.

"Great," Martin muttered. "Like my knees aren't bad enough as it is. I'm late. See you tonight."

If he had known it would be the last time he would ever see them, he might have taken one last look on his way out the kitchen door.

For once traffic was with him as he sped to work. Martin arrived with five minutes to spare. He had barely driven onto the lot before he was driving back out, this time sitting behind the wheel of a SecureCo armored car.

His partner today was Chuck Kaufman. The other man sat in the passenger seat, a worn paperback clutched in his bouncing hands.

The book was four inches thick. It looked more like a dictionary than a novel. Martin noted the name Stewart McQueen printed in large silver letters across the back cover. The author's name was bigger than the title. A pair of glowing demonic eyes stared out from the black background.

"Why do you read that junk?" Riley asked as he drove.

Chuck Kaufman didn't look up. "It's not junk," he insisted as he read. "Besides, you've never read McQueen."

"He wrote *Caterpillar*," Martin said. "A book about a haunted bulldozer that's always driving over everybody. It's people like McQueen who make people like me crawl around on the floor every night looking for the damn bogeyman."

Chuck was no longer listening. Engrossed in his book, he continued reading as Martin drove.

Their first stop was the Orlando Greater Credit Union. Climbing down from the cab, Martin and Chuck rounded to the back of the armored car.

Following standard security procedures, the two men outside and the third man inside the truck used keys and codes to open the back. The bolt clicked and the door opened.

Some of the bags piled in the back were white. Most had taken on tinges of gray. The thousands of dollars they hauled daily quickly discolored the heavy money sacks.

Two dirty gray bags were brought into the bank. They retrieved ten more. In all, it took barely eight minutes before they were back out on the street and on to the next bank.

The rest of the morning went by just as quickly. It was a little past noon, and Martin had begun thinking about the twenty-minute nightly ritual of crawling around Janey's closet and checking under her mattress when something caught his eye.

As he sped down the highway, Martin saw a van in his side mirror.

It looked ordinary enough. Gleaming black paint shone bright in the white Florida sunlight. As it sped up, Martin realized he couldn't see the driver. The windshield was darkly tinted.

The van was driving up in the third lane. Fast.

Martin flicked his attention back to the road ahead.

When he looked into the mirror a few seconds later, the van had skipped over, pulling into the lane adjacent to Martin's. It continued to accelerate steadily.

Some low instinct clicked in the chest of Martin Riley.

"Something's happening," he said cautiously.

"Huh?" Chuck asked. His nose was still buried deep in his book.

The black van pulled abreast the SecureCo truck.

Though the side windows were tinted, too, the angled sunlight shone bright enough for Martin to make out the gloomy interior of the speeding vehicle.

There was no one at the wheel.

Stunned, Martin opened his mouth to speak. The instant he did, the words froze in his throat.

Before his eyes the smooth black side panel of the van began to bulge. It was as if something from within were exerting enormous pressure against the vehicle's metal shell. The bubble swelled like a cancerous growth, extending out toward the side of the armored truck.

And as Martin watched, dumbstruck, a nub appeared in the side of the massive bulge. With impossible speed, it sprouted out into a slender black leg.

It was joined by another, then another.

The eight legs grew with time-lapse rapidity. As soon as they were fully formed, the body popped free of the metal from which it had been born. As it clung to the side of the van, the huge spider legs twitched and stretched, seeming to test their own strength.

Another bulge formed at the top of the round body. This one formed not a leg, but a compact oval.

Slowly, the fat nub at the end of the thorax turned to the armored car. And for Martin Riley, stunned amazement turned to abject horror.

It was a face. Or *half* a face. One eye, a mouth, a nose. Even indentations where the ears should be.

The thing that looked at him from out of that hideous body wore the head of a human being. And its single, soulless eye was staring directly at Martin Riley.

"Sweet Jesus," Martin breathed.

"What?" Chuck Kaufman complained. He was straining across the driver's seat to see what Martin was staring at.

"The thing!" Martin yelled, his head snapping around. "That thing from the paper! It's out there!"

A squeal of tires.

Martin spun back around.

The van was spinning out of control. Dropping back into two lanes of oncoming traffic. It hit the jersey barrier, flipping onto its side, bouncing back over. Sparks flew as it careered into a speeding station wagon. A minivan struck from the other lane, spiraling nose to tail.

Tires screeched as the pileup began.

The SecureCo truck sped away from the crash.

Martin was blinking fear as he studied the mirror.

Cars crashing. Smoke.

All rapidly shrinking in the distance.

No sign of the spider.

A flash of something large in the side mirror. Skittering along the drab green shell of the armored truck.

Martin's stomach melted when he saw the big black legs crawling quickly around the rear, out of sight.

"What the hell just happened back there?" Chuck was asking as he glanced at his own side mirror. His eyes grew wide. "My God!" he breathed.

A tractor trailer had just raced around a distant curve toward the pileup. Too late to stop.

The air horn bellowed as smoke poured from locked tires. Jackknifing, the trailer whipped around, flipping up onto the pile of stacked cars.

The explosion was massive and instantaneous. A plume of orange streaked with curls of angry black erupted high into the clear blue Florida sky. Speeding from the scene, the armored car rattled. With a sinking feeling, Martin knew it had nothing to do with the explosion.

He plowed on.

"Holy shit, Riley," Chuck breathed. His eyes were stunned as he spun back around. "We have to stop!"

Martin was still hunched over the steering wheel, sweat beading on his forehead. Not only did he not slow down, his foot pressed harder on the accelerator.

"Get out your gun," Martin ordered.

"What? Riley, we have to—"

"Get out your gun!" Martin screamed. One hand on the wheel, he wrenched his automatic from his hip holster.

His urgency was a spark that hopped between them. Confused, Chuck pulled out his own gun.

The truck rattled again.

This time there had been no explosion to mask it. The pileup had already vanished behind them.

Chuck glanced at Martin. "What is it?" he asked, realizing now that something was terribly wrong.

A long, torturous shriek of metal erupted from the rear of the truck. It was followed by the sound of gunfire.

The fear now large on his face, Chuck scampered to his knees, sliding open the panel between cab and back.

When he peered through the bulletproof Plexiglas, the shocked gasp that rose from deep in his belly struck a note of raw primal fear.

Something huge scampered freely around the interior of the truck. Crooked legs stabbed like black elbows from a rounded body. And in two of those legs was the third member of their team.

As Chuck watched, the spider lifted the man high in the air, one leg ensnaring his head, the other his chest. When the spider tugged, head went one way, body the other.

Beyond the creature, the twisted door gaped onto the vacant highway. The spider flung the bloody body parts out onto the racing tar.

Behind the steering wheel, Martin saw the decapitated corpse bounce away behind them.

"What do we do?" Chuck begged. He was still staring through the narrow sliver of Plexiglas.

The spider seemed to zero in on his voice. The head with its one ghastly eye turned his way.

"Kill it!" Martin yelled.

As soon as he spoke he heard a sharp crack.

Twisting in his seat, he found that the bulletproof panel had been shattered. Through it, a single thin leg jutted in from the rear of the armored car.

The leg had impaled Chuck Kaufman through the eye, burrowing deep into brain.

Chuck just hung there, slack-jawed. Blood thinned with ocular fluid streamed down his cheek.

And as Martin watched, numb, the first inquisitive tip of the long black leg appeared from Chuck's dead ear.

Martin slammed on the brakes.

The speeding armored car jumped to one side, skipping down the jersey barrier. It screeched and sparked and dug a furrow half a mile long before it finally came to a stop.

Before it had even stopped completely, Martin had popped the door. He fell out of the cab, slamming onto the concrete barrier that divided the two opposite highway lanes.

The fall broke two bones in his arms. Despite the pain, he managed to get up and run...directly into the path of oncoming traffic.

Fortunately for Martin Riley, he didn't feel the impact of the car that struck him. There was a numbness. A sense of lifting, of movement. Then nothing at all.

The force threw Martin back against the concrete barrier over which he'd dropped a moment before.

Even as Martin's lifeless body collapsed to the tar, the concrete block against which he'd been thrown shuddered.

On the other side of the barrier, the SecureCo truck pulled back onto the empty highway.

The gouges in its side were gone. As it sped away, the rear door that had been wrenched apart with inhuman force was once more intact.

It raced quietly away from Martin Riley, who in the last minutes before his untimely death finally realized that his daughter's friend had been right all along.

The bogeyman was real.

12

When Remo and Chiun returned to their rental car after leaving Santa's Package Store, Remo suddenly noticed the newspapers he'd left in the back.

"Oops, I forgot," he said. "As long as we've got mail to send, might as well kill two birds with one stone."

Grabbing up the pile, he quickly skipped through them. With the sewing-kit scissors he'd bought he snipped a few articles. He stuffed the rest of the newspapers in a rubbish barrel at the side of the road.

He returned to the car, placing the articles on the back seat. From the passenger side the Master of Sinanju stared at him in suspicion as he pulled out into the thin traffic.

"You are up to something," Chiun observed.

"Yep," Remo replied. "I'm up to twenty-seven in a twenty-five zone. Lemme know if you see a cruiser. I hear these Florida cops are a real pain in the ass."

Chiun's frown only deepened when he saw Remo's thinly satisfied smile. As they drove, the old Korean tried to sneak a glimpse at the clippings.

Reaching over the seat, Remo snatched up the articles, stuffing them in his pocket.

"This is my hobby, not yours," he warned. "If you want a peek, maybe you could tell me what was so important for you to think about that you couldn't talk to me for a week."

Chiun's face was bland. "I was thinking that you were an idiot," he replied.

"You've thought that for years," Remo pointed out.

"Yes, but I had never devoted the time necessary to delve into the many-layered depths of your idiocy. I was astonished, Remo, to find that in one week I only plumbed the surface. I fear that it is a project that will consume much more than the meager days that remain to me."

"I'll hire a biographer," Remo droned. "And just for the record I don't believe you, and if you keep being nasty I'm never gonna tell you what I'm doing. So there."

"Why should I care what moronic things you do to waste your stupid time?" the old man sniffed. "And perhaps if you kept your dull round eyes on the road and your paws on the wheel you would notice when we are being followed."

Remo had noticed the black van, too.

It had pulled away from the curb with them, trailing them from the liquor store. Remo decided to test to make sure. He slowed. The black van with the tinted windows slowed. He accelerated. The pursuing van kept pace.

"Whoever's driving isn't that inventive," Remo commented. "You'd at least think he'd *pretend* to not be attached to my bumper."

They were passing an office-supply store that advertised a FedEx pickup. Pulling into the parking lot, he steered around the main building.

The van followed close behind.

Cutting alongside the buildings, Remo stopped in the empty back lot. A storage trailer was backed up to the loading dock. Nearby, trash littered the ground around a green Dumpster. Graffiti adorned the store's rear wall.

Once it cleared the side of the building, the black van picked up speed. It squealed to a stop just as Remo and Chiun were climbing from their car.

Side panel and rear doors sprang open.

When the six men emerged from the dark recesses of the van, it was all Remo could do to keep from laughing out loud.

The men looked like extras from a low budget sci-fi movie. All were dressed in silvery white jumpsuits. Matching gauntlets and boots covered hands and feet.

From big plastic holsters that were slung low over their waists, the men removed chintzy weapons that could have been manufactured on a Hollywood back lot. The ray guns were covered with blinking plastic knobs and gold stripes. The men aimed the funnel-shaped ends at Remo and Chiun.

"Halt!" one of the men commanded. His jumpsuit extended up around his head, forming a silvery skull-cap through which peeked his face. Like his companions, a slender microphone stretched out in front of his mouth.

"I wish this dingwipple town would make up its mind," Remo complained to the Master of Sinanju. "Is it trick or treat or deck the halls?"

"Do not ask me," Chiun replied. "I recognize none of this nation's heathen seasons." His narrowed eyes were focused on the ray guns.

Remo had noticed the same thing that had caught the eye of the Master of Sinanju. The blunt end of a very real .45 stuck menacingly from the open end of each plastic gun.

"What were you doing at the liquor store?" the leader asked. A badge on his chest identified him as Major Healy.

"Are you kidding?" Remo asked, his tone flat. "Have you looked around town? With all this Christmas cheer up the yin-yang, drunk's the only way to get through the day."

"Negative," Major Healy said, shaking his head. "That's a nonresponsive answer." His ray gun rose higher. "*Why* were you there?" he pressed.

Remo looked from gun to the major. Finally, he turned his attention away from the gunman completely.

"We need to save one, Little Father," Remo cautioned the Master of Sinanju.

"Why?" Chiun asked disdainfully. "America is not running low on fools."

"They might know something," Remo insisted. "And we've been crossing our wires on this lately. So just make sure you let me save one of them, all right?"

"You may do what you wish with yours," Chiun sniffed. "Just keep them away from mine."

As they argued, Major Healy's head bounced back and forth between them. He leaned back when he found Remo's extended finger pointing an inch away from his face.

"Just so we're clear on this, I'm saving Marvin the Martian here," Remo warned the Master of Sinanju. "Don't kill the one with the really stupid look on his face, okay?"

"I will do my best not to confuse him with you," Chiun said. "However, I make no promises."

"What do you mean, don't kill me?" Major Healy said, sneering. "In case you didn't notice, *I'm* the one with the weapon."

"Oh, yeah," Remo said. "Yoink."

All at once the major felt a lightness to his gloved hand. When he looked down, he found that his gauntlet was empty. More horrifying, when he glanced back up, he found where the handgun had gone.

Remo held the gun in both hands. "Haven't you heard toy weapons promote real violence?" he admonished.

As he spoke, he squeezed. The plastic that encased

the handgun turned brittle and cracked. Underneath, the very real metal gun seemed to grow rubbery. With a groan of metal Remo twisted the gun until barrel kissed stock. When he was through, he tossed the horseshoe shape over his shoulder. The gun landed in the overflowing Dumpster on a pile of cardboard boxes.

"Swish," Remo Williams said, smiling.

A shocked expression blossomed on Major Healy's face. He fell back, bumping hard into the side of the black van.

"They are hostile!" he yelled. "Enforce directive two and eradicate the enemy!"

The other five men were arranged in a fanning arc. At the shouted order, the group tightened around Remo and Chiun. Gloved fingers clenched firmly on triggers.

The man nearest Remo almost fired. The instant before he did, he saw a flash of movement. The world became a blur.

Remo grabbed the gunman by the collar of his silver space suit. The man went from zero to sixty in half a heartbeat. So abruptly was he launched that the g-force pulled back his face into a smiling grimace as he screamed through air.

"To infinity and beyond!" Remo exclaimed as he swung the man straight into the side of the van. Van went bong. Head went splat.

"Pay attention," Chiun warned. "You will not lay blame at my sandals if the wrong fool turns up dead."

As he spoke, the old Korean's hands flashed out, long nails perforating the belly of the man nearest him. So fast and precise did they move that not a mark or tear appeared in the space suit. The man realized something was wrong only when he felt his organs grow heavy inside his suit. With an audible slurp, organs slipped from the razor slit Chiun had sliced in the man's abdomen. Like a frog negotiating its way through a snake, the wet bag of organs slithered into the thighs of his trousers. By the time the blood began to bubble out the tops of his boots, the man had already pitched forward onto the ground.

Remo was inserting the broad plastic end of a ray gun into another man's mouth. "Anyone wanna tell me who they work for?" he called to the others.

"Don't tell him anything!" the major commanded, cowering near the van. "We've got the prime directive to uphold."

"Suit yourself," Remo said, slapping the gun butt. The weapon formed a new holster in the gunman's cerebellum.

There were only two men left. Quaking in his space boots at the side of the van, Major Healy suddenly realized which way the solar wind was blowing.

"We're compromised!" he yelled, diving into the back of the van. "Initiate self-destruct!" Frantic hands rolled the side panel door shut.

Remo and Chiun had taken hold of the two remaining men. Human cargo in hand, Remo windmilled right, Chiun, left. When they let go, the men whirled like loosed tops. Twin spinning blurs, the two men twirled straight into each other, bodies meeting with a bone-shattering crunch. They struck with such force that their bodies fused into a single fleshy unit. An undertaker would need an electric carving knife to cut the men apart.

Remo spun away as the silver-wrapped bundle of arms and legs collapsed to the ground.

The van door through which Major Healy had disappeared remained closed. The cab was empty, the engine silent. As he approached the side door, Remo heard the sound of knees scuffing across the floor.

"Ground control to Major Asshole," Remo called, reaching for the silver handle. As he did so, he heard a small click from the interior. A roar flooded in behind it.

A few yards away the Master of Sinanju's weathered face flashed sudden alarm.

"Remo!" Chiun shouted. Even as he yelled, his kimono skirts were billowing as the old man raced for cover.

For Remo, it was already too late. The explosion came too fast for him to flee.

The van erupted in a ball of flame. And as the panels blasted apart with horrifying force, Remo felt his body being thrown back by the leading edge of the mighty shock wave.

13

There wasn't time to dive for cover. No time to outrun the blast that had erupted from the van's interior.

Remo didn't even try to fight it. There was no point. It would be impossible to resist a force so powerful.

When the hot leading wave pummeled his chest, he allowed himself to be flung backward, joining with the force of the fiery, violent surge of energy.

All around him swarmed deadly daggers of hot twisted metal. The remnants of the van moved with him, keeping pace. For what he had to do Remo knew there was no margin for error. He would either survive or he'd be shredded to hamburger by the shards of flying metal.

As he soared through the air, fingers of flame raced out after him, singing the hair on his bare forearms. No matter. The fire was irrelevant. The flames would recede before they caused any real damage.

The roof of his rental car flew beneath him. As it whipped by, Remo was already stretching out the toe of one loafer. He caught the upper door frame of the car.

Flex, push.

His speed increased. Even as the force of the explosion began to die he continued to accelerate.

The Dumpster flew up. Remo caught the lip with one extended hand, latching on tight. Up and over, he whipped behind the safety of the waste receptacle, his soles brushing lightly to the trash-covered ground.

Metal fragments pounded the far side of the Dumpster.

Beside him crouched a familiar wizened figure.

"What, Remo, did you learn from the one you saved for questioning?" the Master of Sinanju asked blandly.

Remo's face was sour. "From now on I'm saving a spare," he groused.

The shock wave had passed. By the time Remo and Chiun stood, the explosion had rattled off into the woods behind the building.

The black van was little more than a burning skeleton of a frame on four charred wheels. The cooked remains of Major Healy jutted from his smoking silver space boots.

"Well don't that just beat all," Remo griped as Major Healy's burned body sizzled and spit.

Near the remnants of the van lay the bodies of the other five, their space suits now streaked in black.

Chiun was already heading for their own car. Reluctantly, Remo followed.

Their own vehicle was relatively undamaged. Most

of Chiun's side had been raked and blackened from the blast, but it was still driveable.

When Remo drove around the building no one seemed interested in the muffled explosion that had just issued from the far side.

"We're lucky this is Florida," he said. "They must've thought someone's still blew up."

He decided to risk mailing the piece of metal they'd found at the liquor store. Parking quickly, he raced inside the office-supply store. Buying three envelopes, he stuck the shard of strange black metal in one. He quickly dashed off a note to Mark Howard on another before filling it with the newspaper clippings. He stuffed everything inside the third, larger envelope, addressed the whole mess to Smith and left it all in the reliable hands of Federal Express.

"No cop cars yet?" Remo asked when he hopped back behind the wheel of their battered rental.

Above the strip mall the curl of black smoke from the burning van thinned as the fire died out.

"No," Chiun replied. "Given the confusion this town has with your Western holidays, perhaps the local constabulary is occupied at their televisions waiting for that man with the lifted-up face and dyed eyebrows to drop a ball on that dirty city to the north."

"I don't think we should push our luck," Remo said.

Leaving the lot, he drove a few miles down the road. Once they were out of Yuletide, he found a lonely diner. At the pay phone out front, he stabbed out the multiple 1 code that would reroute the call to Smith's desk. The CURE director answered on the first ring.

"Remo?" Smith asked sharply.

"In the singed flesh," Remo replied. "Something weird just happened down here."

"I know," Smith replied. "I take it you have seen the news reports."

Chiun stood beside Remo. Hands locked on to opposing wrists, his arms formed a single knot of bone.

Remo glanced worriedly at the Master of Sinanju. "I know I'm gonna regret this," he said cautiously to Smith, "but what news reports?"

"I assumed that was why you called," Smith said. "There has been a major traffic accident involving more than three dozen cars near Orlando."

Remo frowned in confusion. "Just because I took this nothing assignment doesn't mean I'm gonna start playing meter maid now, Smitty," he warned.

"Unless it is on the advice of the handsome Prince Regent," Chiun interjected loudly. He dropped his voice. "Is Smith's heir on the phone, as well?" he hissed.

"No, Chiun," Remo sighed. "It's just Smith. You wanna say hi?" He held out the phone.

Chiun leaned back from the receiver, his face fouling. "Why would I want to talk to that creaky old pinchpenny?" he asked, just low enough that Smith could not hear. "Him I already work for."

He turned his face to the sky and began examining the clouds.

"The accident does not matter," Smith pressed, steering back to the topic at hand. "It's the *cause*. A passenger in a car driving in the opposite direction was videotaping the northbound lane seconds before the pileup. He taped the vehicle that spun out of control into the oncoming lane of traffic."

"Sell it to Fox," Remo said. "What's it got to do with me?"

"You don't understand," Smith insisted. "On the footage he taped was a—" he hesitated, at a momentary loss for words "—a *thing*," he concluded, unhappy with the term.

"What sort of thing?" Remo asked. He found himself growing troubled by Smith's anxious tone.

"For lack of a better explanation, the thing taped resembles an enormous arachnid." The CURE director seemed embarrassed to even utter something so ludicrous.

"Arachnid?" Remo asked, his tone flat. "As in spider?"

"It is only visible for a short time," Smith persisted. "Just before the crash it can be seen crawling along the side of an armored car. Presumably, it jumped over from the vehicle that caused the pileup. The footage lasts until it tears its way into the back of the car. At this point the camera operator shifts focus to the crash."

"How did it tear into an armored car?" Remo asked doubtfully.

"I don't know," Smith admitted tightly. "It appeared as if with nothing more than its legs it somehow managed to rip open bulletproof metal."

The strain was evident in his voice. Harold Smith had seen many things that challenged his rigid perceptions of reality during his time as head of CURE. And in spite of being witness to so much, each new occasion remained hampered by his sturdy pragmatism.

"It's gotta be a fake, Smitty," Remo insisted.

"It came in too quickly to have been doctored."

"Fast doesn't matter these days. Every pizza-faced high-school drip can whip up *Star Wars* special effects in two seconds on their home computers."

"No," Smith disagreed. "Not this fast. And according to experts who have examined it, the footage has not been digitally altered. Therefore until it is disproved we must assume that it is genuine."

At first, the Master of Sinanju had been pretending to ignore the phone conversation. Smith's words, however, had apparently sparked interest in the old man. Though still looking at the sky, he edged closer to the phone, one shell-like ear cocked in Remo's direction.

"Where's the armored car?" Remo asked.

"It vanished," Smith replied. "There was a crew of three onboard. All dead."

"Now the thing drives?" Remo demanded skeptically.

"While I have made several logical leaps thus far, that is not one of them," Smith said crisply. "It is possible that a human accomplice somehow seized the cab of the vehicle while the creature turned its attention on the rear."

Remo shook his head. This was just too incredible.

"How is this possible, Smitty?" he asked. "Something as crazy as that just doesn't crawl out of the woodwork and go 'boo.' If that thing was running around in the woods out there somewhere, it would have been found already."

"Not necessarily," Smith said. "Although not quite so farfetched, there have been cases similar to this recently. For many years it was thought that all of the large species of animals had been discovered. Many experts assumed that even the most remote locales were now accessible thanks to transportation and technology. Yet there have been several new species discovered in the past few years."

"I've seen junk like this on PBS, Smitty," Remo dismissed. "It's all microbes and see-through fish."

"That is not the case," Smith explained. "There have been large mammals, as well. Species of goats and gorillas thought extinct were found within the past decade alone. Also a heretofore unknown relative of the horse was recently discovered in Asia. Not to mention our own experience with the Apatosaur in Africa."

"I guess," Remo said slowly. "But if this thing's been living in the Everglades all these years, I doubt it's crawled out now just to hijack a Brinks truck."

"I agree," Smith said. "Since it steals, it is safe to conclude that it has been trained to do so."

"It just gets better and better," Remo droned.

"While I admit that it is improbable, the videotape I have seen forces me to explore possibilities that I would dismiss under other circumstances."

"I'd *still* like to," Remo sighed. "You think Siegfried and Roy have an alibi?"

Smith ignored him. "I suggest that you and Chiun find someplace to view the footage. Most news outlets are playing it virtually nonstop. If you encounter this creature, I want the two of you to have all the information that is available on it."

"Speaking of info," Remo said, "I might have something in that department."

Remo quickly told Smith about the frictionless metal fragment Chiun had found at the liquor store. He concluded by mentioning Major Healy and the other costumed gunmen.

"That is odd," Smith said once he was through. "I will send the piece of metal for analysis as soon as it arrives. As far as the men you describe, I am at a loss."

"At this point I don't know what's going on," Remo said. "Hell, maybe they're part of the spider-training team. Those Halloween getups could be their way of hiding in the open."

"Perhaps," Smith said. "In any event, they are likely connected, given the nature of their attack on you. I will have Mark look into them."

At the assistant CURE director's name, Remo suppressed a thin smile. "There's something in the envelope I sent for him," he said. "Give it to him when it shows up, okay?"

"Very well," Smith agreed slowly.

"For now, I'm gonna find a motel. I'll call you once we've seen the show."

Turning, he hung up the phone.

When he glanced at the Master of Sinanju, the old man was nodding sadly.

"You will listen to Smith's fairy stories but you dismiss the tale of Master Shiko," Chiun said.

"The yeti guy? How can I dismiss it? Unless you've been beaming radio waves into my head, I haven't even heard it yet."

"If I thought there was a chance you would actually listen for once, I would try that method," the Master of Sinanju replied. "I will inquire of Smith if radio signals can penetrate solid granite."

"Yeah, okay. I get it," Remo said. "I've got a thick skull. Ha-ha. Can you give me the *Reader's Digest* version? I'm kind of in a hurry." He palmed the car keys.

Chiun shook his head. "No. I will tell you when you are ready to make a true effort to listen." Turning, he padded away from Remo to their rental car.

Remo was relieved, grateful to dodge an ancient Sinanju legend.

"Just as well," he said, trotting to the driver's side. "We've got to find a TV. Besides, no offense to Master Shiko, but no matter what I think about this spider thing anymore, I sure as hell don't believe the abominable snowman exists."

Climbing into the car, the Master of Sinanju's papery lips formed a sad smile. "Master Shiko was just as certain that it did, my son," he replied somberly. And in a voice only he could hear, he whispered, "You are both wrong."

14

Colonel Zipp Codwin had come to NASA the hard way. While still a pup, he'd paid his way through college flying crummy little biplanes for cash. Barnstorming, crop dusting, anything he could do to turn an honest buck. Sometimes, when things got tight and he was really strapped for cash, the bucks turned less honest. But he'd done it. Zipp Codwin had paid his dues and succeeded.

College led to the Air Force. Air Force led to a spot at NASA.

During the days of the post-Sputnik space race, when the United States was locked in its most desperate competition with the Soviet Union, Zipp had proved he had the right stuff a hundred times. A hundred *times* a hundred times. Yet he always seemed to come in a day late and a dollar short.

Sure, he'd circled the Earth a couple of times. But he wasn't the *first* man to do it. In a twist of fate that still ate through his belly like acid, that honor went to a Russian. A damn-blasted Russkie had beaten Zipp to space.

The moon belonged to Neil Armstrong and a couple other brownnosing pissants who knew how to suck up to brass. Plain and simple. Thanks to his give-'em-hell personality, Zipp never even made it there at all.

He hadn't even had the good fortune to be blown up with Gus Grissom or lost in space with Apollo 13. Good Lord-in-a-laundry-basket, they made a goddamn movie out of that one. With Tom Hanks, for Christ's sake! *Tom Hanks!*

The fabled decade of exploration ended with less than a whimper. All the Mercuries, Geminis and Apollos became ancient history and Zipp Codwin's beloved NASA surrendered the front page to pantywaist civilian groundlubbers.

It was pathetic. The one agency that had stood toe to furry toe with the great Russian bear and made that goddamn Bolshoi bruin blink was surrendered to a passel of nerds who thought that space exploration meant flinging a couple of blinking tin cans called Voyager out of the solar system. By the time the *Challenger* went boom, ol' Zipp Codwin had long since hung up his helmet and space suit.

Zipp drifted. For a time he became an aeronautics consultant for Lockheed, Boeing and a few of the other giants. Pure window dressing, of course. As one of the dinosaurs from the old days, he was pretty much relegated to the status of cocktail-party curiosity.

That life was hell for a man who had been trained

to strap a rocket to his ass and fly screaming into the smarmy, smirking face of God himself.

In a quirk of fate, Zipp was sent to Washington by one of his bosses during the big defense-industry mergers. He happened to find himself in front of a committee chaired by one of his flyboy buddies from the old days. Turned out there was an opening at NASA, his pal put in a good word and before you could say strafe the weasel, Zipp Codwin found himself back at the agency he'd left two decades before.

When he arrived, he found that it was worse than he thought. Geeks prowled the halls of Canaveral as if they owned the joint. In the old days they were there, sure. But damn if they didn't know enough to keep their voices, eyes and technobabble down when in the company of their superiors—their superiors being the men who were willing to risk their cullions in the cold heart of space.

But even that was another story. Some of the men these days were women. Real, honest-to-Jebediah gals of the female persuasion. And the men weren't real men, either. They were all studious, bookish types. Not a Tailhooker among them. The nerds were running the asylum. And thanks to them, the program suffered.

All that was happening at the best damn space agency on the face of the bluest damn ball of rock in the solar system was a couple of moldy-oldy shuttle missions a year.

Shuttle flew up. Shuttle puked out some crummy

weather satellite or half-busted telescope. Shuttle flew back down.

If there was *real* excitement on a mission, the shuttle would have to wait an extra day because of some damn farty windstorm out in California.

It was awful. But the money just wasn't there anymore for anything grand. Zipp had hollered himself hoarse looking for more scratch from the miserly buttwads on the Potomac, but they stubbornly refused to surrender an extra damn cent.

Zipp had been forced to use extreme measures every now and again in order to boost cash flow. In this regard, the slew of PR flacks he kept around came in handy.

Clark Beemer was a good one. Dumb as grandma's mule, but dang if he couldn't come up with a winner. The rock he'd used as proof of life on Mars was a classic. Netted a healthy chunk of change there. And the fact that the public had fallen for it was proof enough to Zipp Codwin that there was still an appetite for the junk NASA was peddling.

The next project would have been just as ambitious. In a few months' time it was going to be revealed that one of NASA's cosmic listening posts had intercepted coherent signals of extraterrestrial origin. Men in the bowels of the Kennedy Space Center were currently working to create those alien signals by splicing and overdubbing old 8-tracks. With a mathematical symbol buried in the recording, ol' Zipp Codwin had intended to stand on the dais in front of a roomful of reporters and, with a straight face, swear to the Lord God Almighty and all his children in the choir that the signals were real and that all NASA needed was a few extra million to decipher exactly what they meant. By the time the world found out they consisted of nothing more than old Carpenters songs played backward, the cash would be in the bank and NASA and Zipp would be moving on to the next scam.

Of course, that was what the plan *was*. With the discovery Pete Graham and his Virgil probe had made in that Mexican volcano, all bets were off.

Mr. Gordons was the score to end all scores.

The uncreative android with the survival craving had blown completely off the radar everything else Zipp Codwin might have had in mind to solve NASA's fiduciary concerns.

Sure, the initial meeting had been rough, what with Gordons trying to strangle him and all. But after that encounter in the hallway outside Graham's lab, things had begun to drop into place for Colonel Zipp Codwin.

"Will you help me find a way to destroy my enemies?" Mr. Gordons had asked once he'd allowed himself to be escorted—in spider form—back to Graham's lab.

"Sure thing, sonny boy," Zipp had said. "Anything you want. That's what family's for."

The truth was, he would have promised that monster the moon if it kept it working on behalf of the National Aeronautics and Space Administration.

With only a vague promise of assistance from the head of NASA, Mr. Gordons had gone about securing the infusion of cash that would help haul the space agency out of its thirty-year doldrums.

Zipp had started him out small. Just to see if he could hack it. To Colonel Codwin's delight, the android inside the Virgil probe was more than up to the challenge.

"This is beautiful!" Zipp Codwin had exclaimed as he pawed through the nine hundred thousand dollars in cash Gordons had liberated from a newly opened supermarket.

"Beauty is not a concept that I recognize," Mr. Gordons had said. In the guise of the Virgil probe, he stood before Zipp's desk, his long legs tucked beneath his body.

They were in Codwin's spacious Kennedy Space Center office. Model replicas of capsules and rockets from various ages in NASA's history were mounted in glass-lined cases all around the walls.

Colonel Codwin held up a hundred-dollar bill. "Then let me explain it to you," he beamed. "This, my boy, is beauty at its most pulchritudinous."

By this point an entire face had formed on the front of Virgil's thorax. Zipp had gotten used to talking to the head that stuck out of the probe.

With his lone eye, Gordons looked at the bill.

"It is no more than paper stained by ink," the android said. "While the design is slightly different than it was before my confinement, presumably to discourage replication, it remains uncomplicated."

Zipp got a sudden flash of hope. "Can you print your own cash?" he had asked.

"Affirmative," Mr. Gordons replied.

Lights of joy sparked bright in Zipp Codwin's eyes.

"But I will not," Mr. Gordons had finished.

The colonel's heart fell. "Why in the name of hot holy hell *not?*" Zipp asked.

"I have done so before," Mr. Gordons had replied. "To do so again would be uncreative."

And that ended all discussion on the subject. Zipp had to settle for simple robberies.

The past week's tests proved Gordons's mettle. Zipp Codwin had quickly decided that the nickel-and-dime stage was over. It was time to move on to bigger and better things.

That morning, he'd sent Gordons out to find an armored truck. Any would do. As for the how, where and when, the android had been left to his own devices.

When he saw the footage on the news, Zipp Codwin nearly had a stroke. There was Gordons—as big as life—crawling along the side of the armored car.

Fortunately for NASA, Mr. Gordons had improved on the design of the probe he had assimilated. Gone was the awkwardness of a wind-up toy. Gordons had given Virgil a fluidity of motion that it had never had before. He had also used a spider he had seen spin-

ning a web in the lab as a template to remake his
image. The Virgil probe was no longer merely remi-
niscent of a spider; it looked like the real dang thing.
Furry legs, smooth body and all.

Zipp had been a little worried that the armored car
stolen so publicly was making a beeline straight for
him, but he soon found that Gordons had made some
cosmetic alterations en route from Orlando. He
learned this when he drove back from lunch and
found a Mr. Coney ice-cream truck parked in his
space.

"What the hell is this?" Zipp bellowed when he
saw the ice-cream truck. It had an open counter with
pictures of sundaes and cones painted on the side.
There was no driver. "Security!" he howled.
"There's a goddamn frozen-pudding peddler parked
in my space!"

"Keep quiet," advised a voice that seemed to
come from somewhere in the truck.

Zipp's face turned purple. "Who the hell do you
think you're talking to, boy!" he screamed. He stuck
his head in the open window. There was no one in
the cab.

"I am talking to a human whose neck I will snap
if he does not quiet down," said the now familiar
voice.

It seemed to be coming from the dashboard. When
Zipp looked closer he saw that, instead of a volume
control knob for the stereo, there was an eye. It was
looking at him.

"Oh," said Zipp, finally realizing to whom he was talking.

He ushered the truck to the building that housed Pete Graham's lab. There the Virgil probe detached itself from the vehicle. When it crawled up out of the open door in the back, Zipp Codwin's eyes grew wide. The floor of the truck was filled with sacks of money.

Operating capital. Gordons had gotten his first big score for NASA. And he'd managed to do it under the noses of every law-enforcement official in central Florida.

Suddenly, the possibilities that had been present in the earliest days of the space agency flooded back. In that moment images of lunar cities and Martian colonies and starships exploded bright and beautiful in Zipp Codwin's retired Air Force brain.

"Son," he said to the probe that stood patiently beside him, "if I wasn't so dang-blasted sure the current Mrs. Codwin would rake me over the coals in the settlement, I'd ditch her saggy old behind and hitch up with you!"

And, unable to keep his exuberance in check, he flung his powerful arms around the torso of the Virgil probe.

FOR SECURITY REASONS Colonel Codwin had kept knowledge of Mr. Gordons limited to a tight inner circle.

Graham's team, which had flown Virgil to and

from Mexico, wasn't a problem. As far as they were concerned, its return from the depths of Popocatepetl had been nothing more than a bizarre malfunction. The only men other than Zipp himself aware of the probe's true nature were Dr. Graham himself and the PR guy, Clark Beemer.

When the time came to haul the money out of the ice-cream truck that had once been a SecureCo armored car, Graham and Beemer were conscripted to do the honors.

"I don't know if it's such a good idea to just stack it here," Pete Graham ventured. Panting, he dropped the last dirty sack onto the pile.

There was dried blood on the exterior of the bag. Graham tried not to think about how it got there.

"This is NASA, boy," Zipp Codwin dismissed. He was sitting on a mound of sacks. Around his ankles he had dumped a pile of bills. "No one's gonna suspect we're involved in anything dirty. Hell, most folks'd probably be surprised to find out we were still around."

The Virgil probe was back in the corner of the room. The three men paid it no attention while they worked.

"I don't know," Beemer said worriedly. He used his sleeve to wipe sweat from his forehead. "This last robbery made a big splash on the news. Somebody might figure out that the spider doing all the stealing is ours. And if it *does* get out, I'm not sure we can spin our way out of it."

His voiced concern was met with a metallic shriek from behind them. All three men whipped around.

The Virgil probe was reaching up to the ceiling with one of its slender spider legs. It had just ripped a security camera from the wall. The device tore free in a spray of bright sparks.

"Hush up, ya dagburn fool," Zipp hissed. "You're pissing him off." He rubbed the purple bruises on his neck, remnants of the last time Gordons had gotten upset.

But Virgil didn't seem to be paying attention to them. It was more concerned with the camera in its claw.

"What are you doing?" Graham asked.

"This one is correct," Mr. Gordons said. "I am incomplete. I have been concealing myself in a shape not adequate to camouflage. To maximize my survival I must adopt a form more inconspicuous."

The leg expanded until it enveloped the small camera. There was a grinding of metal during which some small parts fell to the floor. What remained when he was through, Mr. Gordons pressed to his face.

When he removed his makeshift hand, a second eye had joined the first. Both eyes looked at the three NASA men.

"Survive...survive...maximize survival...."

As he spoke, all eight legs folded up underneath the Virgil probe. Its torso floated to the floor like a metallic soap bubble. When it landed, the legs were immediately absorbed into the main body. At the same time, the body itself began to compress, collapsing in on itself.

It looked for all the world as if the probe were melting.

"How can he do that?" Beemer asked in wonder. "Virgil's got to be five times bigger than that."

"If you're measuring the actual distance from leg tip to leg tip and top to bottom, it's more like ten times," Pete Graham whispered excitedly. "But the components of Virgil are light and spread thin. He can somehow manipulate those components into a more compact unit. The mass remains the same. It's just formed into a different shape."

Zipp Codwin looked at the shrinking form of Mr. Gordons. "So it's like he's crushing the Virgil in one of those car compressors they have at junkyards?"

Graham nodded tightly. He was staring in rapt attention at the amazing transformation taking place before them.

It was obvious now what Gordons was doing. The shape had begun to grow familiar. Arms, legs. The head still remained as a command unit above the newly re-formed torso.

When Mr. Gordons stood a moment later, he was completely remade. Circuits blinked at strategic points around the metal frame. Clusters of multicolored wires were visible at all the major joints. But in spite of the high-tech gloss, the form he had taken on was clearly recognizable.

"My God," Clark Beemer murmured.

"Dang if he don't look human," Zipp breathed.

"Thank you," Mr. Gordons replied. "It is the optimum manner in which to conceal myself among you. According to my projections the human population should be well in excess of six billion by this time. This form will help me to blend in with greater success. In addition to this, my experience has taught me that my enemies have a lower degree of success recognizing me when I have assumed the human form."

When he was through talking, he brought up his arms.

The metallic hands seemed to shudder. And before their eyes, the fingers on each of the android's hands compressed into single units. The new hands flattened and lengthened until they had grown into familiar shapes.

"There was an element of my program that once allowed for the incorporation of organic material," Mr. Gordons explained. "That has been damaged irreparably."

Pete Graham liked the sound of that. Especially given the fact that Mr. Gordons now seemed to have two long, curving knives in place of hands.

Near the stacks of money was a sofa. The android turned his attention to it now.

It was an old leather number that had been kicking around the lab for years. When he had first taken over this NASA lab, it reminded Pete Graham of the couch he'd had back at his dorm at MIT. He had fought off multiple attempts by the staff to remove it.

Mr. Gordons leaned into the sofa with his hands.

The blades became blurs. Slicing turned to tearing, and before Pete knew what had happened his old sofa had been stripped of every last bit of leather. It sat on the floor like a skinned fish, all stuffing and springs.

When he stood, Mr. Gordons's hands had resumed their human shape. In them were clasped the strips of leather.

As the three men watched, Gordons folded his hands over his chest, pressing the upholstery to his body. With a soft hiss the leather disappeared.

Just like that. Disappeared. Absorbed into the metal frame like water into a paper towel.

"What the ding-dang?" Zipp said. "How did he—?"

Before he could complete the thought, the leather reappeared.

It showed up first on the forearms. Bleeding up from below the metal surface. Digested and assimilated, it was softer now. A perfect carbon copy of human skin. It had lost its faded brown, resurfacing in a bland baby pink.

Rapidly, the thighs and torso were covered. The rest of the arms, legs, hands and feet followed. Last was the head.

When the metamorphosis was complete, Mr. Gordons stood before the three NASA men, naked and whole.

"Oh my..." whispered Clark Beemer.

Zipp Codwin's mouth hung open wide. "How—how does he have *hair?*" he asked Pete Graham.

Mr. Gordons answered for the scientist. "Threads contained within the sofa material provided adequate source material." A mechanical facsimile of a human hand brushed back the sandy blond hair. "It is quite lifelike. I require clothing to complete my disguise. Yours will suffice."

He pointed at Clark Beemer. The public-relations man didn't even argue. Terrified eyes focused squarely on the man before him, he began stripping off his clothes. He handed them to the android. Gordons put them on.

"I am now fully functional," Mr. Gordons said once he was dressed. "It is time."

There was a long pause during which none of the men said a thing. It was Zipp Codwin who finally realized that Gordons expected something of them.

"Um, time for what?" he asked. He had grown strangely comfortable talking to Gordons in his spider form. This human thing was going to take some getting used to.

"To implement your plan," Gordons said in his smooth, mechanical voice.

Zipp glanced at Beemer and Graham. "My, um, plan?"

"Please do not tell me that you have not developed

a plan of attack I might use against my enemies," Mr. Gordons said. "I do not wish to have to rip your medulla oblongata from your skull as an example." His lips were parted in something that was almost but not quite a smile.

"Whoa, there, son," Zipp said, hastily throwing up his hands. "I gotcha. Wrong wavelength before. *Plan.* You want the plan I've come up with for you. Well, about that. See, I haven't had the time to fully flesh it out."

"You have had six days, eight hours and twelve minutes in which to complete your task," Mr. Gordons said. "In the meantime I have done all that you wish. I have stolen one million, thirty-four thousand, seven hundred eighty-seven dollars and thirty-three cents for you to use as you wish."

"For *science*," Zipp stressed, lest anyone get the impression that he was in this for personal gain.

"How you make use of it is irrelevant. I have held up my end of our bargain. It is time for you to reciprocate."

Zipp shot a look at Graham. "Help me out here," he whispered sharply.

Graham jumped. "Me? Oh, ah, well..." His eyes darted around the room as he tried to come up with an answer Mr. Gordons would find acceptable. "Maybe you don't have to face these enemies at all. You're just looking for safety. To survive. We could, um, send you to someplace where you're sure to be safe. You—that is, the Virgil probe—are designed to survive in an inhospitable alien climate. If we send you to Mars or a Jovian moon you'd be safe."

"Are you out of your mind?" Zipp Codwin snapped, smacking Graham on the back of the head. "I need him."

"Negative," Mr. Gordons said to Graham. "Mars will likely be inhabited by humans within the next three hundred years. It is possible that the descendants of my enemies will come there. While colonization of Jupiter's moons is unlikely, they are not suitable to my needs. I am a mechanical being. Were I damaged somehow, the parts to repair me would not be available on an uninhabited world. Even if replacement parts were sent with me, they would not last long enough, since it is not possible at the present time to ship supplies from this planet on such a vast scale. Remember, my life span is far greater than that of humans."

"Life span?" Beemer asked. He was shivering in his underwear.

"I am self-aware," Gordons said. "Therefore I live." His mechanical voice turned even more cold as he looked back to Zipp Codwin. "What is your plan?"

Zipp gulped. "It's such a good plan, I don't want to ruin it by blurting it out too soon," he dodged. "Gimme another day to think. Just one more. Is that good for you?"

Gordons's blue eyes were ice.

"You had better think fast," he warned. "During

each of the robberies you have involved me in I left a small piece of the Virgil probe. When discovered, the fragments will be traceable back to NASA. As a result of my very creative plan you will soon have enemies like mine. In your case it will be the authorities. If you do not aid me, I will leave you and this agency you revere at their mercy.''

Zipp Codwin felt as if he'd been kicked in the gut. The room spun around him. "Not *NASA!*" he gasped.

If it was possible for an android to display smugness, Mr. Gordons did so now.

"I calculated an eighty-three percent probability that the agency for which you work was more important to you than your own life," Gordons said. "I am pleased to know that I was correct."

"You were correct, dammit," Zipp snapped. "Okay, okay. These enemies you keep blabbing about. Who are they and where are they?"

"Some of my memory degraded while I was inactive. I do not know where they are located, but their names are Remo and Chiun. They are practitioners of an ancient martial art that, as far as I have been able to ascertain, predates and surpasses all others. These two men are unlike any I have ever encountered and have caused me to cease functioning at full capacity six times before. I would further caution you that they will most likely be alerted to the participation of the Virgil probe in your illegal activities not long after the normal civilian authorities uncover the clues I have left. This, Administrator Zipp Codwin of the National Aeronautics and Space Administration, makes it all the more imperative that you help me sooner rather than later. That is, assuming you wish to keep this agency from being dismantled by the United States government piece by piece.''

And with that, Mr. Gordons turned on his heel and walked from the room.

The way he moved was unnerving. There was a deliberate, gliding slowness to his newly formed feet. No uncertainty, no experimentation. He just slid forward and was gone.

When the door closed gently behind Mr. Gordons, a shell-shocked Colonel Codwin turned to Beemer and Graham.

''Cold, calculating son of a bitch,'' Zipp muttered. ''Hate to say it, but he's a man after my own damn heart.''

''What do we do?'' Clark Beemer asked nervously.

Zipp shook himself from his trance. He looked at Beemer. ''First thing, go and get some pants on,'' he said to the half-naked PR man. ''For God's sake man, this is NASA.'' He took a deep breath, crossing his arms. ''Second, we figure out how to help our friend Gordons kill those two pals of his. All in the name of good old-fashioned American interplanetary exploration, of course.''

15

Remo found a hotel near City Point, fifteen miles south of Yuletide. After calling Smith to give him the number, he and Chiun settled down in front of the TV.

Smith had been right. The cable news outlets seemed to have put the footage of the creature's attack on the SecureCo armored car on an endless loop of tape. The sequence repeated ceaselessly as somber-faced newscasters commented on it in deeply serious voices.

The head of the armored-car company was interviewed. Various law-enforcement officials and entomologists were on hand to offer their perspectives. Even the governor of Florida was questioned about the spider at a statehouse press conference.

One cable station even hauled out a pair of Hollywood producers who a few years before had made a film about a giant mutated lizard that destroyed New York City.

Everyone seemed to be interviewing everyone else and, from what Remo could see as day bled into the dark hours of night, no one knew anything.

He hit the mute button.

Remo didn't need to hear what they were saying. The footage—what there was of it—spoke for itself.

For the twentieth time Remo watched as the massive spider scampered along the side of the SecureCo truck. As it worked to tear open the back door, its long legs were shielded by its body.

The results of its efforts were evident soon enough. The door wrenched apart, and the huge arachnid scurried into the back through the wide opening.

After this, the now out-of-focus camera bounced rapidly, following the path of the abandoned van. The van bounced off the jersey barrier and rolled out into the oncoming lanes of traffic. Just as the first speeding car crashed into it, the image cut out.

Quietly, Remo clicked off the TV.

Seated on the floor next to him, the Master of Sinanju had been studying the screen carefully. He seemed to be absorbing every movement of the creature as it crawled around the outside of the armored car.

"It moves funny," Chiun pronounced as the picture faded to black.

"Nothing funny about that," Remo said grimly. His expression was dark as he shook his head. "And did you happen to notice how that van looked like the one the Rocket Revengers blew up? They *must* be tied in somehow."

A leathery hand waved away any interest in the

crashed vehicle. "The men are irrelevant," Chiun said. "It is the beast that is troublesome."

"Gotta go with you on that one," Remo agreed. "I have to admit I'm not thrilled at the idea of having to tussle with a bug that big. What do we do, have one of us pin it down while the other one squashes it?"

Chiun's brow was furrowed. "Whatever else this creature might be, it is new to Sinanju," he intoned seriously. "Without the wisdom of the past to guide us, we should learn all we can about it before we race off to engage it. Perhaps even leave it to a later Master to exterminate."

Remo was surprised by his teacher's reluctance. It was an attitude he did not share.

"Nah," he dismissed. "We've gone up against worse. As long as we don't wind up snagged in its web like Vincent Price, we'll be golden."

"Did you *see* a web?" Chiun challenged.

Remo was surprised at his scolding tone. Impatience sparked the depths of the old Korean's eyes.

"I was just kidding, Chiun," Remo said.

The Master of Sinanju closed his eyes patiently. An intense world-weariness descended on the dry skin around his creased lids. "Please, Remo, make an effort to involve your brain, as well as your mouth, when you are thinking. I will not be here forever to guide you."

The fatherly care with which his words were spoken made Remo feel suddenly very small. And concerned.

"Are you all right, Little Father?" he asked, worry tripping his voice. He thought of the week's worth of near silence he'd been subjected to by the old man.

Chiun's eyes opened. Though the skin around them crinkled like old parchment, they remained youthful. "Of course I am all right," he retorted. "But I will not always be so. Anyone can see that my days have long grown short."

Remo fidgeted uncomfortably. "There's nothing wrong with you," he dismissed.

"Now," Chiun said, shaking his head. "But not forever." An awkward silence momentarily descended. "Have you forgotten your visitations from your brother?" the old Korean asked quietly.

Remo felt a chill in the hotel room that had nothing to do with the air-conditioning.

The old Asian was referring to Remo's ghostly visitor from the previous year. The small Korean child had foretold that the coming years would be difficult for Remo Williams.

The little boy had appeared a half-dozen times to Remo, and it was only after he was long gone the last time that Remo found out who he was. The boy who had haunted his days was Chiun's natural son, Song, who had died in a training accident before Remo was even born. Since Remo was Chiun's spiritually adopted son, the old Korean considered him brother to the biological son he had lost years ago.

"Of course I haven't forgotten," Remo said softly. "I just don't like to think about it that much."

A fleeting sternness touched the Master of Sinanju's wrinkled visage. "Is that so?" he asked. "Can I assume you were not thinking about it when you slew the homicidal ballfooter but a stone's throw from Fortress Folcroft, knowing that it would upset Emperor Smith? Have you not been thinking about it when you've used every opportunity to antagonize the Prince Regent? Was it far from your thoughts when you watched our home burn to the ground?"

Remo's shoulders sagged. "Okay, so it's passed through my mind from time to time." He raised a warning finger. "But I'm bugging Howard on my own time," he stressed.

"So you say," Chiun replied thinly. "In any case you were warned that these times preceded your ascension to Reigning Masterhood. You must understand that when that time comes, your responsibilities will be far different than they are now." The old man's tone was serious.

Remo was now reasonably certain why Chiun had been so quiet after their talk in the Folcroft hallway. He, more than even Remo, understood the truth behind Remo's hastily spoken words.

Remo knew that there was nothing more sacred to his teacher than his duties as Reigning Master of the House of Sinanju. And even though it pained him to even consider a time when Chiun would not be Master, Remo understood that one of the most weighty tasks as Master was to choose a successor who understood all the great burdens his station entailed.

Burying the sadness he dared not reveal, the younger man nodded. "I understand, Little Father," Remo said softly.

At his pupil's gentle tone, the harder lines of the old man's face softened. "You are a good pupil, Remo, as well as a good son," he said. "And despite what I and others have told you over the years, you have a good brain, too. It merely lacks focus."

Remo's smile bloomed with childlike pride. "You really think so?" he asked.

Chiun rolled his eyes. "Of course not," he droned. "When I first met you I considered wadding up cotton in your ears at night to keep the mice out. I was merely saying so to boost your self-esteem."

A cloud formed on Remo's brow. "Mission accomplished," he grumbled, folding his arms.

Chiun turned his attention back to the blank TV screen. "I saw no web from this spider-that-is-not-a-true-spider that moves funny," the old man said. "And if it is different in this one way, it could be different in others."

"Like being as big as a Buick, for one," Remo suggested thinly.

"Yes," Chiun replied without irony. "If we are to meet this creature about which you know nothing, do not let its resemblance to a thing you know confuse your reactions to it."

Remo understood the Master of Sinanju's concerns.

Yet they seemed unwarranted. "Not a problem," he said.

As he spoke, the room phone jangled to life. Floating to his feet, Remo scooped up the receiver from the nightstand next to the bed.

"Yello," he said.

"Remo, Smith," announced the CURE director's breathless voice. "The creature has been spotted again."

Remo was instantly alert. "Where?"

Smith couldn't keep the troubled anxiety from his voice. "Ten miles from your location," he said. "A bar called the Roadkill Tavern. Local authorities were just alerted. As far as anyone knows, it's still there."

The older man quickly spit out directions. With a final caution to be careful, the CURE director broke the connection.

Remo slammed down the receiver. When he spun toward the Master of Sinanju, Chiun was already rising to his feet, a serious expression on his aged face.

"You heard," Remo said quickly.

"Yes," Chiun said seriously as he swept to the door. "I only hope that you did, as well."

And in a flurry of green-and-red silk, he was gone.

The old man's concern was infectious. Feeling a pang of unaccustomed disquiet, Remo raced out into the night after the elderly Korean.

16

The girl had gotten into the Roadkill Tavern with fake ID. Had to have. There was absolutely no way she was the legal limit. Fake ID and maybe a pretty smile had gotten her through the door.

She was seventeen at best. Maybe a year or two younger. No amount of booze or makeup could hide the truth from the eyes of the shadowy figure who sat in the corner booth. After all, he was an expert.

A warm beer sat on the table before him. Not too stale that the waitress would get annoyed at him for taking up valuable real estate. He knew how to pace his drinking while remaining inconspicuous. Afterward, when the police started asking the inevitable questions, people might remember there was someone sitting there for a few hours—maybe even come up with a vague physical description—but they wouldn't be able to pin down any specifics.

It was a talent honed from years of experience.

As he sat alone watching the girl at the bar, he tapped a single index finger on the dirty tabletop.

A smile above a halter top. Maybe she had a face, maybe not. It didn't really matter. He'd known it the moment she stepped through the door. She would be the next.

Click-click-click.

The metal pad recessed in his fingertip drummed a relentless staccato on the table.

He alone heard the noise. The jukebox was so loud no one else could hear the sound of Elizu Roote's tapping finger.

A faint reddish blush of anticipation brushed the flesh of his otherwise pale cheeks as he watched the boozy young face of the girl he intended to murder tonight.

IN THE PARKING LOT outside the Roadkill, Clark Beemer hunched behind the steering wheel of the black NASA van. He was trying desperately not to be noticed.

When someone passed by the van, Beemer's eyes grew wide behind his dark sunglasses. He fumbled with the radio, tugged at the upturned collar of his trench coat—anything to distract, to give the appearance that he belonged here.

This wasn't fair. Just because he happened to be in on the big, bad secret at NASA, why did *he* get tapped to chauffeur around the scary robot?

Clark had been standing right there when Zipp Codwin asked Mr. Gordons to drum up some more operating capital. Even after the thing had turned himself into something that looked human. Even after

Gordons had threatened Codwin and all of NASA. One thing about Zipp—he had guts.

Codwin's earlier argument held true. NASA needed the money, and Gordons had needed NASA for repairs in the past. But now there was the additional problem that Gordons had created. With the clues he had left behind, the authorities might already be zeroing in on the space agency.

"Safer from a survival standpoint for you to minimize your time here, son," Zipp had insisted. "Let the brains like me and Graham figure out how to solve your problem. Ol' Clark here'll take you on your rounds tonight."

So that was it. Clark Beemer wasn't the brains. While the only other men with knowledge of who and what Mr. Gordons was stayed back in the well-guarded safety of the Kennedy Space Center, Clark was forced to take to the road with that creepy, emotionless tin can.

He heard a shuffling in the rear of the van.

Since that afternoon at NASA, Mr. Gordons had retained his human form. Like a regular person, he had ridden to the bar in the front of the van with Clark. Once Beemer had parked at the very distant edge of the lot, the android had gotten up and slipped into the back of the van.

More shuffling. A soft grinding of metal.

"Why didn't they let you go alone?" Clark muttered to himself as he sank further into his own shoulders.

A cool mechanical voice answered his question.

"There is a fifty-six percent probability that Administrator Codwin did not want you in his vicinity. That, coupled with the eighty-five percent probability of his not wanting me there, either, made his decision to send you with me a reasonable one."

When Clark turned a peeved eye to Gordons, he nearly jumped out of his skin.

The android had reverted to his spider form. This time the not quite smiling face that jutted from the body of the creature was flesh colored.

"Why do you look like *that* again?" Clark asked, panting with sudden fright. One hand was pressed to his chest to steady his rapidly beating heart.

"In order to mask my true features," Mr. Gordons said. The flatness of his tone never varied. "Necessity forced me to maintain the shape of the Virgil probe throughout the assimilation process. Even though I am now operating at one hundred percent efficiency, I have found that this shape is effective as camouflage. Humans who might otherwise be curious about me are frightened into submission when they see me in this guise. I believe this is due to the fact that most human beings harbor a visceral fear of insects in general and arachnids in particular, would you not agree?"

Not waiting for a response, the Gordons spider scurried around on clattering metal feet. Displaying its furry rear end, the massive creature rapidly crawled to the rear of the van. It popped the door.

Clark felt the van rise on its shocks as the heavy android slipped down to the parking lot.

There was a skittering of feet that seemed to fade in the distance. Clark allowed himself a relieved exhale that lasted only until the huge creature sprang up beside his open window. Gordons leaned his face in close.

"Do not leave," the android instructed. "I'll be back."

With that he sank back onto his metal legs and began scurrying to the bar. Clark watched Gordons crawl quickly through the shadows between the many parked cars. He disappeared around the side of the building.

Clark didn't even realize that he had placed his hand back over his thudding heart.

"I don't know what *visceral* means," Clark whispered, "but you sure as hell got the fear thing down cold."

Pulling his trench coat collar higher, he hunched farther behind the wheel.

THE FLIGHT Stewart McQueen had taken from Maine to Florida had been as pleasant as it could be for the most famous novelist in America. Only ten people in the first-class cabin approached him to say they were interested in becoming writers, too. A miraculously small number considering how many usually pestered him.

It never failed to amaze McQueen. Young, old, educated, morons. Everyone he ever met swore that they could be writers just because they knew a few English words and could—when pressed—actually spell some of them. None of them realized that few professional writers stumbled into the job as a lark or a second career. Writing was an obsession that started young and, more than likely, never panned out.

On his way off the plane, the pilot bounded from the cockpit to pitch him an idea. McQueen brushed him off. The same went for three hopeful flight attendants.

As he walked through the airport, McQueen pulled his Red Sox baseball cap low over his eyes. Even so a handful of people spied him as he made his way through the terminal. Some asked him questions about agents and publishers. Most were autograph seekers who shoved dog-eared copies of some of his own thick paperbacks under his sharp nose.

McQueen dodged them all and hightailed it outside.

The woman who rented him his car made him autograph her copy of *The Gas Mileage,* a terrifying sixteen-part serial thriller he'd written a few years before. It was all about prison inmates, supernatural powers and an evil cadre of killer cars that got only eight miles to the gallon.

In the farthest airport parking lot, McQueen stopped his rental car. Fishing in his luggage, he pulled out a police scanner he'd brought from home. Hooking it up, he latched it to the dashboard with a pair of roach clips.

Most of the sightings of the creature had taken place east of Orlando. He struck off in that direction. By the time he began prowling the streets, night had long taken hold of the Florida peninsula.

McQueen didn't believe in God. Satan, however, was another story. Given the content of his books, the Prince of Darkness buttered his daily bread.

As he rode along through the enveloping black night, eyes peeled for signs of strange movement, ears alert to the staticky squawk of the scanner, Stewart McQueen found himself uttering a soft prayer to the king of all that was unholy.

"Dear Angel of the Bottomless Pit, your Satanic Majesty and Father of Lies. Hi. It's me again. I know there's not much left of my eternal soul, but whatever's there is yours. Just give an old pal a break here, would you?"

Hoping that would be enough to kick start Old Bendy into lending a scaly hand in ending his current bout of writer's block, McQueen raised his penitent head. The instant he did so, a horrifying thought suddenly occurred to him.

His head snapped back down so fast, he smacked it off the steering wheel.

"But when I finally do die, just don't stick me in the same pit as John Grisham," he pleaded. "I know he *has* to have the same deal with you as me. Hail Satan, and amen."

THROUGH THE SLIDING peephole in the storage room behind the bar, Juan Jiminez peered at the shadowy figure.

The stranger had picked the darkest booth in the Roadkill. According to the bartender, he'd been there for more than two hours. Just sitting and staring.

As he studied the mysterious figure, Juan felt a puff of hot breath on his neck.

"You think he's a cop?" an anxious voice whispered.

Juan pulled his eyes away from the peephole.

Ronnie Marzano was standing on his tiptoes trying to see through the opening. His black-rimmed eyes were worried.

"I don't know what he is, but he ain't no cop," Juan said with snide confidence. Without another glance out into the bar, he slid the cardboard shutter back over the opening.

Ronnie blinked hard as he turned his anxious gaze back to the storage room. "Yeah?" he said. "I hope you're right. I got a lot riding on this."

At that, Juan snorted. "*You* do?" he mocked.

There were five more men arranged around the room. Each joined in the derisive laughter.

Ronnie felt like the odd man out. The other five were Cubans, like Jiminez. All six had come to the U.S. ten years ago, floating on a waterlogged boat made from rotted wooden planks lashed to four rusty oil drums.

There was a camaraderie derived from shared hardship among those six that Ronnie could never be a part of. Not that their friendship was anything he really needed. All Ronnie really wanted out of this deal was some free blow and a couple of bucks for his trouble.

A stack of corrugated cardboard boxes lined one wall of the big storage room. Each box was filled with two dozen tightly wrapped plastic bundles. More than a million dollars' worth of cocaine, smuggled by Juan Jiminez into the United States from South America. Ronnie had done his part by setting up the meeting between Jiminez and a local distributor out of Miami.

As Jiminez walked back across the room and plopped into a wooden office chair, Ronnie tracked him with his eyes.

"I'm the one who sets up the meetings here," Ronnie reminded the Cuban. "I'm the one whose neck's on the line."

He left out the fact that his brother-in-law owned the bar. Ronnie also neglected to mention that the heat had been threatening to turn up on the Roadkill lately. Word had begun to filter out into the surrounding neighborhood about what was really going on at the dingy little bar.

Ronnie rubbed his tired, bloodshot eyes. "I gotta go to the can," he mumbled.

Leaving the group of armed Cuban expatriates, he ducked through an ancient door that led into a short hallway. Down at one end was the main bar area. In the other direction were the rest rooms and an emergency exit.

Ronnie headed for the bathrooms. He was pushing open the men's-room door when he noticed that the exit at the end of the hall was open a crack. Through the opening bugs flitted around a tired parking-lot light.

"Someone skipped out on their tab," he muttered as he walked over to close the door.

An ancient cloakroom was next to the door. As he passed by the deep alcove, Ronnie saw a hint of movement from the shadowy interior.

Suddenly cautious, he stopped before the room.

"Who's in there?" Ronnie asked.

It was quiet for a moment. So quiet that Ronnie thought he had imagined the movement. He was ready to chalk it all up to jangled nerves when a face appeared from the darkness.

The man was short. Had to be, since the face was only about five feet off the floor. The rest of his body remained obscured in shadow.

"Where is the money?" the stranger asked. His voice was flat, without any intonation at all. Almost mechanical.

"Huh?" Ronnie asked, his brow furrowing.

And in the moment he uttered that single, confused syllable, the rest of the man appeared.

Ronnie sucked in a shocked gasp.

The human head was grafted onto the most frightening creature Ronnie Marzano had ever seen. Spiky black hair covered the bulbous body. Four of eight legs had carried the beast out into the hallway. The rest were still hidden somewhere in the shadows beyond. The monster had to be huge.

Ronnie had seen the news reports of the giant spider on TV all day. Until now he'd assumed it was a hoax.

He wanted to run. Fear kept him from fleeing. Ronnie fell dumbly back against the wall.

"I have been sent to collect money," the spider said. "According to the human who sent me here, this drinking establishment is utilized as a secret exchange by elements of the subculture that traffics in illegal narcotics. Yet, despite this fact I am unable to detect particulates in the air that would indicate a large quantity of cash. Therefore, I ask again, where is the money?"

Ronnie gulped. It was hard to breathe.

"Not here," he managed to say.

"This is unacceptable," the spider said, its voice cold.

The flesh-colored face looked down the hall.

"I detect slight airborne concentrations of an addictive drug derived from the leaves of the coca plant," Mr. Gordons said. "This drug generates money." The flesh-colored face turned accusingly to Ronnie. The tiny curls at the corners of the human mouth seemed to mock the drug dealer.

"It's n-not here *yet*," Ronnie stammered.

"How soon will it arrive?"

"I'm not sure exactly. Soon," he promised.

Gordons considered the information. "Very well," he said all at once. "Do not move."

Ronnie wasn't about to disobey. He remained stock-still against the wall as the spider skittered backward into the shadows of the cloakroom. There came a strange scraping of metal from out the darkness. When it was over seconds later, a man emerged calmly from the shadows. Ronnie was horrified to see that he wore the same face as the spider.

"Take me to where the money will be," Mr. Gordons said.

Ronnie dared not refuse. His legs felt as if they were dragging lead weights as he brought the man—who a moment before had been a giant spider—to the back room.

The Cubans looked up as the door squeaked shut.

"Who the hell is this?" Juan Jiminez demanded.

The man with Ronnie Marzano looked harmless in a bland sort of way. His blue suit was a little too perfectly tailored, his face too smooth.

"Hello is all right," Mr. Gordons said. "I would be able to offer you a drink, as this is an establishment that specializes in the selling of fermented-grain beverages, but unfortunately I am without the funds to do so."

Juan's brown eyes were clenched with tight suspicion. "Who you bring back here, Marzano?" he asked Ronnie very, very slowly. "This some kind of cop?"

Already the rest of the men were fanning out. With

guns drawn, they surrounded the stiff-looking stranger.

"I am not a police officer," Mr. Gordons answered. "And I must ask that you cease your current course of action, as it could be perceived as a threat to my survival."

"Bet your ass it's a threat," Juan snarled. "And you're going down with him," he said to Ronnie.

Ronnie Marzano was standing next to Gordons near the door. "Please, Juan," he begged, shaking his head.

But it was already too late. The moment Jiminez threatened to endanger the survival of the man standing next to Ronnie, the drug dealer's fate was sealed.

Mr. Gordons moved his arms out to either side of his body, the fingertips angled toward the floor.

As Juan watched, the man's arms were suddenly very long. Much longer than human arms should be. There was something shiny at the ends of them. And when the stranger bent his arms at the elbows, the shiny something of his left hand was flying very quickly in Juan's direction.

The steel knife blade of the android's hand thunked deep into Juan Jiminez's forehead, splitting apart the hemispheres of his dead brain. At the same instant, a second blade shot through the skull of another Cuban drug dealer.

There was a moment of shock during which their leader's lifeless body slid from the gleaming silver appendage of the intruder. But it lasted only an instant.

As one, the remaining four men whipped up submachine guns. Shocked fingers clenching triggers, they opened fire.

The first barrage sliced Ronnie Marzano to ribbons. He slid to the floor in a bloody tangle.

The same bullets should have transformed the intruder into hamburger. They didn't.

Though they fired point-blank, the men were stunned to find their target still standing. Hot lead pounded into the man's chest. Still, he showed no visible reaction.

Bullet holes peppered the wall behind him. Already screams were audible from the bar beyond.

Standing in front of the barrage, Mr. Gordons didn't flinch. While the men fired, he calmly raised his hands, still in the shapes of twin daggers.

The nearest drug dealer was only a few feet away. Like giant scissors, the blades snapped together. Unfortunately for the man, his neck was between them.

As the decapitated head thudded to the floor, the intense burst of gunfire burped to silence. The remaining three men quickly gauged the situation. Flinging down their guns, they ran screaming out into the bar.

Gordons followed.

He caught the last man just outside the door.

The blades that were Gordons's hands slashed right and left. The drug dealer surrendered arms and legs.

The other two men had already raced out the door, along with the other bar patrons. Gordons didn't pursue them.

It was unlikely now that the humans negotiating the purchase of the drugs would arrive with their currency. There was also a nearly hundred percent probability that the authorities would be arriving soon. Mr. Gordons had failed in his mission.

Feeling no disappointment, the android turned from the main bar floor back to the rear hallway.

He found a human blocking his way.

"You ruined my night," the man drawled. "Only fair I get to ruin yours, too."

The young man who stood before Gordons was exceptionally pale. The flesh around his soft cheeks was so white it was almost blue. A shock of white hair sprang up from his scalp. It had been short during a stint in the military. Much longer now, it jutted up like curling, demented horns.

Elizu Roote raised his hands shoulder high, his palms directed toward Mr. Gordons.

At first, the android ignored Roote. Knife blades shuddering as they re-formed into hands, he continued to stride back toward the exit. But when Roote's hands opened, revealing the tarnished gold pads that were buried at the tips of his fingers, the android stopped dead.

He tipped his head. "Are you biomechanical in nature?" Mr. Gordons asked with childlike curiosity.

The question had barely passed his lips before an

audible hum filled the air. The android's optical sensors detected ten distinct flashes at each of the young man's fingertips. Jumping forward, they formed a single white bolt. With a crackle the electrical arc surged across the space that separated Elizu Roote from Mr. Gordons.

The shock pounded the android hard in the chest.

There was no way Gordons could avoid it. Indeed, his metallic frame made him a lightning rod.

Gordons stumbled back into the bar, his face contorting into a parody of human shock. And as his joints seized and his body stiffened, a soft smile of demonic satisfaction kissed the pale white lips of Elizu Roote.

STEWART MCQUEEN WAS driving aimlessly through the streets of City Point when his police scanner squawked to life with news of the commotion at the Roadkill.

He had a street map taped to his dashboard. At a glance he saw he was only two blocks away.

Thanking his lord and master the Prince of Darkness for his guidance, the world-famous novelist pressed down hard on the gas, tearing off in the direction of the bar.

CLARK BEEMER WATCHED with a sinking feeling as the people flooded out the front door of the Roadkill.

Clark started the NASA van's engine, his weak eyes trained on the back door of the bar.

When Gordons failed to materialize, Beemer grew even more anxious. But when he heard the sound of approaching sirens, he panicked.

Knocking the van into drive, he twisted the wheel, flying across the lot. Frightened people scattered from his path as he goosed it out into the street.

Bouncing off the curb, Clark Beemer raced away from the bar. As the PR man tore off into the night, he hoped that Florida's famously strict laws were muddy on the punishment for being accessory to a killer mechanical space spider.

STEWART MCQUEEN ARRIVED at the Roadkill moments before the police. He screeched to a halt in front of the bar and bounded for the entrance.

The novelist didn't know what to expect when he flung open the battered door. In spite of all the strange, paranormal events he'd written about in his long career, he was ill prepared for what he found.

Toward the back of the dimly lit saloon a ghostly white young man appeared to be firing bolts of lightning from his fingertips. The arcing current was pounding against a figure that was sprawled back against the bar.

Despite the apparent amazing abilities of the first man, it was the second figure that shocked McQueen more.

The thing appeared to be half man, half spider. Twisted arachnid legs jutted from a sparking torso, thrashing as if in pain with every surging burst of power.

When Roote attacked, Gordons had tried to assume a shape that would frighten the man into retreat. With his circuits overloading, the transformation hadn't been fully successful.

As McQueen watched, the powerful hum that seemed to rise up from Roote slowed.

Confusion marred Elizu Roote's pale face.

His power charge was weakening. Cutting the juice, he wheeled from Gordons. Staggering slightly, the thin young man disappeared down the shadowy hallway and was gone.

Mr. Gordons reeled away from the bar. His face showed no emotion as his spider legs flailed in space. Pitching forward, he fell against a chair.

Extra furry arms kept him from falling. He pushed himself back to his feet, staggering for the door.

Near the entrance to the Roadkill, Stewart McQueen shook his head, snapping himself from his trance. Racing over, he grabbed Gordons up under his human set of arms. The writer was relieved when he received no shock.

A soft word croaked up from the belly of the android.

"...survive, survive, survive, survive..."

Gordons didn't seem to be aware of where he even was.

Stewart McQueen nodded tightly, struggling to

support the android. He was amazed by how heavy Gordons was.

"I can help you to survive," McQueen promised. "Just remember, one hand washes the other."

He hurried the android outside, dumping him into the back of his rental car. McQueen tumbled in behind the steering wheel.

With fresh images of *New York Times* bestsellerdom dancing in his head for the first time in months, Stewart McQueen thanked the prince of all that was unholy before tearing off into the night.

17

Remo had to swerve a dozen times to avoid fleeing cars. They were barreling up the middle of the road away from the Roadkill Tavern and into oncoming traffic.

One of the vehicles in particular headed straight for him up the double yellow line. Twisting the wheel to one side, Remo scraped sparks from the sides of three parked cars. The menacing black shape tore past them.

"Wasn't that another one of those boohawdle vans?" Remo growled as he pulled back onto the road.

Chiun was carefully scrutinizing the escaping van in the side mirror. "One ugly American vehicle looks the same as the next to me."

Given what they had seen already, Remo was reluctant to let the van get away. Hoping that their giant spider wasn't caged inside it, he continued down the road to the bar.

When they pulled into the parking lot a minute later, the police had just arrived. Remo waved his FBI

ID under as many noses as was necessary to gain them admittance.

Inside, the two Masters of Sinanju noted the fresh black burn marks on the floor. There were two of them. Side by side, they traced the approximate oval shape of a pair of shoe soles.

Remo and Chiun exchanged a quick glance. They had seen similar marks before.

It was Remo who shook his head dismissively.

"Can't be," he insisted. "He's dead. Besides, look at this." He indicated the severed limbs lying on the floor near the bar. The rest of the drug dealer's corpse lay in a bloody heap nearby. "This is something different."

Chiun nodded sharply.

There was greater police activity in a room behind the bar. When Remo and Chiun stepped through the door, they found an even grislier scene. One man's head looked as if it had been sliced off by a portable guillotine.

As Remo examined the corpse, he glanced at the Master of Sinanju. "If I didn't know better, I'd think this was your handiwork, Little Father," he commented.

Chiun shook his head. "This butchery was done with an implement," he said, his face registering disgust.

Remo nodded. "Not a single blade, either," he said. He noted the slight irregularity on either side of the neck. "Looks almost like a big pair of scissors."

As he stepped around the body, he felt something under the heel of his loafer. Turning, he scuffed his foot across the floor. Chiun's gaze tracked the movement of his pupil.

On the floor were tiny black flecks, so small they would have been invisible to the average naked eye. Crouching, Remo gathered a bit of the residue on one finger, rubbing it between thumb and forefinger. His fingertips barely registered the presence of the frictionless material.

"More spider poop," he pronounced, dusting the thin black powder from his hands. "And just what the hell kind of spider sheds metal anyway?"

Tipping his head low, he found a few larger fragments scattered beneath a desk and chairs that sat back against the wall. Judging by the many bullet holes in the wall, they had apparently been blown off the creature.

Remo rose, fragments in hand and a dark cloud on his face. "Dammit, we should have followed that van. You get a look at the driver?"

"Of course," Chiun sniffed.

"And?" Remo asked after a brief moment of silence during which the old man said nothing.

Chiun shrugged. "He had a big nose, big hands and big feet. I would say he was a typical white."

Remo's lips thinned. "He wasn't driving with his feet, Chiun," he said.

"I merely extrapolated from that which I could see," the wizened Korean replied. Eyes growing conspiratorial, he pitched his voice low. "Although I have toiled in this land lo these many years, Remo, it remains a mystery to me to this day how you people are able to tell each other apart."

"Yeah, our lives are just one wacky *Patty Duke Show* episode after another," Remo said. "Guess we're screwed."

He found a plain white envelope on the desk and dumped the black fragments into it, stuffing the envelope deep in his pocket. Hands clenching, he turned back to survey the macabre scene.

He was thinking about how hard it would be to track an eight-legged opponent. Did eight legs mean it could run four times faster than a man?

"Of course," Chiun observed all at once, "there are always those numbers to differentiate one of you from the next."

"What numbers?" Remo asked, turning slowly.

"The identifying numbers on the back of the vehicle that drove directly at us," Chiun replied. "You know, Remo, the numbers that you failed to note since you were preoccupied with the task of not even glancing at the driver."

"You got the license-plate number?" Remo asked.

"Of course," Chiun said. A knowing sadness touched his weathered face. "And need I point out yet again that my eyes will not always be here to see for you?"

The dark lines of Remo's face grew firm.

"Nope," he said, shaking his head. "You're not

sucking me in with that now, Little Father, so you can just save the morbid stuff for another day. I've had enough lemonade making lately. For the moment my life's gonna be about the here and now—not some far-off time when everything's supposed to come crashing down around my big white ears. And right now I've got a bug to squash."

Face resolute, he went off in search of a phone.

Behind him Chiun considered his pupil's words.

Remo hadn't spoken in anger, merely with determination. And in his heart of hearts, the Master of Sinanju knew that his son's resolve was correct. The future would come in its time and would be whatever it would be.

Nodding silent agreement, the old man padded off after his pupil.

THE MIDMORNING SUN BURNED fiery hot over Cape Canaveral. The sunlight dragged across the half-opened venetian blinds, slicing perfect yellow lines across the hard-edged face of Administrator Zipp Codwin.

Zipp sat behind his sparkling white desk, his sharply angled chin braced on one bare-knuckled fist. His free hand drummed the desk's surface.

This kind of waiting was more than tedious to an old flyboy like himself. It was made all the worse by the A #1 screw-up of them all, that PR flak, Clark Beemer.

Not that everything had been going swimmingly.

In truth at first the NASA administrator and Pete Graham had made little progress on their plan to defeat Mr. Gordons's enemies. The thing that made it most difficult was the fact that Gordons himself seemed so unstoppable. If he couldn't kill the two guys he feared, how could Zipp hope to?

At least, that had been his thinking at the outset. Of course, he had abandoned such thoughts early on. He was Zipp Codwin, after all. He was a larger-than-life hero from another age who had truly gone where no man had gone before.

As the night hours had crept toward dawn, a plan had begun to take shape. It wasn't perfect, and it might not work. But it was an old-fashioned NASA-style plan.

Of course, Gordons might not approve. Zipp was bracing himself to bear the terrible wrath of the android when something far worse than being throttled by a pissed-off robot happened. That idiot Clark Beemer had returned to Canaveral. Alone.

Something had gone wrong with the latest robbery, and the public-relations asshole had beat a hasty retreat, abandoning Gordons at the scene. Zipp didn't even have time to wring the little coward's neck, so desperate was he to get to a TV.

The news coverage about the latest spider sighting was bland and uninformative. No mention of Gordons being captured and, most important of all, no mention of NASA.

Zipp breathed a heavy sigh of relief.

The agency was safe. At least for now. But the most valuable asset he'd had in his corner since assuming the top spot at America's space organization was MIA.

Without Gordons he was dead in the water. He couldn't go forward with his plans to refinance NASA, and he couldn't help eliminate the android's enemies.

His problems were held in stasis for a few hours, postdawn. They had worsened a few short minutes before.

He had just been informed that a pair of FBI agents was on the base. Fearing the worst, Zipp refused to allow anyone else to speak with them. He ordered the men brought to his office.

He was sitting in the smothering sunlight at his desk when a sharp rap sounded at his office door.

"Come!" Zipp called.

His secretary peeked her head inside the room. "Those men you wanted to see are here, Colonel," she said.

"Yes, yes," Zipp waved impatiently. "Let 'em in."

When the two men entered his office, Colonel Codwin was sure someone somewhere had gotten their wires crossed. There was no way these two could be FBI.

The first one was a skinny young guy in a T-shirt. The other was a wrinkled Asian in a kimono who looked older than the man in the moon. When they got to the desk, the young one flashed his laminated FBI identification at Codwin.

As Zipp carefully inspected it, the contents of the NASA administrator's desk caught the eye of the Master of Sinanju.

The desk was an ultramodern teardrop shape. Arranged before the blotter were dozens of model rockets. They seemed poised to launch an invasion of some tiny plastic planet.

His eyes trained with laserlike focus on the display, Chiun pushed his way past Remo. Slender fingers scooped up one of the small models.

The toy was divided into three stages. When Chiun pulled at it, two of the stages separated. When he pushed them together, they clicked back into a single unit.

Behind the desk, Zipp finally turned his nose away from Remo's ID, nodding acceptance.

"Welcome to NASA, gentlemen," he said. Standing, Zipp extended his hand. He offered a smile so strained it looked as if his underwear was six sizes too small.

Chiun ignored the administrator. He was too busy studying the rocket in his hand.

"Yeah, yeah," Remo said, interested in neither Zipp nor his offered hand. "Where do you keep your vans?"

There was a flicker at the far edges of Zipp's painful smile. "Vans?" he asked. "I think you're mistaking us for General Motors, son. We're your space agency. We don't do vans, we do shuttles, rockets and satellites.''

"Look, Flash Gordon," Remo said to Codwin, "I saw the size of this joint on the way in. Unless you pinheads zoom around here in portable jetpacks, you've got to use cars to get around. Where are they, and are there any missing?"

Zipp bristled at his words. "You sure you're FBI?" he questioned suspiciously.

"We're from the less tactful branch," Remo explained. "We're the part that uses toy rockets for suppositories when we don't get the answers we want."

Zipp glanced at the Master of Sinanju. The old man had just removed the nose cone of his rocket. Chiun blew on the module, simulating wind, as he lowered the capsule for splashdown in an invisible sea.

"You gentlemen are making it difficult for me to be polite," Codwin warned.

"Look, I've met three of your vans so far," Remo said. "One blew up on me, one caused that highway pileup yesterday and the third one almost ran me off the road as it left a multiple-murder scene last night. We tracked its plate to here. Polite went out the window the minute those loons in the first van tried to barbecue me. Now what's the deal?"

Zipp's smile collapsed. "I was afraid of this," he said in somber tones as he sat back in his chair. He steepled his fingers under his razor-sharp nose. "A couple of our vehicles have turned up missing recently. I ordered an investigation. At the faster, better, cheaper NASA we do not tolerate any wastefulness when it comes to taxpayer dollars."

When Remo snorted at that, Zipp bit his tongue.

"No matter what anyone might *think*," Codwin said, barely containing the acid in his tone, "NASA has undergone some severe belt tightening these past two decades. These days Congress is so cheap when it comes to our budget we can't afford to lose any equipment at all. Even vans."

Beside Remo, Chiun let out a whooshing sound. Guided by a sure hand, his rocket strafed the armada that was arranged for launch on Zipp's immaculate white desk. Most of the other toy models failed to survive the attack. As those few that remained upright teetered like wobbly bowling pins, the NASA administrator jumped across the desk, sweeping up the rolling rockets in both arms. A few clunked to the floor.

"I keep those here as souvenirs," he snarled at the Master of Sinanju. "Why don't you just take that one."

"They are free?" Chiun asked craftily.

"Sure," Zipp barked. "Take it."

Bending at the waist, the old Asian snatched up two of the rockets that had fallen to the floor. These disappeared inside the folds of his kimono. The first remained clutched in his hand. Spinning from the desk, he began flying it around the room. It attacked the fronds of a potted plant that sagged near a bookcase in the corner.

"You sure he's with the FBI, too?" Zipp asked.

As he spoke, another rocket tipped out of the pile in his arms, dropping to the gray carpet.

"He meets the Bureau's quota for odd-couple pairing." Remo nodded. "I had my choice between him, the superskeptical female doctor who never believes my crazy theories or the black guy who's always two weeks from retirement."

"Huh," Codwin grunted. His eyes still trained on Chiun, he drew the models across the desk, dumping most of them into a half-empty drawer. "If that's all, I have work to do. Space doesn't explore itself, you know."

"Actually, there's something else," Remo said. He dug in his pocket, removing the envelope he'd picked up at the Roadkill. Taking out one of the larger black fragments, he dropped it in Zipp's callused palm. "You have any idea what this could be?" he asked.

Codwin studied the jagged object carefully. When he touched the surface with an exploratory finger, a gunmetal-gray eyebrow rose on his lined forehead.

"Where did you get this?" Zipp asked.

Remo hesitated. Even after the previous day's news reports, he was uncomfortable admitting his mission.

"It was left at a crime scene," he said.

"Hmm," Zipp said, handing the fragment back to Remo. "We're not exactly a forensics lab here, but we're not lacking in brilliant scientists. I think I've got someone here who might be able to help you." He stabbed a finger on his intercom. "Mitzi, I'm bringing my guests down to see Dr. Graham. Tell him they've got some stuff they've collected from a crime scene they'd like to have examined.''

When he looked up at Remo there was a glint of something new in his pale blue eyes. A kind of knowing smugness. His tightly smiling mouth displayed a line of barracuda teeth.

''Come with me,'' the NASA head offered.

18

"By the way, Zipp Codwin's the name."

They had crossed the broad expanse of a tarmac to enter another big building on the Canaveral grounds. The NASA head let his famous name hang heavy in the air between them.

As they walked, Remo was supremely disinterested. "Blame your parents," he said, not looking Zipp's way.

The eyes beneath the steel-gray hair darkened. "Zipp Codwin," Zipp Codwin pressed. He pointed at his own chest. "*The* Zipp Codwin."

Remo glanced at Chiun. The Master of Sinanju was keeping pace with both men.

"Don't look at me," the old man said, his eyes downcast. He was studying a tiny window in his plastic rocket. "I do not even know what a Dipp Codpiece is."

"You ain't alone," Remo muttered.

"You don't remember me," Codwin growled, his painful smile collapsing to a more comfortable scowl. "Damn that whole shuttle program. Kids around the country remember the name of some blown-up schoolteacher who wasn't anything more than a piece of glorified luggage, but they don't know the names of the real pioneers who built the whole damn program.''

"Okay, Piss—'' Remo began.

"That's Zipp,'' Zipp interrupted coldly.

"Whatever," Remo said dismissively. "I get the drift. You were some kind of astronaut when the moon was still in diapers. Now let's just aim your rocket boosters into the *current* century where you can help the nice men who don't give a crap in a hat what your life story is.''

Zipp's scowl grew so tight it threatened to cave in on itself like a collapsing dwarf star.

"Son, there used to be a time when folks'd go ass over knickers at the chance to meet a bona fide spaceman.''

"We're thrilled," Remo said, deadpan. "Aren't we, Little Father?''

Chiun wasn't even listening. Plastic rocket in hand, he was soaring skyward. "Whoosh," the elderly Korean said.

"I suppose I shouldn't keep getting ticked that folks don't remember me," Zipp muttered. "It's been thirty damn years since we've done anything significant around here." He instantly regretted speaking the words aloud. "Not that we're not still important," he quickly amended. "It's just that our purpose has changed over the years.''

"I'll say," Remo agreed. "You've changed from

an extravagant waste of money that used to do stuff once in a while to an extravagant waste of money that doesn't do anything at all ever. NASA's just a black hole the government shovels tax dollars into."

"That isn't true," Codwin insisted hotly. "NASA is a vital and, I might add, underfunded agency. And thanks to me, you can be certain that your tax dollars are wisely spent."

"Not mine," Remo said as they walked. "Don't pay 'em."

"Hear! Hear!" Chiun sniffed at his elbow. As they continued down the long, sterile hallway, his rocket flew parallel to the floor.

Codwin's steely eyes narrowed. "Are you telling me that neither of you pays taxes?"

One hand still flying the model, Chiun used the other to stroke his thread of beard thoughtfully. "A tax collector visited my village once when I was a boy."

"Uh-oh," Remo said. "You never told me that. What'd those money-grubbing villagers do, boil him in a pot?"

"Of course not," Chiun frowned. "We are not barbarians. My father allowed him to leave in peace. He merely kept his purse." He tipped his head. "And his hands. I believe he had them bronzed and sent them along to Pyongyang. We weren't bothered by another tax collector as long as my father lived." There was a tear of pride in the corner of one hazel eye as he resumed flying his rocket.

"Even so," Zipp droned flatly, suspicious eyes trained on the old man, "taxes are our lifeblood. Without money this agency couldn't function."

Remo snorted. "Said the head of the agency that can't even land a Tinkertoy on Mars."

Zipp's face clouded. "The media likes to dwell on the negatives," he said through tightly clenched teeth, "but the truth is we've had many great successes lately. There was the ice that might or might not be on the surface of the moon that we almost found, some close-up pictures of a big rock in space and a new generation of space plane that could be off the drawing board by the year 2332. And don't forget, we even sent Senator Glenn back into space."

"Yeah, but then you had to ruin it by bringing him back down," Remo said. "And we're not here for the sales pitch."

Nostrils flaring, Codwin only grunted.

They took an elevator to a lower level, exiting into an antiseptic hallway. Down the corridor and around the corner, Zipp led them through a door marked Special Project Director, Virgil Climatic Explorer, Dr. Peter Graham.

The man inside, a twitchy twenty-something with shaggy hair and pasty skin, was perched on a lab stool. Graham's tired eyes jumped to the door when the three men entered.

"Pete, these men are with the FBI," Zipp announced. "They have something they want you to examine for them."

"Yes," Graham said, his eyes shifting back and forth from Remo to Chiun. His nervous voice cracked. "Some crime-scene evidence?"

Remo handed the scientist the envelope. "You know what this stuff is?" he asked.

"Nope," Graham insisted with absolute certainty.

"You wanna try looking inside the envelope first?" Remo suggested.

"Oh." Pete Graham dumped a few of the black fragments into his hand. "Nope," he stated once more.

Beside the seated scientist, Zipp Codwin's lips thinned disapprovingly. "Pete here's the best in the business," he said tightly. "If he says nope, I gotta believe it's nope."

One of the benefits of Remo's Sinanju training was the ability to detect when someone was lying. Heart rate, perspiration, subtle mannerisms—all helped determine if a subject was being untruthful. It was clear to him that these two men were lying about something. Given what he'd seen of their operation, he was willing to chalk it up to the lies men told to cover up rank incompetence.

He was about to press further when a muted electronic beep issued from the pocket of Zipp's jacket. When the NASA head answered his cell phone, his angled face grew puzzled.

"It's for you," Codwin said, handing the phone to Remo.

"Hello?" Remo asked with a frown.

"Remo, Mark," Howard's familiar voice said excitedly. "Someone thinks they saw the spider. She saw someone helping it into the back of a car. Weird thing is, she says it looked like a man, but with a bunch of arms like a spider."

Chiun had grown bored with his toy. At Howard's words, the plastic spaceship vanished inside his robes. His face serious, he listened in on Remo's call.

"Where's Smith?" Remo complained.

"He asked me to call," Howard said. "Remo, I know this woman's story sounds kind of out there—"

"No, Zitt Hatpin is kind of out there. You're light-years past him. Let me talk to Smith."

"Hush, Remo," Chiun admonished.

"Whatever it was, she swore she knew the guy who helped it get away," Howard pressed. "It was Stewart McQueen."

A shadow formed on Remo's brow. "Stewart McQueen? Isn't he the guy who writes all those crackpot horror books about killer clowns and possessed farm equipment?"

"He used to," Howard said. "Until he got hit by a car. I heard on TV he's got writer's block. Anyway, because of the stuff he writes and the fact it's almost Halloween, the cops didn't believe her story. Didn't hurt she was at a bar. But I had a hunch so I did some digging. Turns out a car was rented down there last night under one of McQueen's pseudonyms. He's already turned it back in. And he bought an *extra* ticket for the plane ride home."

"You think he managed to sneak a giant spider into first class?" Remo said doubtfully.

"He snuck *something* on," Howard insisted. "He's back at his home in Bay Cove, Maine, by now. Dr. Smith wants you to check him out."

Remo felt someone pressing in close behind him. Hot breath whistled from pinched nostrils.

Zipp Codwin was leaning in, straining to listen to what was being said. Beyond him, Pete Graham cowered in the corner, chewing nervously on his ragged fingernails.

Remo turned a withering eye on the NASA head. "How'd you like a trip back to the moon?"

Zipp hitched up his belt with both hands. "Well," he said proudly, "technically I was never on the moo— Oh."

Crossing his arms huffily, the NASA administrator turned away from his visitor.

"Is there a problem?" Mark Howard asked.

"No," Remo grumbled. "Tell Smitty we're on our way."

"I'll have the tickets waiting for you at the airport," Howard promised. He cut the connection.

Remo handed the phone back to Codwin.

"Looks like you clowns are off the hook," he said. "You and the rest of NASA can go back to pretending to work while the rest of us have to do the real thing."

Turning from Codwin and Graham, Remo and Chiun quickly left the lab.

When the ping of the elevator doors closing issued from far down the hallway, Pete Graham finally worked up the nerve to speak.

"Did I do okay?" he asked weakly.

Zipp responded by cuffing the scientist in the back of the head.

"You're as big an idiot as that Beemer," the NASA head growled. "Not that it matters. Thanks to those two, we know where Gordons is now. The capsule's splashed down. We just have to go retrieve it."

"But the FBI's involved," Graham argued. "How are you going to get by them?"

For the first time, Dr. Pete Graham saw something that approached a genuine smile on the face of Zipp Codwin. It was like some demonic grinning ice sculpture come to life.

"NASA has resources that you don't know about," Codwin said malevolently. "And dang-blast it to all high heaven, it's not like they don't deserve it. I mean, they don't pay taxes." His voice was flirting with the quivering edges of outrage. "I mean—Lord God Jeebus Almighty—*tax cheats*. At NASA there's nothing lower. No wonder Gordons wants them dead. Well, that tin can's about to get his wish."

Spinning sharply on one hard heel, Colonel Zipp Codwin marched boldly from the research lab.

19

Stewart McQueen knew that it was the intervention of Old Scratch and all of his hellish minions of evil that brought him safely back home to Maine. The front door accepted the writer's key, and the security system—which was wired around the entire mansion—yielded to his special access code.

His gimpy leg ached. Limping under the weight of his precious bundle, the novelist steered his mutant spider-man into the living room.

Mr. Gordons had fallen silent during the plane ride up from Florida. Good thing, too. It was hard enough to hide all those extra furry legs under an overcoat, but McQueen doubted he could have avoided extra attention if the creature had continued to mutter "survive, survive" over and over again as he had on the car ride to the airport.

Once on the ground in Maine, McQueen had been startled when he started to help his monster up from his first-class seat and discovered that the spider legs had disappeared at some point during the flight. All that was left were the two human appendages. When McQueen looked closely, he could still see the slices in the blue fabric of the jacket through which the extra legs had jutted.

He was home now, and his creature still had but two arms as Stewart McQueen dumped Mr. Gordons into his old living-room chair. A thick cloud of white dust escaped into the air as the heavy bundle settled into the cushions.

Coughing and limping, McQueen collapsed exhausted to the high-backed Victorian-era sofa.

"We made it," the novelist gasped to himself. He blinked away the sharp pain that suddenly gripped his knee.

As if in response, a noise sounded deep within the chest of his guest. It was as if he was trying to speak, but the words wouldn't come. Even his lips failed to move.

Stewart strained to hear what he was saying. It came slowly, as if echoing up from the depths of a dark well. The same word, repeated over and over.

"...survive, survive, survive, survive..."

McQueen's shoulders slumped. "Not again," he sighed.

"...survive, survive, survive..."

The word grew louder. He had been quiescent during the flight, but it now seemed almost as if the spider creature had been recharging its batteries.

All at once Mr. Gordons snapped alert. His eyes opened wide, as if seeing his surroundings for the first time. His head twisted to one side.

On a stand next to the chair was a television remote

control. As the word *survive* cut out, Gordons lifted his right hand and dropped it on the sleek black device.

There was a crack of plastic.

When he took his hand away a moment later, all that remained was the shattered casing and two crushed batteries. The guts of the remote had been absorbed into Gordons's hand.

His head twisted again, right then left. He seemed to be absorbing every minute detail of the room he was in. At last he turned his flat gaze on Stewart McQueen.

"I am not home," Gordons pronounced.

"Home?" McQueen asked, still amazed by what his monster had done to the remote control.

Gordons resumed scanning his surroundings. Artificial cobwebs hung from beamed ceilings. Above the black stone fireplace, a pair of carved gargoyles stared back at him.

"This is not NASA," Gordons stated. "It is an environment unfamiliar to me. Where am I?"

"You're at *my* home," McQueen explained. "In Maine. I rescued you from that bar. You were pretty beat up."

Gordons seemed to be remembering, accessing those parts of his stored memory not damaged after his deadly confrontation at the Roadkill Tavern.

"I encountered an entity of a nature unknown to me," he said. "From what I was able to ascertain before and during his attack, he was a cybernetic being.''

"Yeah,'' McQueen nodded. "He seemed to pack a real wallop.'' A hopeful glint sparked in his eyes. "You wouldn't happen to have his address, would you?''

"No.''

"Too bad,'' McQueen said. "That guy had inspiration written all over him. Just like you.''

Standing, the android examined his arms and hands. "There are no words inscribed on my body,'' he disagreed. "Nor would the presence of such a disfigurement be effective camouflage. As for the cybernetic man I encountered, he is irrelevant. I do not have the time to engage another enemy. My primary targets remain the same.''

"Targets? What targets? Hey, that's my computer.''

Gordons was at the desk in the corner. "I require components to complete repairs.''

Placing his palms firmly on either side of McQueen's PC, the android's hands began to shudder. As the writer watched, fascinated, the hands seemed to melt through the chassis, disappearing inside the machine. They rested that way for a moment, bare wrists fused to metal. A few crunches and whirs later, the hands reappeared, apparently as good as new.

The same couldn't be said for McQueen's computer. The device now sported two perfectly round holes in each side.

"Hey, the first drafts of my next fifteen books were stored on that thing," the novelist complained. "I wrote them before I got hit by that car. That's three weeks' worth of work you just ruined."

Gordons didn't seem to care about the great loss to modern literature. Bringing one hand back, he rabbit-punched forward, shattering the computer screen. He began rooting around inside the monitor for parts.

"It's okay," McQueen quickly declared. "Take whatever you want. I can always type up a couple more books. Usually takes me about two days to do three hundred pages anyway." He bit his lip with his rodentlike incisors. "Although lately it's been a little harder than it used to. That's why I went to find you. A real live monster could maybe help to shake things up for me. Um, you are a monster, aren't you?"

"I am an android," Mr. Gordons explained.

He ripped two green motherboards from the interior of the shattered monitor. When he turned to face the novelist, McQueen saw that a wide gash had opened in the being's stomach. The computer components disappeared in the freshly created slot. After they were accepted inside, the wound sealed back up behind them. So, too, Stewart McQueen noted, did the creature's dress shirt.

"Android, huh?" McQueen said, trying to hide his disappointment. "I don't know about that. Kind of sci-fi, you know what I mean? The readers might complain if I start shoving robots into my books."

"I must go," Gordons announced abruptly.

Without another word he started across the room.

"Whoa, there, Charlie," McQueen blurted, jumping to his feet. His leg nearly buckled beneath him in his dash to get out in front of the departing android.

"My name is Mr. Gordons, not Charlie. And if you do not step from my path, I will assume that you are an enemy to my survival, as well."

"I'm not an enemy," McQueen argued. "I *saved* you. And I can help you with whatever you need. I'm *loaded*. You want computers? I can feed them to you three squares a day. You want sanctuary? You got it here. This is still a small town. No one knows I brought you here."

"Even if that is true now, it will not remain so," Gordons disagreed. "My enemies have the resources to locate me if they so desire."

"Then let me help you stop them," McQueen pleaded.

He dropped to his knees. Tears immediately welled up in his eyes. Most from the buzz-saw pain in his injured leg.

Gordons seemed to consider his words. "The resources of NASA are far greater than yours. It is unlikely that you will be able to assist me. However, the information I have absorbed from your computer's hard drive indicates to me that you are a creative individual. This is a trait that I lack. Perhaps it would be wiser from a tactical standpoint to accept your offer. If you fail, I will always have my fallback position with Colonel Codwin and NASA. Two lines of attack are always preferable to one.''

"Sure," Stewart McQueen agreed. He had no idea what the hell the screwy robot was talking about. Probably had a few gears loose in the old noggin.

As the novelist dragged himself back to his feet, Mr. Gordons crossed back into the room, walking over to the TV.

Bringing his arm up, he punched his hand through the top of the television. The set flickered on.

McQueen was standing upright now, grasping the door frame. "Just 'cause you broke the remote, there's still a control panel on the front of that thing," he panted.

A grainy image appeared on the screen. It seemed to have been recorded on a very old videotape. Ghosts of other images played in the foreground and background.

"Given time, I could resolve the picture quality," the android said. "This is an old image, taken by me just prior to an earlier encounter with my enemies. I am translating it from partially damaged files into a video context that is comprehensible to your limited ocular system."

"It's fine," McQueen said.

The pain in his leg was nearly forgotten. He hobbled forward, amazed by the android's abilities.

On the TV screen were two men. Despite the ghosts and the grainy grayness of the picture, they appeared to exist almost three-dimensionally. One was a young white; the other was a very old Asian. They were strolling through what appeared to be some sort of amusement park.

"That thing you do," McQueen mused thoughtfully as he stared at the picture, "where you take the parts of stuff and incorporate them into you...?"

"My ability to assimilate," Gordons suggested.

"Yeah, that," McQueen said. "I have an idea that might knock your pals off their game. How big an object can you assimilate?"

There was no bravado in the android's voice. "How big an object do you wish me to assimilate?"

McQueen flashed a ferretlike smile. He glanced around at the gloomy Gothic surroundings of his dusty mansion. There was an evil twinkle in his eye.

"How about a haunted house?" asked the world-famous horror novelist.

FOR SECRECY'S SAKE, Mark Howard had driven across the New York border to Milford, Connecticut, mailing the small metal fragment Remo had collected in Florida from there. The package had been picked up and was well on its way to a laboratory for analysis by the time Mark made his way back inside his Folcroft office.

He noted the small envelope that sat on the edge of his desk as soon as he opened the door.

The morning had been so hectic that he hadn't even bothered to open the second envelope Remo had addressed to him. There was a note scrawled on the outside. With a frown, Howard reread it: "Nothing to do with what we're working on, Prince. Just leave this in my room. R."

Mark collected the envelope. It was fat but soft.

Envelope in hand, Mark headed down to Remo and Chiun's quarters. He unlocked the door with his Folcroft passkey.

The common room was tidy. Probably Chiun's doing. Remo didn't strike Mark as a neat freak.

He crossed over to Remo's bedroom door.

Fumbling around the corner, he flipped on the light. He was halfway to the bureau when he stopped dead.

Jaw dropping, Mark swung his head slowly around.

All four walls were covered with scraps of paper. Mark couldn't believe his eyes.

B. O. Anson Dead!

B.O. KO'd By Runaway Golfball.

FORE!

LAPD Denies Involvement.

The headlines blared from every corner. Since Anson's death, Remo had to have collected every newspaper and magazine article he could find. On many of the articles, pictures of Anson's grinning face and dead eyes stared out at the room.

Mark couldn't believe what he was seeing. Four walls dedicated to the death of B. O. Anson. A shrine to Anson's murder. He realized with a sinking feeling that this was precisely the sort of thing a serial killer would do.

All at once he remembered the envelope in his

hands. With anxious fingers, Mark tore open the bulging envelope.

More articles on Anson's death spilled out, these ones from Florida papers.

Mark glanced up once more. Jaw clenching, he shook his head in disbelief.

This was worse than stupid. It was dangerous. Remo had crossed a line far worse than before.

Going over to the nearest wall, Howard began the laborious task of pulling down the many clippings.

20

"It is time," the Master of Sinanju announced abruptly.

They were on the flight to Maine.

Remo glanced around the cabin, a concerned expression on his face. He assumed that Chiun had seen another passenger of Vietnamese descent and was about to embark on a fresh round of candy-corn-inspired ethnic cleansing. When Remo saw no Asian faces, he didn't know whether he should be relieved or even more worried.

"Time for what?" he asked cautiously.

"Time for you to listen," Chiun said. "For I am going to tell you the dark tale of Master Shiko and the truth behind the infamous yeti of the Himalayas."

"Oh. You sure you don't want to assault any of the other passengers?" Remo asked hopefully. "I think I smelled a Frenchman back in coach." He rose halfway to his feet.

With one bony hand the Master of Sinanju drew him back down into his seat.

"Now, this did take place but a few scant centuries ago," Chiun began. His singsong voice took on the familiar cadence of storyteller. "It was during that period of time after which Master Shiko had already trained a Master to succeed him, but before his time of ritual seclusion. Since his heir had not yet chosen a pupil of his own to pass on the ways of Sinanju, Master Shiko had not yet relinquished the title of Reigning Master, even though he had already ceded most of his responsibilities to his young protégé."

In the seat beside Chiun, Remo shifted uneasily. His teacher's words were a reminder of something he didn't want to think about right now.

If Chiun sensed his pupil's discomfort, he didn't show it. He continued with his story.

"Even though Shiko was in but the waning days of his first full century and still technically true claimant of the title Master, his health was not as it had once been. His infirmity was not the result of age alone," Chiun quickly pointed out, "but was due to an encounter several years before with a cult of fire-worshiping Ghebers in Persia."

"Gabors?" Remo asked. "Like Zsa Zsa and Eva?"

Chiun's papery lips pursed. "There are medications, Remo, for children with wandering minds. I will ask Emperor Smith to write you a prescription." Not desiring another intrusion, he continued. "The Ghebers were a once-powerful sect of Zoroastrians, thought extinct by Sinanju."

This triggered something from far back in Remo's memory. "Those Zeroequestrians were astrologers, weren't they?" he asked. "I remember Sister Irene saying that that's what the three Wise Men were way back in grade-school religion class."

Chiun shook his head impatiently. "As usual the carpenter's maidens have dropped in a single fact to float in the pool of their fictions. Yes, some were that. Others were much, much more. And that they were Zoroastrians is irrelevant. That they were from Persia is what matters." He continued his story. "In the sunset of his life Master Shiko was summoned to perform a minor service for a Persian emir. The emir wished the Master to remove a band of cutthroats that was terrorizing the lowlands of his kingdom.

"Now, under ordinary circumstances, though still Reigning Master, Shiko would have remained in Sinanju to mend the nets and watch the children play, allowing his pupil, whose name was Hya-Tee, to go in his stead. However, since Persia was the place where he had met great hardship, Shiko did not wish to risk endangering his pupil so early in his life, Hya-Tee having seen a mere forty-five summers. And so in his age and infirmity did Master Shiko take up his bundle and travel to the distant land of the Persian emirs."

Remo shook his head. "If Shiko was in such crummy shape, shouldn't Hya-Tee have insisted that he go instead?"

"There are Apprentice Reigning Masters and there are Reigning Masters," Chiun replied evenly. "In your experience, Remo, which one has the last word?''

At this Remo couldn't argue.

Satisfied, Chiun resumed his tale. ''Now, it should be known that, although in failing health by Sinanju standards, Shiko was still better than any mere man. His bones were old, his sight was poor and some have said that his mind was beginning to precede his body into the Void, yet all of this mattered not when it came to the task he was to perform. In Persia he did impress the court of this lesser emir with his displays of speed and skill. And this was as it should be, for in his youth Shiko was as able as any Master who had come before, save only the greatest of the line. Verily did Shiko slay the murderous highwayman and, receiving payment in full, did he begin the long trek overland back to Sinanju.

''It was during his journey home that Master Shiko did make a most grave mistake. Flush with his success and the accolades he had received at court, Shiko did see himself for what he once was. In the clouding mind that sometimes comes with the sicknesses of age he once more became the man of his youth. Rather than take the longer, safer path that he had used for his earlier journey to Persia, he did take the less certain route he had employed several times as a young man.

''And lo did Shiko abandon the wisdom of age and travel did he up the treacherous route through the Himalayas. His path did bring him to Nepal and past the rude buildings that would one day rise up to become what is now the famed Tengpoche Monastery, which sits in the shadow of Chomolunga, the highest mountain in all the world.''

In spite of himself, Remo had found that he was being drawn into the story. But at this, he had to interrupt.

''Wait,'' he said. ''If it's in the Himalayas, that's gotta be Mount Everest, not Chumbawumba.''

Chiun raised an annoyed eyebrow. ''The civilized half of the world doesn't recognize that new name,'' he said frostily.

''Okay, but it is Mount Everest we're talking about?'' Remo asked. ''I just want to be clear.''

''*I* am talking about Chomolunga,'' Chiun sniffed. ''What filters through to your brain is of no consequence to me.''

''Okay,'' Remo said, satisfied that they were indeed talking about Mount Everest. He settled back down.

Chiun didn't even have a chance to pull in another breath before Remo was interrupting again.

''Wait a sec, I thought K2 was tallest now.''

Chiun's face puckered. ''What is that?''

''A mountain. I think it's in India somewhere.''

''If it is in India, then that ugly thing is not its true name. No doubt the white who first saw it laid claim to it and replaced the good Indian name with that K9 appellation.''

''K9's a dog, Little Father,'' Remo said. ''But

you're right. The Indians wouldn't have named it after something that'd be confused with a dog. Cow's more their speed." His face brightened. "Say, you know if there's a Mount Bossie anywhere in India?"

"No," Chiun said dryly. "Are you quite finished?"

"Yeah, I'm done," Remo nodded.

The Korean's narrowed eyes seemed not to believe his pupil. Nonetheless, he forged ahead.

"Now, it was here in the shadow of Chomolunga where Master Shiko did come upon a gathering of Sherpa monks. They had heard that the Master of Sinanju was approaching their pathetic excuse for a monastery and had come out to greet him. And on the slippery path to Kathmandu, they did beg him stop. Surrounded were these monks by men of the new squalid Sherpa settlements, and the look of fright was full on all their ugly flat Sherpa faces. However, Shiko could see only the faces of those nearest, for his eyes were weak by now. But heard he the trembling fear in their voices.

"And these monks did speak in quavering voices, and they did tell of a terrible beast that had been attacking their settlements. They claimed that this creature did live in the forested regions near the snow line and did only venture down to prey on them. The beast was of great size with fearsome large hands and feet. The color of snow was this terrible creature, and was thus nearly invisible to the eye until it was too late. Many had died, they said.

"'Why does this beast attack you, O quivering Sherpas?'" the aged Master Shiko did ask.

"'He fears our nearness, great Master of Sinanju,' the monks did reply. 'For until our arrival these mountains were his home and his alone. At unsuspecting moments he does leap from concealment, casting our people from the mountainside to the rocks of the ravines far below. We fear he will kill us all, thus reclaiming that which he sees as his.'"

At this, Remo broke in once more. "You're saying they were new to the mountain, right?" he asked.

"That is correct," Chiun replied.

"Hmm," Remo said. "Maybe there was no abominable snowman," he suggested. "Maybe they were just slipping on the snow and falling over the side of the mountain."

In an earlier day Chiun would have been annoyed at yet another interruption. However, this time a thin smile slithered across the old man's parchment lips.

"That is partly true," he admitted, nodding wisely. "These first Sherpas had only recently migrated from the eastern Tibetan province of Khams to settle in this mountainous region. If Shiko's mind was as clear as that of the young Master he was pretending to be, he would have realized that these clumsy clods were not used to living on mountains and were merely slipping and cracking open their own thick Sherpa heads. But, alas, this did not occur to Master Shiko. He did have mind enough to know, however, that Sinanju had met many things known to quail the human heart. Some have been real—like dragons, minotaurs and gorgons.''

"Gorgons?" Remo asked skeptically. "Aren't those the snake-haired chicks that turn you into rock?''

"There are limits to my patience, Remo," Chiun warned.

"Sorry," Remo sighed.

"So some monsters have been real while many more have been false things, created by man to explain or excuse his own weaknesses. In the age during which Shiko lived, there were few real monsters left. And though he had spent much time on these paths as a young man, in both winter and summer months, never once hearing of such a fantastic creature, Shiko was nevertheless intrigued by this tale, for he was still in the blush of false youth following his success in Persia. Throwing wisdom to the wind, he agreed to undertake the task of hunting this new beast. The Sherpa monks did pay him in gold and, after ritualistically sprinkling the ground around his feet with holy water and flowers, they did send him off on the hunt.

"Ordinarily, a Master would have embarked on such an expedition alone, but even in his delusional state Shiko realized that he would need someone to carry the tribute paid him by the monks. In addition to this, a fierce winter had late descended on the Himalayas. Men were needed to carry his supplies, and so it was decided that a group of young Sherpas would accompany him on his journey.

"They traveled on mountain paths, around Solu Khumba and up toward Kala Patter, which lay in peaceful slumber beneath the watchful gaze of mounts Lhotse and Nuptse. The trails were treacherous, and many were the times that Master Shiko's swift hand saved one or another of his retinue from falling to their deaths. They had trekked far, and Shiko was beginning to lose hope that they would ever find the creature they sought. But on the first day of the third week, they spied the beast's tracks."

In the seat next to the old Korean, Remo's face grew intent. The sounds of the plane engines and the general passenger sounds faded as he listened to Shiko's tale.

"Giant were these prints in the snow," Chiun continued. "Five times larger than any man's. They followed the trail to the thinning edge of the trees. And at dusk on the very day on which they discovered the tracks did they spy the creature." The old Korean tipped his head sadly. "Such was it recorded by Shiko, Remo," he said, his voice low. "However, in point of fact it was the Sherpas who claimed to see the beast. Shiko's eyes being what they were, he could not see to where they pointed. Yet he followed. For months they did follow a jagged course, up mountains and down. The beast remained before them, ever out of reach. And during this time Shiko failed to notice that the men with him—men who had at first fallen with nearly every other step—had slowly become more surefooted.'' Chiun paused momentarily, eyeing his pupil.

Remo said not a word. He didn't have to. A knowing look had settled on his face.

Chiun nodded. ''You understand what Shiko did not,'' he intoned. ''For although the deceitful monks claimed to be in search of a monster, what they really wanted was a way to keep their clumsy fellow Sherpas from falling off their silly mountains. And so it was that by the time Shiko's party had finished scouring the hills around Pokhara valley, the Sherpas had become the most skilled mountain climbers in the world outside of Sinanju. Even so, Shiko in his foolishness did not know the truth. Eventually, his health failed him and he was carried back to the Tengpoche Monastery, there to die.''

''Bastards,'' muttered Remo, who understood that the skills of the Master of Sinanju sustained the village. ''They took advantage of an old man. Everybody's out looking for a freebie. I'm surprised Shiko's student what's-his-name, Hat-Trick, didn't kack every last one of them.''

At this, Chiun nodded. ''Back home in Sinanju, Hya-Tee heard of his teacher's sickness. He did undertake the long journey to Chomolunga, there to find his Master in his final hours of life. On his trip up to the monastery, Hya-Tee did note the ease with which the Sherpa people journeyed about the mountainside. At the bedside of his Master, Shiko in his dying

breath told Hya-Tee of the beast that he had been
hired to kill. At that moment did Hya-Tee understand
the truth.''

"I'm confused," Remo said. "If Hya-Tee knew
what happened, why didn't he wipe out the Sherpas
then and there? I mean obviously he didn't, 'cause
they're still good at climbing mountains today.''

"Alas, it would have been an easy enough thing if
it were but a matter of removing the men who had
accompanied Shiko on his fruitless quest," Chiun explained. "But upon returning to their villages, they
did instruct their females and children the proper way
to tread on mountain snow and ice. The people of
other settlements were taught, as well. By the time
Hya-Tee arrived there, the skill had been passed to
every Sherpa. Still, Hya-Tee could not allow such
thievery to pass unpunished. He learned the names of
the men who had been with Master Shiko on his
pointless hunt, and for a time after the death of his
old Master, Hya-Tee became the embodiment of that
false creature Shiko had sought. He prowled the night,
invisible in the snow, casting to their deaths the original thieves who did steal from Sinanju.''

"Good." Remo nodded, crossing his arms in satisfaction.

"It was more than good—it was right," Chiun
said. "At first the Sherpas knew fear. But over time,
fear became respect. Eventually all did realize the
debt they owed to Sinanju. When the last thief had
met his just end, Hya-Tee did show himself. And said

he, 'Thieving Sherpas, you have stolen from foolish Master Shiko and thus from Sinanju. To steal from us is to steal the food from the mouths of our children, for it is the work of the Master that sustains the village. Therefore, on this day and every time this season comes again for as long as you live in these mountains, Sinanju demands payment. The skills you have stolen will not be shared with outsiders, lest you incur the wrath of the shadowy beast of your own creation.'

"And thus it was agreed," Chiun said. "Every spring to this very day, the monks of Tengpoche do send a stipend to our village. Hya-Tee returned home to Sinanju, there to inter the body of his dead Master. As the years went by and this tale was passed down from one generation of Sherpas to the next, Hya-Tee's name became distorted. However, his legend is such that men around the world today speak his name."

Finished with his tale, he fussed at his robes.

Beside him, Remo frowned. "Hya-Tee. I don't know—" The light dawned. "Yeti," he said, his eyes widening. "You're saying a Master of Sinanju is the abominable snowman?"

"I am saying that Hya-Tee exacted proper penance and is remembered for it," Chiun replied blandly.

"All right, so what's this got to do with the eight-legged bank robber we're after?"

"It is of particular relevance," Chiun said. "Remember, Master Shiko sought a monster that he could not see."

"It's not the same," Remo pointed out. "Everyone says they've seen a spider."

"And this is the lesson of Master Shiko," Chiun nodded wisely. "Just because many say they see a thing, that does not make that thing real. Trust your eyes not theirs."

"*We've* seen it," Remo suggested.

Chiun shook his head. "I have seen *something*," he replied, folding his arms. "What that something is I don't know. In any case, that television image was not clear. It is always wise to make no assumptions about what you think you know about your opponent until you've actually seen it with your own eyes. Such has it been since the time of Master Shiko." He pitched his voice low. "In point of fact, it was like this even before Shiko," he admitted. "Most Masters who came after him agree that we are fortunate the senile old fool didn't sell the entire village out from under us for a handful of magic beans."

The old Asian settled comfortably back in his seat, interwoven hands resting on his belly.

Remo bit his cheek thoughtfully. The sounds of the cabin seemed suddenly louder.

He had seen the image on the TV with his own eyes. It had certainly looked like a spider. But in truth the camera had been wobbly and the image had been fleeting.

When was a spider not a spider?

His face tight with somber reflection, he pondered Chiun's words for the rest of the flight to Maine.

21

When they landed in Bangor, Remo called Smith for directions before renting a car at the airport. They drove east to Bay Cove. With a twice-delayed flight and a long drive, the late-afternoon shadows were already growing long.

It was the end of the autumn-foliage season in New England. Nature had painted the trees along the winding roads in vivid shades of red and yellow. By the time they arrived in the small seaside community Stewart McQueen called home, Chiun had his window rolled down. The old Korean sniffed the chilly October air with satisfaction.

"This place reminds me of my village," the Master of Sinanju said as they took the winding main road past quaint cottages decorated with lobster traps and sea-stained buoys.

"I don't smell shit," Remo said as he studied the road signs.

Chiun ignored him. "My quest for a new home still continues. I have seen many pictures. The Prince Regent has been most helpful."

"I think Smitty wants us out of Folcroft," Remo

said. "The artist formerly known as Prince is just following orders."

He turned off the main drag onto a shaded side street.

"Yet you persist in your recalcitrance."

"I don't want to live in Maine, Chiun. It's colder than all hell. Besides, we've done the East Coast thing already. I'm putting winter behind me."

"We will see," Chiun said, settling back into his seat.

Remo followed Smith's directions, turning off the small lane and onto a tree-lined cul-de-sac. They looped around to the end. When he stopped before the gates of Stewart McQueen's mansion, his eyes grew flat.

"You gotta be kidding me," he said as he looked up at the unsightly Gothic mess that was Stewart McQueen's home.

The four-story structure slouched like an architectural bully at the end of the sparsely populated street. The round windows of the gabled attic rooms were like malevolent eyes of doom, staring out across the neighborhood. A widow's walk with rusted rail clung precariously to the slate roof. Gray shingled walls in desperate need of paint were adorned here and there with half-nailed shutters.

Around the property, autumn seemed to have come earlier than in the surrounding region, for any trace of leaves had been stripped from the handful of trees whose clawlike roots were fixed to soil. Bare black branches scraped the sky.

In the front seat beside Remo, the Master of Sinanju's button nose crinkled in distaste as he viewed the house.

"What is this place?" Chiun asked unhappily.

"I think the nuns would call it a living testament to the decline of American literature," Remo suggested. "Either that or it's the Munsters' summer house."

The two men got out of the car.

A pair of black metallic bats decorated the stone posts to which was fixed the rusting front gate.

"Cameras in the bats' eyes," Remo pointed out as they strolled up to the gate. He had detected the soft clicks and whirs of delicate machinery.

"What manner of man lives in such a dwelling?" the Master of Sinanju asked. Standing on tiptoe, he was peering intently up at the bats.

The bats didn't look back. Remo and Chiun were now below their range. The dark, smoky eyes stared out across the deserted street.

"The guy's a superrich horror writer," Remo explained. "I saw on some tabloid show how he had his place done up to look like a haunted house." Hands on his hips, he peered through the bars of the gate at the house beyond. "Can't say it looks better in person than it did on TV."

With a soft harrumph of disapproval, Chiun dropped back to his soles. "The gate is electrified," he announced, tucking hands inside his kimono sleeves.

"Whole place is, judging by the hum I'm getting off it," Remo replied. "He must have a major security system. So what do you say, Little Father," he asked, turning to the Master of Sinanju, "through it or over it?"

Neither course proved necessary. As Remo and Chiun stood on the sidewalk before the gate, a gentle click sounded at the heavy bolt. The electrical charge that hummed through the fence powered down to silence. With a forlorn groan of rusted metal, the heavy steel gate rolled slowly open.

Remo glanced at Chiun. "This might be a good time to remember not to take any balloons from killer clowns who want to lure us into the woods," he said dryly.

Chiun's face was serious. "Stay alert," he warned. With that the old Korean slipped through the gates.

Remo followed him inside.

As they walked away, high up on the gateposts behind them, the heads of the two bat sentries swung around.

The eyes of the metal creatures were directed at the backs of the two men as they made their way up the walk.

When Remo felt the telltale waves from the cameras on his back, he arched a curious eyebrow.

"I thought those things looked solid," he commented. "Didn't look to me like the necks could swivel."

He glanced over his shoulder. But when he did, the bats were once more facing the street, away from Remo and Chiun.

"What the hell?"

As a frown took shape on Remo's face, the front gate abruptly swung closed without so much as a creak. The hum from the electrified fence rose in the chilly air.

"Isn't this the part where Shemp sees the ghost, but Moe and Larry are too busy moving furniture to notice?" Remo asked the vacant air.

As if in response, a low moan rose from the house, painful and protracted.

As they headed up the flagstone walk, Chiun and Remo both saw the small speakers hidden under the lip of a narrow ledge just above the eaves. The protracted moan echoed to silence, replaced by the distant, desolate howl of a wolf.

A blanket of rotten leaves was spread across the dead brown grass. Thorn bushes and creeping ivy decorated the front of the house around the porch.

The front steps were bowed and rickety. Up close Remo could see that they were deliberately made to look old and battered. They seemed sturdy enough underfoot as the two men climbed up onto the broad front porch.

"Abracadabra," Remo said mysteriously, waving his hand as they approached the front door.

The instant he uttered the word, the door creaked open.

"I don't know what you think," Remo said, careful to keep his voice low enough that only Chiun could hear, "but I think we're about to get pounced on by an eight-hundred-pound spider."

"Caution," the Master of Sinanju warned in reply.

Senses straining alertness, the old man breezed through the door. Remo followed.

If the spider was inside, it was not in the foyer. Nor, Remo judged, was it in any of the ground-floor rooms.

From what he could tell there were no detectable life signs. Just the constant thrum of electricity that powered Stewart McQueen's elaborate security system. The whole house seemed to vibrate with coursing energy.

The two men had taken only a few steps inside the house when they felt the rush of air at their backs. Spinning, they were just in time to see the front door slam shut.

To Remo's trained eyes, it moved faster than any mechanical device should have allowed. The entire house rumbled from attic to basement, such was the force with which the door cracked shut.

Remo bounded back over to the door, grabbing the handle. He expected to shatter the simple lock with ease, but when he took hold of the tarnished brass knob, a surprised look blossomed on his hard face.

"There's no dead bolt," he said.

The Master of Sinanju frowned. Joining his pupil at the door, Chiun tapped the knob with a single slender finger while placing the flat of his palm on the door's veneer. His leathery face grew amazed.

"This is no longer a door," the Master of Sinanju said as the solid vibrations returned to his bony hand.

It was as if upon closing, the entire door had merged with the frame around it, becoming one with the wall itself. They formed a single, solid unit.

"It's altogether ookey," Remo suggested. "Wanna take the whole wall down?"

Chiun shook his head. A look of strange puzzlement had taken root on his face. His ears were trained on the rooms around them as they walked out into the big foyer.

Though only an anteroom, the foyer was larger than an average living room. A warped wooden rail stretched to the second-floor landing, balusters missing at irregular points. A big vase filled with dead flowers sat on an old oak stand thick with dust. The lace doily that hung in tatters from beneath the vase was yellow with age. A ratty Oriental runner stretched across the floor from the sealed front door to the hallway that lay adjacent to the main foyer.

They had barely reached the staircase when they felt the surge of displaced air above their heads.

Their senses tripping alert, instinct took over. Remo jumped left, Chiun leaped right.

They had barely bounded to safety before the big

crystal chandelier that had been hanging from the foyer's vaulted ceiling crashed to the floor.

The heavy weight tore through the lower section of the bannister, ripping wood to pulp and screaming into the bottom steps. Glass cracked and scattered into dank corners.

A cloud of dust rose into the musty air.

As the sound was swallowed up by the darkest reaches of the big old house, Remo turned a level eye on the Master of Sinanju. "Now, *that* was not right," he said evenly.

By the look on Chiun's face, the old man agreed.

Ordinarily, Remo and Chiun would have detected the faint grinding of mechanical parts that would have warned them a trigger or release had been activated. But in this case there was no such sign. It was as if the chandelier itself had made a decision entirely on its own to drop on their heads.

"Do not become distracted," Chiun cautioned. "All is not as it appears here."

"If you're saying it's not looking and acting like a creepy haunted house, then I've gotta disagree," Remo said. He looked down at the twisted chandelier. It blocked the route to the staircase. "Looks like someone doesn't want us going upstairs."

"Or else that is precisely where they wish us to go," the old Korean pointed out.

Remo considered his words. Given what they'd seen so far, it was possible that the house was using reverse psychology on them.

"I don't know about you," Remo grumbled, annoyed, "but I'm not about to start trying to figure out what some wrecking ball reject wants me to do."

And curling his toes he launched himself up over the broken chandelier.

Chiun followed suit. The two men landed lightly, side by side on the fifth broad step.

Ever cautious, they began climbing the stairs.

To their right as they ascended, portraits lined the broad, curving staircase. Though not antiques, they had been carefully treated to look as old as the house itself. Each was of a single man made out to look like a famous character from horror fiction. There was the Wolfman, the Mummy, Frankenstein's monster and a dozen more that Remo didn't recognize. He noted that the face on each of the paintings looked the same. When they reached the Dracula painting at the first landing, it finally struck him.

"That's the guy, Little Father," he said, snapping his fingers. "Stewart McQueen. I'd know those teeth anywhere."

Pausing, Chiun glanced at the Dracula painting with thin disgust. "I do not know why you in the West revere this Walachian so," he said unhappily. "He was a stingy tyrant and not even a true vampire. It was a happy day when Sultan Mehmed hired Master Foo to remove his miserly head."

"You talking McQueen or Dracula?"

"He was known as Vlad the Impaler," Chiun said dryly. "And before you ask, I am not a walking history lesson. If you are interested, look it up in the scrolls yourself.''

He spun on his heel.

As Remo was turning from the painting, something suddenly caught his attention. A flash of movement. When he snapped his head back around, he saw that the black eyes of the Walachian ruler had twitched to one side.

Remo took a startled step back. The movement came as a shock to his highly trained senses, for he had not perceived any living thing behind the wall.

He wheeled to the Master of Sinanju, stabbing a finger at the portrait. ''Chiun, did you see what I—''

He didn't get a chance to finish his question. The old man's face was a mirror of his own shock. As he jumped forward, the Master of Sinanju's long nails unfurled like deadly knives of vengeance. Slashing left then right, he reduced Dracula's face to a mass of canvas tatters.

Behind was nothing more than an oak-paneled wall.

No. More than that. As Remo listened, he heard the distinct creaking of floorboards. The sound seemed to be coming from a hollow behind the wall.

A secret passage.

''Okay, Remo's had enough fun at the wacky shack,'' Remo muttered angrily.

Grabbing the portrait, he flung it to the stairs.

Pulverizing fists shot into hard wood. It cracked and splintered. Grabbing at the edges of the new-formed hole, Remo yanked. An entire panel tore away.

Beyond was a narrow hallway, just wide enough for a man to walk along. Without a glance at his teacher, Remo slipped through the two-foot-wide opening. The Master of Sinanju came in behind.

The passage was illuminated by a few bare bulbs. It appeared to loop around the second story of the house. The far ends disappeared around sharp corners in both directions.

"You get a sense of which way he went?" Remo asked.

"He who?" the Master of Sinanju said thinly. "I sensed no life signs from this chamber."

"Yeah, but you heard the floor creak," Remo pointed out. He glanced around. The electrical hum was stronger in here. He felt the short hairs rise on the back of his neck. "Maybe all this electric junk is some sort of force field or something. Could have kept us from getting a bead on him."

"Or *it*," Chiun cautioned.

"No bogeyman living here, Little Father," Remo said firmly. "Just some nutcase writer. Let's try this way."

He struck off to the right.

Unlike whoever had preceded them through here, neither man made a sound on the warped boards as they slid stealthily down the long corridor.

They had traveled only a few yards along the passage when the strange electrical charge that filled the dank air around them abruptly grew in pitch.

Remo stopped dead.

"Maybe this wasn't such a hot idea after all," he said, his voice thick with foreboding. "What say we amscray?"

His answer was a shocked intake of air, then nothing.

And in the moment of that single gasping breath, the distinctive beat of the Master of Sinanju's heart vanished.

Remo wheeled around.

Chiun was gone.

He was vaguely aware of a panel closing in the floor. But even his supersensitive eyes had difficulty adjusting to the speed with which it snapped shut.

His heart knotting in his chest, Remo fell to his knees, attacking the floor.

He soon discovered that this wood was not like the paneling he had just broken through. Each pummeling fist was absorbed by the floor. Although the wood appeared solid, it was like punching marshmallow. Though his hand fired down with punishing force, he failed to make a single dent.

Worse than that, there was no longer any hint of a trapdoor. As though one had never existed.

The first hint of panic began to ring in Remo's ears.

As concern for his teacher grew, he was vaguely aware that his hands were slick with some wet substance. At the same time Remo heard a soft gurgle in either direction.

He snapped his head left.

The walls were excreting some slippery liquid. At first glance it looked like blood. But the smell was wrong.

It was oil. It seeped out invisible pores above the trapdoor.

Somehow the house had known that Chiun would attempt to grab on to something when the passage opened beneath him. It had prevented him from doing so by greasing everything within reach.

Remo hopped to his feet. Thoughts only on Chiun, he raced for the opening they had used to enter the passage.

He'd start his search on the first floor and move to the basement if necessary. To find Chiun, he would tear the entire house down brick by brick.

When he reached the spot where the opening had been, Remo froze.

It was gone. Somehow the jagged hole he'd torn in the paneling had healed itself.

And on either side of the narrow passage, the walls began to thrum, as if with a pulsing life force all their own.

Whatever was happening, it wasn't good.

Remo slashed out a hand at the wood.

It absorbed the blow.

He tried again. Still nothing. The paneling that had

shattered so easily two minutes before now seemed impervious to his attacks.

A click and a whir behind him, followed by a low rumble.

Remo didn't turn. He didn't need to look to know that the walls were closing in.

There wasn't a sense of hydraulics. Just the inexorable move of the wall toward his back.

And as the passage constricted, threatening to crush Remo to paste, a single camera winked on at the far end of the corridor, its somber lens focused on the dramatic final moments of life of the younger Master of Sinanju.

22

At first he had an impossible time orienting himself. All around him the world was shaded in black.

But after a time, shapes began to form. Angled shadows rose right or left, indicating where walls and ceiling were.

Mark Howard was at Folcroft. As usual. That much he knew. But he couldn't quite place exactly *where*.

He started walking.

As he headed down the long hallway, each footfall was thunder only he could hear.

When he felt the first kiss from the icy rush of air, he knew what it preceded.

Come for me....

The disembodied voice echoed forlornly off the shadowy walls. It seemed to be inside his head, as well.

He had heard the voice before. In this same place. But as far as he knew, it wasn't a voice he recognized.

The hallway grew longer with each step. He passed a window. In the tree beyond, an owl blinked inquisitively, its eyes washed in purple from the strangely deformed moon.

Release me....

A door. Mark had seen it before. Each time he visited this hallway, he managed to get this far. With growing dread he knew that it would soon be over.

It was a patient's door. Crisscrossing wires were buried in the small Plexiglas rectangle.

Mark crept forward. The thudding of his shoes faded, overwhelmed by the pounding of his own heart.

The door was solid, unbreakable.

He touched the handle. As usual, no sense of cold or warmth. For a moment he considered turning it.

Some unexplainable inner dread held him back.

He released the knob.

The instant he let go, there issued a timid scratching from inside, as from a dying animal. Whatever it was, it gave the sense that captivity was sapping its vitality.

Holding his breath, Mark moved to the window.

Though it was dark inside, he could still glimpse a few familiar shapes. A bed. A dresser.

The rustle of movement.

He leaned in close, his heart beating a chorus in his ears.

Movement no more. For an instant he thought it might have been imagined.

And in that moment of doubt, it sprang at him.

When it shot up from the shadows, Mark fell back. It pounded the window, cracking the reinforced mesh.

"Release me!" the beast shrieked.

The features were feral. Not human, not animal. It was all hatred and rage.

Howard skittered back on all fours, slamming the wall. He blinked. The instant he did, the darkness turned to gray, quickly fading up to white. And even as the light returned, the beast continued to slam the door, demanding release.

Pounding, pounding, pounding...

KNOCK, *knock, knock.*

Mark opened his eyes.

It took him a moment to realize where he was.

Four walls. Close enough to touch.

Folcroft. This was where he worked now.

A dream. *The* dream. Again.

He rubbed his head where he had bumped it against the wall. His office was so small that his chair barely fit behind his desk. During his first month here, he had hit his head against the wall at least twice every day.

Knock, knock, knock.

"Mr. Howard?" a timid voice called from the hall.

Okay. He was back. The dream was rapidly becoming nothing more than a disturbing memory.

In the battered oaken desk before him was a raised computer screen. Howard felt near his knee, depressing a hidden stud beneath the desk. The monitor whirred obediently down below the surface.

"Come in," he called, clearing the gravelly sleep from his throat.

The wide face of Eileen Mikulka, Harold Smith's

secretary, peeked into the small room. "Good evening, Mr. Howard," she said cheerily. "I was just passing by on my way home and I thought I'd remind you about your meeting with Dr. Smith."

Mark smiled. "I know. Thanks, Mrs. M."

She warmed to the familiarity. Assistant Director Howard was such a nice young man. Not that her employer, Dr. Smith, didn't have his good qualities. It was just that it was nice to have such a pleasant young fellow at Folcroft.

"He's a stickler for punctuality," she said. "Which isn't a bad thing. It's just the way he is. Anyway, I wouldn't want you to get in trouble."

"You're a little late for that," Mark said quietly, sitting up. He rubbed the sleep from his eyes.

Standing in the doorway, Smith's secretary smiled.

"You'll do fine here," Mrs. Mikulka promised. She cast a glance at Howard's desk. "It seems funny to see that again after all these years," she commented. "That was Dr. Smith's desk for such a long time. I was surprised when he had me send workers to bring it up from the cellar for you. I didn't know he'd kept it. It isn't like Dr. Smith to be sentimental over something like a dirty old desk. I guess it just shows that you can never know everything there is to know about a person. Good night, Mr. Howard."

She backed from the small office and shut the door.

After she was gone, Mark Howard nodded silent agreement.

"Not if you want to live to tell about it," he said softly.

Shaking the cobwebs from his brain, Mark got to his feet, struggling around the desk that was far too big for the cramped room.

THE SUN HAD SET over Folcroft. Outside the sanitarium windows it was almost dark as Mark made his way through the administrative wing of the building. He met only one other employee, an elderly janitor with a bucket and a mop.

As far as staff was concerned, night wasn't much different than day. Dr. Smith limited the staff in this wing of the facility to a skeleton crew. The fewer eyes to see what was going on, the better.

The way Smith told it, either he or his secretary could handle Folcroft's affairs virtually alone. When he had mentioned this fact to Howard, it was the only time Mark had seen the old man express real pride in his work.

So while the doctors and nurses and orderlies worked in the medical wing, Mark Howard generally walked alone through the empty second-floor hallways.

This night, the emptiness was unnerving.

As he made his way up the hall, he tried to soften his own footfalls in an attempt to keep from reminding himself of his disturbing recurring dream. He was grateful for the muffling effect of Smith's drab reception-room carpeting.

On his way to the office door, Mark glanced at his wristwatch.

"Uh-oh," he said when he saw that it was four minutes after six.

Expecting to be chewed out for his tardiness, he rapped a gentle knuckle on the door even as he pushed it open.

As usual Smith sat behind his broad desk. Through the one-way picture window behind the CURE director, the thinning black trees of Folcroft's back lawn surrendered their burden of dark leaves to dusk. Beyond the trees the choppy waves of Long Island Sound were gray and cold. At the same time in a few short days, the end of daylight savings time would bring nightfall an hour sooner.

Smith's face was stern.

"I'm sorry I'm late," Mark said as he clicked the door shut. "It won't happen again."

He was surprised when Smith did not so much as raise a disapproving eyebrow. His hard expression never wavering, the CURE director beckoned the young man forward.

"Is something wrong?" Mark asked as he slipped into his usual straight-backed chair.

"The report you got this afternoon on the metal fragment Remo found in Florida," Smith said, not answering the question. "The results were conclusive?"

It was an odd question. They had discussed the lab report only an hour before. Afterward Smith had said that he was going to do some research. By the sounds of it, he had found something that was not to his liking.

"Yes," Mark replied. "It was a special alloy created to be virtually impervious to intense heat and chemical abrasion." He shook his head, confused. "Is everything all right, Dr. Smith? I sent it by courier to one of your approved labs. If you want it retested, I can send it to one of the others."

"The lab is not the problem," Smith said darkly. He sank back in his chair, a dim shadow in his gloomy office.

Howard detected something in the older man's tone he had never heard before. It was deep concern. Bordering on fear.

"I have been doing some digging," Smith said somberly. "There are few applications for such an alloy. Since one is space exploration, proximity obviously dictated that I should start with NASA. I have concluded that this is indeed the likeliest source."

"Remo said they couldn't identify it," Howard frowned.

Smith was not dissuaded. "That is unlikely," he said. "Look at this." He pulled his chair in tight to his desk. The old man looked down over his monitor like a modern sorcerer searching for augers in the realm of cyberspace.

Curious, Mark circled around the desk.

On the monitor was a picture Smith had found at a science magazine's Web site.

The subject of the photograph was a giant robotic spider. Underneath the picture a caption identified it as the Virgil probe, part of a new generation of NASA space-exploration technology. Technical data filled the screen all around the picture. Small images of Neptune and Venus had been plugged in around Virgil, red arrows detailing atmospheric and climatic information.

Knuckles leaning on the lip of the desk, Howard glanced down at Smith.

"I don't think that's what we're after, Dr. Smith," Mark cautioned slowly.

"You are correct," Smith said gravely. "Our adversary is far more dangerous than any of us realized." He glanced up at Howard. "You have analyzed some of CURE's operations database. Have you reached the section on Mr. Gordons?"

Mark shook his head. "I don't think so," he admitted. "What's his first name?" he asked, hoping to jog his memory.

"He—or rather, *it*—doesn't have one," Smith explained. "Gordons is an artificially created entity built by the space program. He has the form of a man, but he is not human. He was meant to be utilized for interstellar exploration, but he escaped from his lab years ago and has been at large ever since. CURE has encountered him on numerous occasions over the course of the last two and a half decades."

As he stood beside Smith, Mark Howard's face was perfectly flat. Moving only his eyes, he looked from the picture of the Virgil probe to the CURE director's serious face.

"I'm not sure what to make of this, Dr. Smith," he ventured cautiously.

"I know it sounds absurd," Smith agreed, "but

you need only review the material we have collected on Gordons to see that it is true. In point of fact, science has nearly caught up with his design in the years since his creation. There have been great advances in robotics, computer science, artificial intelligence and miniaturization. At the time of his creation he might have seemed like science fiction, but science fact is rapidly catching up with him.''

Mark already knew from experience that CURE dealt with things that seemed somewhat out of the ordinary. And the truth was Mark Howard himself somewhat fit the mold of extranormal phenomena.

''All right,'' he offered. ''I'll review the Gordons data. But if what you're saying is true, he'd technically be an android. A machine in human form. What does he have to do with this?'' He nodded to the image on the computer.

''Gordons is more than just a simple android,'' Smith said, exhaling. ''He was programmed to survive. It is a command that supersedes all others. In his quest to survive, he is able to assimilate all materials from his environment necessary to fulfill that function. During Remo and Chiun's last encounter with him six years ago, they disposed of Gordons's brain housing in a Mexican volcano. At the time I had hoped that his metallic components would melt in the magma. If not, it would not matter so much, for he was finally isolated. Left in a place where there was no hope of assimilating the material, he would need to remake himself.''

In a flash Howard had a moment of intuitive clarity.

"The Virgil probe," the young man announced. "It's supposed to be used on hostile planets. They would have had to simulate an alien environment to see if it worked. NASA must have brought it to that volcano for testing." He nodded to himself, not waiting for a response. "They sent it down there and it found something it didn't expect. Whatever was left of your Mr. Gordons must have assimilated the probe."

"It appears that is the case," Smith agreed. "I have reviewed NASA's internal data. They brought Virgil to the Popocatepetl volcano late last week. It was only a few days after it was brought back to the United States that the first spider sighting took place in Florida. I am almost certain we are dealing with Gordons." He glanced up at Howard. "However, Remo and Chiun are unaware it is him."

The assistant CURE director's brow creased. "But they'll be safe, right?" he asked, his voice troubled. "I mean, they've beaten this thing before."

"Mr. Gordons is no ordinary foe. Yes, they have succeeded in neutralizing him in the past, but not without great difficulty. And I fear complacency might be their enemy this time. If they are certain in their belief that Gordons is dead, the risk to them increases."

Mark straightened, a determined cast to his soft jaw. "Then I'll fly to Maine and warn them."

"You would not reach them in time," Smith said. "They are already on the ground there."

Standing beside Smith's desk, Mark Howard felt a

surge of impotent frustration. He clenched and unclenched his hands, unsure what to do.

Outside, night had taken firm hold. The grounds beyond Smith's one-way picture window had been swallowed up by an impenetrable cloak of blackness.

"There must be *something* we can do," Howard insisted.

Smith nodded. "Yes, there is," he said. Still seated, the older man looked up over the tops of his rimless glasses. "We will remain at Folcroft and use CURE's resources to uncover who at NASA is responsible for the events in Florida. Someone there has been directing Gordons in the guise of the Virgil probe. If Remo and Chiun succeed in Maine, we will send them back to Florida to deal with his accomplices."

"And if they fail?" Howard asked.

Smith didn't miss a beat. "Then CURE will be without its enforcement arm and you will have gotten your wish."

Turning from his subordinate, he began typing swiftly at his computer keyboard.

Smith's words were not said as a rebuke. Still, they stung. Mark was at a loss for words. He turned woodenly.

Feeling the weight of his own earlier suggestion on his broad shoulders, Mark Howard quietly left the office.

23

The darkness through which he fell was complete. There wasn't so much as a trace of light for his eyes to absorb.

Slipping through this shaft of utter darkness, Chiun kept his arms bent slightly, his fingers extended.

He didn't know what to expect. When the trapdoor had opened beneath him in the secret passage upstairs, he couldn't move out of the way quickly enough. It was the same strange sense he and Remo had gotten from the falling chandelier. There had been no triggering of hinges or hasps. It was as if the trapdoor had made the decision to open up and swallow him entirely of its own volition.

As he rocketed through empty space, a sudden pressure against his eardrums told him something flat and solid was racing up toward his feet. The tube was sealed.

He expected to drop onto the invisible floor, but the instant before he hit, the ink-black tube through which he was plunging split like a yawning mouth.

Dim light flooded the tunnel. Chiun caught a flash

of a slick black wall as he was spit from the tube. Free, he plunged out into open air.

Chiun's kimono became a billowing parachute as he floated to the dirt floor. On landing, his sandal soles made not so much as a single scuff.

He quickly scanned his surroundings.

He had fallen into the basement. The high brick walls were ancient. Icicles of dry mortar hung from between the bricks.

The room in which he'd fallen appeared to be sealed. There was no sign of window or door.

The floor beneath his feet was level, but two yards off it began to slope rapidly downward into a separate alcove. Shadows drenched the farthest recesses of this pit.

There were no signs of life anywhere in the room. Still, his experiences thus far in this strange house were enough that he would not trust all to be as it should.

Senses straining alertness, Chiun turned to the nearest wall. He hadn't taken a single step toward it when he detected sudden movement behind him.

He wheeled around.

From the darkness of the alcove a long, low figure was slithering into view. Dark and menacing, it moved swiftly on short legs across the dirt floor.

A second creature emerged behind it, followed by a third. Elongated mouths smiled rows of viciously sharp teeth. As powerful jaws opened and closed experimentally, the darting beasts lashed the air with fat, pointed tails.

Chiun took a cautious step back from the familiar shapes.

The creatures advancing on him appeared to be crocodiles. But appearance alone was deceiving.

That these were not ordinary crocodiles was apparent to the Master of Sinanju. For one thing there were no life signs emanating from them. And though they made a good pantomime of living motion, their movements nonetheless were more jerky than the real thing. Their squat legs shot into the floor like fired pistons, propelling them forward. There was not the grace natural to all living things.

Even as the animals crept toward him, Chiun demonstrated his contempt by tucking his hands inside his kimono sleeves.

Raising his wattled neck, he addressed the four walls.

"Fools," he spit, his voice dripping scorn. "Your mechanized beasts are no match for Sinanju."

His words brought an odd reaction from the crocs.

All three animals stopped dead in their tracks.

With agonizing slowness, the lead animal raised its head, looking up at him. Deep within its shiny dark eyes came a click and a whir. Chiun had no doubt that whoever was controlling the beasts was looking at him now.

Artificial eyes trained square on Chiun, the crocodile's mechanical mouth opened wide. The old Korean saw that the rows of white teeth were sharper than any knife blade.

Jaw locked open, the creature paused. For a moment Chiun thought that it might have broken down. But all at once a tinny sound issued from the black depths of its mouth, like a poorly reproduced recording of an old radio show.

"Hello is all right," said the crocodile. And far back along its powerful jaws, its mouth curved up toward its eyes in a parody of a human smile.

Standing above the beast, Chiun felt his very marrow freeze to solid ice. Hazel eyes opened wide in shock.

And in that moment of stunned amazement, the crocodile darted forward, its machine jaws clamping shut around Chiun's exposed ankle with the force of a snapping bear trap.

REMO GAVE UP trying to attack the walls. If he had more room to negotiate in the ever narrowing chamber, he might have been able to break through. As it was, the only dents he had succeeded in making had quickly healed themselves.

The rear wall of the secret passage continued to slowly close in behind him. He was now only a few seconds from being crushed. But a few seconds was all he needed.

Far down the corridor the red eye of the security camera continued to watch dispassionately.

On the floor around Remo's feet were a few of the

chunks of paneling that were left after he'd forced his way inside the chamber. With the toe of his loafer, he drew the longest one toward him.

"First thing," Remo snarled. Leaning sideways, he scooped up the wooden fragments. "I don't like an audience."

His hand snapped out. The chunk of wood whistled down to the far end of the narrowing corridor.

The dart pierced the lens and the camera burst apart in a spray of white sparks.

Behind him the compressing wall creaked as if in response. He felt it begin to move in faster.

Remo released more breath, deflating his lungs.

He'd have to work fast.

Whoever had designed this place might not have been very creative. They had gotten Chiun with the floor and they intended to get Remo with the walls, but it was possible they had left one avenue open.

Thrusting his hands straight up, Remo hopped off the floor, curling his fingers over the upper edge of the wall.

The dust on the two-by-four framing was thick.

Feet dangling in space, he began shifting his weight from hand to hand, rocking his body from side to side. As the walls continued to close in, he quickly picked up momentum, his feet swinging toward the ceiling.

It was tough to work in such a confined space. Even so, his toe had just brushed the cheap pine when he heard a fresh noise in the passage.

Somewhere distant, an intercom speaker clicked on. A tinny voice called out to him.

"What are you doing?"

It was thin and metallic. As he swung back and forth, Remo could not help but think he'd heard that voice before.

"Given our past relationship I had an understandable desire to witness your demise," the faceless speaker continued, "but you have impaired my ability to see you. Perhaps you are already dead. Given the nature of the very creative trap in which I have ensnared you, there is a high probability that this is the case."

Remo couldn't believe what he was hearing.

It *couldn't* be. It wasn't possible.

Yet given the circumstances it offered the best, if not the least troubling, explanation.

"I will assume for now that you are not dead," suggested the voice. "I will continue to permit this passage to close in on itself, thereby insuring your demise."

With that the speaker clicked off.

As far as Remo was concerned, nothing more needed to be said. He had already heard enough.

With a final wrench he flipped himself ceilingward, releasing his grip on the two-by-four.

His body was propelled up from the passage and into the tight space between two parallel floor beams. His speed was such that the entire length of his body became a punishing force against the brittle wood. The pine cracked obediently.

As dry kindling rained down inside the passage, Remo was already slipping up inside the dark crawl space. He burrowed through insulation and broke through underflooring, emerging—battered and dusty—in a third-story bedroom.

When he glanced back down through the hole he'd made in the oak floor, he saw nothing but blackness. The walls had closed in, sealing the corridor.

Another few seconds and he would have been dead.

His thoughts flew to Chiun. The old man didn't know what they were truly facing. And with their opponent, a few short seconds was the difference between life and death.

Hoping that his teacher had fully embraced the lesson of Master Shiko, Remo raced from the bedroom.

THE CROCODILE HAD FIRED forward much faster than it should have. Chiun felt the rush of compressing air as the jaw snapped shut around his bony ankle.

In the instant before it bit through flesh and bone, he jumped. His pipe-stem legs cut sharp angles in the musty cellar air. He landed in a flurry of robes, twirling to face the mechanical crocodiles.

Bodies low to the ground, the animals were scurrying across the dirt floor after him.

Understanding who his true foe was now, he kept his entire being alert as the animals advanced.

"Your adopted son is dead," the lead crocodile said.

Chiun paid no heed to the words or the mouth from which they emanated. He had no reason yet to believe them.

As the lead crocodile and its companions crawled toward Chiun, the animal continued to speak.

"He has temporarily impeded my ability to see his body, yet I have calculated a near one hundred percent probability that my stratagem to kill him has succeeded. I tell you this now, for I find that in times of emotional loss humans are more likely to make mistakes. An error by you now would give me the advantage, thus assuring your demise, as well."

Chiun knew that the voice alone didn't necessarily mean that his enemy was here. While he could be hidden in one of the crocodiles, he was just as likely controlling them from some remote location.

The crocodile lunged forward, its jaws snapping shut.

Hopping over the savage champing mouth, Chiun's heel touched the back of the crocodile's head.

It seemed like the gentlest of nudges, yet the animal's face rocketed down into the hard-packed dirt. There was a twist and groan of metal. When it rose back up, the crocodile's snout was bent straight up in the air at an impossible angle, obscuring its eyes.

"I am curious to know if you are like other humans," the crocodile said around its twisted mouth. "Has the death of Remo, for whom you have an emotional attachment, made you more likely to make a fatal mistake?''

The disconcerting smile stretched up the long mouth of the crocodile. As it did, the jaw creaked slowly back down, re-forming into its original shape. With a satisfied thrashing of its fat tail, the croc shot forward again.

It nearly found its mark. Not because of its speed but because Chiun had become distracted by something else. Something at the far end of its whipping tail.

At the last moment the aged Korean bounded from between the clamping jaws. He landed square on the beast's back.

The crocodile twisted around after him. Even as it did so, the other two animals thrust their heads forward, all flashing jaws and razor teeth.

Chiun ignored them all. Hopping through two more sets of clamping jaws, he negotiated a path straight down the lead animal's spine. At the far end of its whipping tail he found what he was looking for.

A thick black cable ran out from the tail's nub. Snaking away across the floor, it vanished into the darkness of the pit from which the animals had come. Two more wires extended up into the room, connecting to the other crocs.

As the lead crocodile contorted its body to snap at its unwanted passenger, the old Asian leaned down. With one long fingernail he snicked the cable in two.

The animal immediately froze in place, its jaws open wide.

The other two crocodiles were scampering toward him. Flipping around behind them, Chiun used flashing nails to sever their cables, too. The crocs stopped in midlunge, collapsing to the floor in twin coughs of soft dust.

As soon as their umbilical connection was severed, the three cables that extended up out of the alcove began to thrash around the floor like fat black snakes. With desperate slaps they lashed the dirt in search of their severed ends.

Before the cords had a chance to reconnect, Chiun kicked two of the huge animals to the far side of the room, out of reach of the grasping cables.

He bent for the last crocodile. Swinging it by the tail, he brought it against the nearby wall.

Crashing metal pulverized brick and mortar. The wall to the sealed-off room collapsed out into the main cellar.

Tossing the broken shell of the big robot animal aside, the Master of Sinanju sprang through the hole. Thinking only of Remo's safety, he flew for the stairs.

24

Stewart McQueen watched the action taking place inside his mansion from the safety of the tidy furnished loft apartment above his carriage house. As he studied the remote image on his TV screen, his lip was curled in nervous concentration, revealing sharp rodent's teeth.

Mr. Gordons had suggested that the writer remain hidden in the remodeled carriage house while he dealt with his enemies in the main house. Something about his enemies being able to detect human life signs.

At first McQueen wasn't sure he should believe the claims Gordons had made about the men who were after him, especially when he got a look at the pair who showed up at his front gates. But after watching them smash through his home, Stewart McQueen was starting to think he might not be safe even in this separate outbuilding.

Gordons had hooked the security system into the TV, allowing McQueen to see everything. He watched the men enter, climb the stairs and break into the booby-trapped secret passage. When the old one was dumped down into the crocodile pit and the walls began to close in on the young one, McQueen was certain they were both as good as dead.

But then things started to go wrong.

First the young one managed to break the camera that was trained on him. No small feat, considering he did it with a wood chip the size of a pencil thrown down a corridor thirty feet long and two feet wide.

The old one wouldn't be so lucky. He had survived a two-story fall, but there was no way he could last in the basement crocodile pit.

McQueen's confidence evaporated when he saw the old one leap over the head of his fiercest faux crocodile. The animal's camera eyes twisted around just in time to see the Asian—riding the croc's tail like a surfer on a board—snip the wire that connected the animal to the rest of the house. After that, this image went dead, as well.

Sitting in his loft on the edge of a neatly made guest bed, McQueen chewed his nails nervously.

"What's happening?" the novelist asked his TV.

"I am attempting to ascertain that now," said a voice from the television's speaker.

Mr. Gordons had wormed his way like a virus through the electrical system all over the grounds.

"Are they dead?" McQueen asked anxiously. "I thought you'd know if they were dead."

"Visual inspection has failed," Gordons explained. "Although I am possessed with the ability to detect things such as heartbeats, perspiration and human odors, this is a function of my primary assembly that is not easily rerouted."

"So you're saying that the house becomes an extension of you, but that your body stays separate?" McQueen suggested. "Like an isolated control unit."

"Essentially, yes," Gordons said.

"Well, that's just great!" McQueen snapped, jumping to his feet. "Those guys are probably running around loose right now, and you don't even know where. What kind of good-for-nothing assimilating android are you?"

"I am the kind of assimilating android who does not accept failure," Gordons replied coldly. "You were supposed to deliver my enemies to me, yet it is possible that you have done the opposite. I need to determine which is the case. Since I am unable to rely on your security cameras, I require your assistance. You will come back to the main house and conduct a visual search for their bodies."

McQueen's eyes sprang wide.

"Me?" he mocked. He shook his head violently. "No way, Jose. If *you're* afraid of those guys, there's nothing you can do to get me back in that house."

The bulbs in three lamps around the bedroom simultaneously exploded.

"On the other hand—" McQueen began.

The voice of Mr. Gordons interrupted. "Wait," the android instructed.

An image appeared on the television screen. It was warped into the bowl shape of a pinhole security camera's transmission. There was no sound to accompany the black-and-white image.

As curls of black smoke rose from the bedroom lamps, Stewart McQueen sat woodenly back on the edge of the bed, his eyes trained with sick fascination on the TV screen.

REMO BOUNDED down the main staircase in two massive strides. He was hopping over the broken chandelier when he heard a painful crash of wood. When he spun for the source, relief flooded his tension-filled face.

The Master of Sinanju was whirling up into the foyer amid the shattered remnants of the basement door.

"You are safe," the old man cried.

"That's open to debate," Remo replied tightly. "That spider isn't a spider after all. It's Mr. Gordons."

Chiun nodded sharply. "He has insinuated himself into this entire dwelling."

Remo still felt the powerful electrical hum all around them. It now seemed even more menacing.

"I think I know how to put a stop to that," Remo said. "But we have to make ourselves a door first."

They found the front door still sealed shut. It reacted to their experimental blows as did the walls in the upstairs passageway. The surface became adaptable, accepting their fists rather than surrendering to them.

But for Remo, two things were different than they had been upstairs. Now he knew who his opponent was, and more importantly, Chiun was at his side.

Working together, the two Masters of Sinanju synchronized their attack. They treated the door like a living thing, setting up a counterrhythm to the steady vibrations the door and wall were giving off.

In a moment the door began to buzz. An instant later it began to shriek. Soon after that the thick steel sheet buried at the center of the reinforced door shattered like an echoing wineglass. The wood collapsed around it, and Remo and Chiun slipped through the new-formed opening.

They bounded down the front steps to the walk.

They had no sooner reached ground than Remo heard rustling from the scruffy bushes beside the steps. He had barely time to turn to the sound when he saw two small black figures dart into view.

They were two feet tall and hideously ugly. When he saw them, Remo didn't know whether he should run or laugh.

The two metal bats that had watched Remo and Chiun's arrival from the stone pillars above the main gates had been given a new purpose as makeshift watchdogs. Metal mouths open wide, they scurried from the underbrush.

They came trailing thin wires. Remo saw that the cords ran back down the walk and up into the gate-posts, connecting the metal creatures with the house security system.

"Oh, this is just too weird," Remo groused as one of the little bats tried to bite his ankle.

"I have discovered the secret of vanquishing these beasts," Chiun intoned. He was skipping back and forth to avoid his own bat. "Promise me that we will buy a home in this province, and I will share it with you."

"No dice," Remo said. "Besides, it's Gordons I'm worried about, not his wind-up dolls."

Leaning, he braced his hand against his bat's head, holding it to the ground. As it snapped and bit fruitlessly at empty air, he grabbed one of its extended wings. With a pained wrench of metal, he tore it loose.

With the curved tip of the wing, he sliced the bat's wires. The creature fell silent.

Seeing that his pupil had found the secret on his own, Chiun frowned unhappily. With an angry exhale of air, he snapped the wires on his own bat. With a sharp sandal, he toe-kicked it back into the bushes.

Wing in hand, Remo struck off across the lawn. Tucking hands inside his kimono sleeves, Chiun trailed Remo as the younger man circled the house.

On the west side Remo found what he was looking for. Thick power cables were strung from a pole out on the street to the corner of the house.

Raising his bat's wing over his shoulder, Remo let it sail. The heavy metal wing sang through the air like a misshapen boomerang, slicing up through the cables. With a snap of rubber and a tiny popping spark it ripped through the wires, burying itself deep in the side of Stewart McQueen's suddenly silent haunted house.

With the power cut, Remo and Chiun circled back to the front walk.

The electrical hum no longer rang in their ears. The looming house now seemed more pathetic than menacing.

And somewhere inside that house, Mr. Gordons was even now in the process of disentangling himself from the elaborate electrical system.

Remo looked over at Chiun, his eyes level. "You hold him down while I pull off seven of his legs," he suggested in a tone flat with menace. "He can run in circles till his battery runs out once and for all."

Without another word, the two men marched back up the porch stairs. When they disappeared inside, the broken front door remained open and silent on the cold Maine evening.

"HELLO! You in there?"

Stewart McQueen desperately slammed a flat palm against the top of his TV. With the other hand he fiddled with the front control panel, flipping from channel to channel.

Nothing. The TV had gone dead.

He had seen the two men march through the foyer. Since the camera didn't angle downward, he lost sight of them when they headed for the door. He realized they had gotten free as soon as the screen switched to an exterior view. From the child's-eye view of his hidden gate bats, he had seen the two of them descend the stairs.

The picture had bounced crazily for a few seconds. That hadn't lasted long. It was a few moments after the bat cameras died that the power went out.

No matter how hard McQueen struck the TV, Mr. Gordons stubbornly refused to respond. He was winding up to give it one last mighty swat when he heard a sound out front.

Squealing tires. The noise was rapidly followed by the sounds of car doors slamming shut.

The TV was forgotten. Limping on his injured leg, McQueen hurried over to the bay window.

From the carriage house he had an unobstructed view of the street.

A black van was parked at the curb. Two men were hurrying from the cab to the back. As McQueen watched, they popped the rear door. A dozen figures dressed in white marched down to the road with military precision. It was dark so McQueen couldn't be sure, but they appeared to be wearing some kind of domed helmets.

He lost the men behind some trees as they hurried up the sidewalk. They appeared again at the locked front gate.

He finally got a good look at them. The men were dressed in what looked like vintage NASA space suits.

In his eerily silent carriage house, Stewart Mc-Queen distinctly heard the sound of a hacksaw.

He did some rapid calculations.

There was a gang of weird-suited spacemen at his gates, an angry android hiding out in his mansion and a pair of unstoppable assassins who could put fear into a metal heart skulking around his grounds.

This was all suddenly sounding more like one of his books than he'd bargained for.

His car was parked in a stall below his feet. A rear garage door opened on a private back road that wound through the woods and dumped out on a city access road behind his estate's high walls.

Writer's block, deadlines and *The New York Times* bestseller list be damned. This was now about survival.

The world-famous author spun from the window. Hobbling to beat the band, Stewart McQueen beat a hasty retreat down the back stairs of the darkened carriage house.

25

The intense silence made it seem as if the dusty old mansion had been smothered in a ghostly fist. Although the thrumming electrical hum was gone, their eardrums still rang with the memory as Remo and Chiun crossed the threshold.

Remo glanced up the stairs down which he'd come a few minutes before. "Big house," he commented. "He could be hiding anywhere."

Chiun shook his head firmly. "Where would you go?" the old man demanded.

Remo considered. "Probably the basement. The fuse box would be there. It'd be easier to connect there if he wanted to run the whole joint. But the way Gordons is, he could hook in at any point if he had to."

Chiun was already breezing past him. "He will be in the basement," he insisted.

"I was only saying that's where *I'd* go," Remo insisted as he trailed his teacher.

"And you are different from an uncreative, unthinking robot in what way?" Chiun asked blandly.

He whirled through the broken remnants of the basement door and ducked down the stairs.

"Don't go on the rag with me just 'cause I'm not moving to Maine," Remo grumbled, following.

Emergency lights on battery backups lit their way.

In the basement Remo didn't comment on the remnants of broken wall or the twisted mechanical crocodile that lay atop the pile of bricks.

They wound around the wooden stairs and headed past the idle furnace.

The cellar beneath the mansion was huge.

In one space off the main room, Remo saw what appeared to be Stewart McQueen's bedroom. There were bookcases, magazines, a TV and a small refrigerator.

A double-wide coffin lined with dirt and shaded by a frilly overhanging canopy was the room's centerpiece. Twin feather pillows rested against the granite gravestone headboard.

"Next time I think I should be reading more, remind me this is where my money goes," Remo said.

Chiun didn't respond. His brow darkening, he held a slender finger to his papery lips. He cocked an ear forward.

Remo had heard the sound, too.

It was a soft metallic groan. The noise rose and fell, like a rusted bolt being unscrewed.

Rounding a corner, the two men found the fuse box. Connected to its face was a pair of fat furry legs.

The body to which the legs were attached was not

visible. They extended through the air and disappeared around a corner. The granite archway into which they vanished opened into a dirt-lined tunnel.

The legs had been spinning in order to unscrew from the fuse box. When Remo and Chiun rounded the corner, the appendages detached and flopped to the floor. Without seeming to be aware of the two Masters of Sinanju, they silently retracted, sliding back into the shadowed recesses of the loamy tunnel.

Remo and Chiun trailed them to the stone arch. The long black legs slithered around the corner and disappeared.

When Remo and Chiun stepped into the archway, the legs were already several yards away. They were being absorbed into the sides of a figure who stood at calm attention in the dark depths of the tunnel.

Over the years Mr. Gordons had assumed many different forms and faces. The face he wore now was the first one they had ever seen on him. He was tall with sandy blond hair and wore a perpetual smile that was not quite a smile. His blue eyes were unblinking.

When they appeared before him, the android didn't express a hint of surprise. As his long spider's legs rolled back into his human torso, he nodded to each man in turn.

"High probability Remo, high probability Chiun. I would offer you a drink, but as it is likely that you intend to cause me bodily harm I have calculated as negligible the odds that you would accept such an offer."

Remo's face was stone.

"You got it wrong, metalman," he said icily as he stepped into the tunnel.

A hint of something that, at least on a human face, might have passed for a frown touched Mr. Gordons's brow.

"That is improbable," the android said. "Unless you have deviated from your previous pattern, you will attack me."

"My son means that we do not intend to cause you mere bodily harm," Chiun explained, circling cautiously away from his pupil. Taking the cue, Remo moved the opposite way. "We intend to dismantle you piece by piece and bury your evil parts in the four corners of the Earth."

The tunnel was wide enough that Remo and Chiun could move to opposite walls as they advanced on Gordons.

With a final whirring snap, the android's spider arms stopped retracting. Each one of them five feet long, they remained jutting from beneath the armpits of his human arms.

"Your statement is incorrect," Gordons said. As they walked toward him, he made not a move. "The Earth is roughly spherical in shape—therefore it has no corners. What is more, it is not I but the two of you who will cease to function this day."

"Sez you," Remo challenged. "So how'd you get out of the volcano, tinman?"

"My family freed me," the android replied simply.

Remo had a mental image of a bunch of toasters and VCRs lowering a knotted bedsheet down into the Mexican volcano where they'd dumped Mr. Gordons.

They were now only a few yards from the android. Remo kept as far from Chiun as possible. Difficult to do in such a confining space. Gordons seemed to realize their problem.

"Your method of attack is flawed," Gordons pointed out. "By separating you think to divide my attentions. But this passage is not wide enough for your plan to succeed."

The words had not passed his lips before he attacked.

The two spider legs whizzed forward, re-forming as they came. By the time they reached Remo and Chiun, their furry tips had been transformed into metallic spearheads.

Remo dropped below the deadly spear. As it brushed over his shoulder, he grabbed onto the shaft with one hand, snapping down with the other. With the side of his palm he severed a two-foot-long section of rigid leg.

Ducking, Chiun mirrored his pupil's movements. When he shot back up he, too, had a spear in hand.

Hissing sparks from their stumps, the injured legs curled back up to the android's chest.

Remo tried to gauge the heft of the weapon in his hand. It was awkward to do. The leg was apparently constructed of the same frictionless material Gordons had left at the scenes of his Florida crimes.

"Use caution, Remo," Chiun warned. Ever alert, he kept his voice low as he advanced with his makeshift weapon. "He is not as he was when last we met."

Remo, too, had noticed the speed. During their last encounter with Gordons, the android was a weakened version of his former self. But this seemed like the Gordons of old.

Although Chiun's words were soft enough that only Remo should have heard, it was Mr. Gordons who replied.

"The old one is correct," Mr. Gordons agreed. "With the introduction of supplementary data, my original program was altered over time. Due to the damage inflicted by the two of you I have decided to go back to my beginnings, reinstalling my original commands. What I once was, I am again."

"You were a tin-plated asswipe," Remo suggested, raising his spear.

Gordons flicked his metallic eyes to the younger Master of Sinanju. And in that sliver of a moment when his attention was diverted, Chiun let his missile fly.

The spear whistled through the dank air, sinking deep into the android's head. A spray of white sparks spit from his face, peppering the dirt floor around his feet.

Gordons reeled, spear jutting from between his eyes like a misshapen extra nose.

It was only when he staggered to one side that they

saw the second set of spider legs. Curled tightly, they had been hidden behind the android's back.

Imminent danger provoked action.

The spare legs shot out from his body. But rather than launch forward at Remo and Chiun, the spider legs plowed into the dirt walls of the tunnel, burrowing deep into earth.

There came a muffled snap of old timber breaking. When the legs retracted, the walls seemed to come with them.

With an ominous groan the tunnel began to collapse in on itself.

As stone and dirt rained down on all their heads, Mr. Gordons fell away, staggering up the far end of the tunnel.

"Remo, hurry!" Chiun insisted. Twirling, he bounded back toward the cellar, away from the dirt avalanche.

Remo hesitated. He clearly wanted to go after Gordons, but he could see that it was already too late. The center of the tunnel was filling in. With a rumble the ceiling began to cave in above him.

With a frustrated snap of his arm, Remo flung his spear through the collapsing wall of dirt. He wasn't sure if his aim was true, but he swore he saw the metal end sink into Gordons's fleeing back. And then the tunnel collapsed fully and the android vanished from sight.

Spinning, Remo leaped back through the stone archway in a cloud of exploding dust. Behind him the thick-packed earth of the tunnel continued to settle in on itself.

Once he saw that his pupil was safe, the Master of Sinanju became a flash of silk. Remo joined his teacher in a mad race for the cellar stairs.

Wherever Gordons was heading, he'd have to surface eventually. Both men intended to be there when the android came up for air.

When they burst into the foyer, Remo's tense face dropped into an angry scowl.

A dozen men were waiting for them, each decked out in the same white jumpsuits as their Florida attackers. Unlike the first group, these men wore round plastic helmets over their heads. Their toy ray guns with the very real .45 muzzles were aimed at Remo and Chiun as the two men appeared through the broken basement door.

Blue patches decorated with the nine planets of the solar system were fastened to their chests. In the center where the sun should be, the legend Space Cadets was stitched in ominous black letters.

"What in the ding-diddly crap?" Remo growled.

He had barely uttered the words when the twelve men opened fire. As the two Masters of Sinanju dodged and weaved, bullets thumped thickly into the wall behind them.

"We don't have time for this," Remo warned Chiun.

"In that case, move quickly," Chiun advised.

The old man skittered right, taking up that line of attack. Reluctantly, Remo moved to the left.

The nearest shooter seemed frustrated by his inability to aim true. He fired madly as Remo waltzed up.

Remo grabbed a palmful of Plexiglas. "I'm in a hurry, Pez head," he said, steering the man's fishbowl into the nearest wall.

Something went crack, and it wasn't the space cadet's helmet. As the Plexiglas globe filled with dark red fluid, the man collapsed to the knees of his space suit.

On the opposite side of the foyer, the Master of Sinanju was using the bright blue patches of two space cadets as makeshift dartboards. He scored perfect bull's-eyes with a pair of extended fingernails.

Shocked gasps hissed from within their helmets.

When Chiun drew his hands away, the tidy little solar systems of their patches were decorated at the center with expanding red nebulae. Clutching chests, the men collapsed like futuristic rag dolls to the floor.

Remo had already moved up the line. Two flattened fingers pierced a domed head, sinking shards of plastic deep into the temple of its occupant. At the same time he launched a toe back in a deceptively gentle move. The rib cage of another attacker was reduced to jelly.

And as he and Chiun moved up their respective lines, the front door of the mansion—and the killer android who lurked somewhere beyond—inched closer.

TWISTED SIDEWAYS in the passenger's seat of the rented van, Clark Beemer was trying to get a good look at the front door of the spooky old house. As he peered into the darkness, he tapped his anxious fist on the dashboard.

Behind the steering wheel, Pete Graham scowled. "Will you stop doing that?" he complained, his youthful voice thick with tension. He, too, watched the door.

The space cadets had gone in a moment ago. With any luck they'd soon emerge in the company of his poor wayward Virgil probe.

Graham had been surprised when Zipp Codwin told him about the space cadets. They were an elite group of commandos hired secretly by the head of NASA with space-agency funds, to be deployed in emergency situations only.

"I'd intended to use them against the more stubborn budget-cutters in Washington," Colonel Codwin had told Graham back at Canaveral. "Maybe their wives, kids, pets. But, son, we have got a dagblummed emergency scenario that's almost as big as our budget woes shaping up here."

And so Graham and Clark Beemer had been sent to Maine with Zipp Codwin's private army to retrieve Mr. Gordons.

As the seconds ticked by and the space cadets re-

mained within the building, Pete Graham's anxiety
level continued to rise. By the time the first gunshots
sounded, his tension was a palpable thing within the
cab of the van.

Graham shot to attention, and Clark Beemer's head
snapped up.

"What was that?" the PR man asked.

"Gunshots, I think," Graham said.

"You think the robot attacked them?" Beemer
asked.

Graham shook his head. "I don't think so. Gordons
is a survival machine. As long as they identified themselves to him like they were supposed to, he wouldn't
see them as a threat."

"So that means there's something *else* in there,"
Beemer said, his voice laced with foreboding. Sick
eyes were trained on the eerie Gothic mansion.

As soon as he finished speaking, something caught
his attention beyond the wrought-iron gate that ran
along the sidewalk next to the van. Since it was night,
Beemer couldn't see clearly. But it appeared as if the
side lawn of the estate had begun to bulge. There was
a small hillock of bowed earth and dead grass where
there wasn't one before.

Gasping, he clutched Pete Graham's wrist, steering
the scientist's attention to the lawn.

When he tracked the path of Beemer's eyes, Graham's eyes opened wide in shock.

In the wash of pale moonlight it appeared as if the
ground were slowly heaving up.

Clark Beemer had seen enough Stewart McQueen movies to know this was in no way good.

"Get us out of here," the PR man hissed.

Pete Graham hated to agree with Beemer, but as the earth continued to bubble the NASA scientist found himself fumbling with the ignition key. He hadn't a chance to turn the engine over when two slender black objects thrust up from the center of the earth-bulge.

The legs sought purchase beyond the mound. Another set appeared, breaking apart the thick clods of dirt. In an instant, Mr. Gordons stumbled up into view.

Standing in the fresh dirt of the newly plowed over lawn, the android seemed disoriented. When he weaved toward the street, Graham saw why.

A foot long tube extended from the android's face. One eye was hanging by sparking wires from its socket.

Gordons stumbled for a moment before falling face first to the lawn.

On the other side of the fence, Pete Graham's jaw flexed. With a look of fresh determination, he put the van in drive. Stomping down on the gas, he flew around the cul-de-sac. Back around in front of McQueen's house, he bounced over the curb and plowed straight through the fence.

A full section of wrought iron detached from its connecting stone columns, crashing down onto prickly shrubs.

Graham came to a stop next to the fallen android. "Get out!" Graham barked at Beemer.

Nodding woodenly, Beemer climbed down from the cab. Together, they helped Gordons to his feet.

Graham noted that it was one of the android's own spider legs sticking out of his face. As they walked Gordons along, the metal of the misplaced leg began to shrink as the android absorbed it back into his system. With a whir and a click, his eye popped back into its socket.

Graham didn't have time to marvel at the complexity of the machine's design. He and Beemer brought Gordons around, dumping him in the back of the van.

As he climbed back behind the wheel, Graham noted that the gunfire in the house was dwindling.

No matter. They had gotten what they'd come after.

Stomping on the gas once more, Graham bounced over the lawn to the side driveway. By the time the shooting finally dwindled to a stop inside, he had plowed through the driveway gates and was hightailing it with his precious cargo back to the safer environs of NASA.

THE BATTLE within McQueen's house was dying down. With twin slaps Chiun merged two of the last space helmets into one. Looking like some alien being with but a single head to direct two distinct bodies, the pair of merged space cadets collapsed to the dusty foyer floor.

There was only one man left.

The last space cadet realized the battle was lost. Twisting his ray gun around, he aimed the barrel at his own domed head. When he squeezed the trigger he was surprised that he didn't hear a boom. It took him a moment to realize why. In order for a gun to go boom, one first needed to have a gun. Somehow his was no longer in his hand.

As his empty white glove clutched the air, an unhappy face appeared before his bowl-shaped visor.

"I got some stars for you, Buck Rogers," Remo said.

He bounced the butt of the man's ray gun off the top of his helmet. The resulting gong penetrated through to the man's rattling brain stem. As his teeth jangled, Remo grabbed him up under the arms.

Chiun had whirled up beside Remo. "What are you doing with this one?" he demanded impatiently.

"I'm sick of going through this all the time," Remo said. "We keep one this time, just in case."

A row of demonic heads was mounted like animal trophies on the wall. Remo hooked the collar of the space suit on the horn of a particularly ghastly creature. As the man squirmed on his hook, Remo and Chiun raced outside.

On the side lawn they found the mound of freshly turned earth and the tire marks that led across the yard from the toppled-down fence to the broken driveway gate.

"Looks like baby's been snatched," Remo said angrily.

Whoever had taken Gordons was long gone. Without hope of trailing the android, they returned to the house.

The lone surviving space cadet was still wiggling high up on the wall. When he saw Remo and Chiun approaching, his eyes grew wide with fear inside his helmet.

Remo pulled him down, popping off his fishbowl.

"Okay, who do you work for?" Remo asked. "And if you say Ming the Merciless, I'm gonna stick this bowl in your mouth and plant petunias in it."

The space cadet couldn't answer fast enough. "Colonel Codwin!" the man gasped.

Remo's face grew dark. "That buzz-cut Ken doll from NASA sent you after us?"

"No," the man said. "We were sent to retrieve a package. But he did tell us to use extreme prejudice if anyone tried to stop us."

"Perfect," Remo grumbled. "A pack of you nits blew themselves up in Florida. He sent them after us, too?"

"That was Alpha Team," the man said, shaking his head. "They were strictly reconnaissance. Taking pictures, surveillance, that sort of thing. The colonel wanted to see who was interested in those giant spider robberies. I didn't know until today that it was a special NASA project."

Remo glanced at Chiun. "So Captain Codface has been pulling Gordons's strings all along."

The old man nodded. "If he so values Gordons, his minions would bring the evil machine back to him."

"Assuming Gordons lets them," Remo cautioned. "After all that's happened, he might not want to go back there."

The spaceman's eyes bounced from one man to the other. "Who's Gordons?" he asked finally.

"You don't even know who you came up here to get?" Remo said. "Is *anyone* at NASA earning his paycheck?" He shook his head. "So what were Zitt's orders?"

"Just to retrieve the Virgil probe—the spider thing that's been on the news—and bring it back to Canaveral. He said that Virgil had developed almost human intelligence and that to insure the solvency of the entire space program we had to get it back or die trying."

"Is that what this whole trip around the moon was for?" Remo asked. "Just to keep the cash flowing in to NASA?"

"I'm not privy to the colonel's private thoughts," the man said. "But he seemed to indicate that. Oh, and he said he had something planned for you if you came back."

Remo's expression hardened. "And I've got something for him. Here's a preview."

He delivered the spaceman's head into the mouth of the nearest convenient monster trophy. Although there was too much head to fit in so little mouth, Remo made it work.

When he was done, **he** turned from the dangling dead man.

"I better call Smith," he said grimly. "He'll want to know who we're up against."

26

"The thing you are after is Mr. Gordons," Smith blurted the instant he heard Remo's voice. The blue contact phone was clutched tight in his arthritic hand. Anxiety filled his lemony voice.

"No kidding," Remo said. "Where were you half an hour ago when we could have used the heads-up?"

Smith sat up more rigidly in his chair. Beside his desk, Mark Howard hovered anxiously.

"Have you already encountered him?" Smith pressed.

"We saw him, all right," Remo said. "And this isn't like the last couple times, either. He's back up to speed."

"Remo is correct, Emperor Smith," Chiun called from the nearby background. "The machine thing did seem rejuvenated. However, he still fears Sinanju."

"Please tell Master Chiun that he has managed to cause much damage over the years, despite that same fear," the CURE director warned. "We cannot take that as consolation."

"Amen to that, Smitty," Remo replied. "And to make matters worse he seemed more like the Gordons we first met years ago—same face and everything. And I'd like to take this opportunity to say that I'd forgotten just exactly what a miserable pile of scrap he was way back then."

"So you were unable to neutralize him?"

Chiun was quick to answer. "*I* landed a crippling blow," he called.

"We put a few dings in the bumper, that's all," Remo said. "I don't know if we could have done more. He got away thanks to Ripp Aspirin and his band of space pirates."

"Remo, Mark and I were in the process of trying to ascertain who at NASA might be Gordons's confederate," Smith said, voice level. "Are you saying that it is Colonel Zipp Codwin who has allied himself with Gordons?"

The CURE director couldn't mask his surprise. Although lesser known than Neil Armstrong or Alan Shepard, NASA's current administrator was one of the pioneers of the early space program.

"You wouldn't be surprised if you ever met him, Smitty," Remo said. "By the sounds of it, that blowhard would get in bed with an invading army of mankind-enslaving space ants just to keep that flapdoodle agency of his afloat. And speaking of stuff NASA does to piss me off, just how the hell did they manage to get Gordons out of that volcano, anyway?"

"They were testing a new piece of equipment in Popocatepetl," Smith explained. "Gordons assimilated it."

"Swell," Remo muttered. "I guess that explains why he thinks his family rescued him. As far as the here and now goes, your guess is as good as mine where he winds up. If he stays with the guys who snagged him, they're probably on their way back to NASA."

Smith pursed his lips. "Did Gordons actually say to you that he felt it was his family who rescued him?"

"Yeah, why?"

"Mr. Gordons has always gone to great lengths to mimic human behavior," the CURE director said. "He has had varying degrees of success, but his attempts have been consistent. For most people the family environment means safety. If he truly considers NASA to be his family, and continues the pattern, it is likely he will go there at a time of crisis."

"I suppose," Remo said.

Smith sat forward, pointing to the door. "I will have Mark arrange a flight from Maine to Florida for you."

Howard nodded sharply at the command. He dashed from the room to make the arrangements from his own office.

As the door swung shut, Smith's face grew somber.

"Remo, the technology Gordons has incorporated into his system from the Virgil probe is more advanced than anything else he has ever assimilated," the CURE director advised. "Just because he looks as he once did, do not assume him to be obsolete. I implore you and Chiun to use the utmost caution against him.''

"Not to worry, Smitty," Remo said. "We know what we're up against. Let's just hope he ran back to the warm embrace of his loving family." His voice grew cold. "But even if he didn't, I'm gonna enjoy paying a visit to his old Uncle Zipp.''

27

At an order from on high, the Kennedy Space Center was closed to outsiders until further notice. No guests or tours were allowed either on grounds or in locked-down buildings. Most of the civilian staff had been given the day off.

A lone space cadet guarded the main entrance. When Dr. Peter Graham and Clark Beemer raced up the road, the sentry waved their van through, quickly calling ahead. By the time Graham squealed to a stop near the command center, Zipp Codwin was already waiting near the door. The NASA administrator was accompanied by a phalanx of armed men.

"Is Gordons okay?" Codwin barked as the two exhausted men climbed down from the cab.

The clipped metallic voice that answered was so close the colonel nearly jumped out of his startled skin.

"I have completed repairs to my damaged systems."

When Codwin whipped around, he found Mr. Gordons standing at the side of the van.

"Oh," Zipp said, trying not to show his surprise. "Good. No, wait a second, you were damaged?"

"Yes," Gordons explained. "In an encounter with my enemies. I was assisted by a novelist in my effort to remove them. I devised a method of attack based on story elements that I found on his computer hard drive. I suspect he was not very creative, for my enemies failed to succumb. As a result of this unsuccessful effort, they now know that I exist. They will come for me. Therefore, I must go."

With that, Mr. Gordons turned and began walking away.

"Whoa, there, son," Codwin said, jumping around him. He bounced along in front of the walking android. "We went through this already. You were gonna let us help you out."

"The element of surprise is now gone," Gordons said. "I trusted another human to aid me, and he failed. At this juncture another such alliance would pose an unacceptable risk to my safety."

"But you were with us *first*," Codwin argued. "And since you left, I've given your problem some thought. I think we can help you get rid of those guys once and for all."

When Gordons abruptly stopped walking, Colonel Codwin knew he had the android on the ropes. Gordons said nothing.

"All the resources of the National Aeronautics and Space Administration have been put at your disposal," Zipp said slyly. "We saved your bacon without even *trying* a couple of times. Doesn't it make sense that with a little effort we'd be able to solve this little problem of yours?''

Gordons considered. ''They are unlike any humans you have met before,'' he said.

''And we're unlike anything *they've* ever met before,'' said Zipp Codwin. Throwing back his shoulders proudly, he drew himself up to his full height. ''We are the goddamnedest sons-of-bitches explorers to ever trod the surface of this benighted rock. We conquered space, for God's sake! And if you need more proof, *we're* the ones who built you, sonny boy.'' He tapped a finger against Gordons's metal chest. ''And you're the finest, most beautiful durnblasted hunk of technology ever to threaten the human race in the name of old-fashioned exploration.'' His eyes were growing moist. ''Oh, God, you got me blubbering here,'' he sniffed.

The colonel pulled out a handkerchief, blowing a massive honk of pride into the finest taxpayer-supplied silk.

As Codwin blew, Mr. Gordons came to a conclusion.

''Very well,'' the android said. ''I will accept your assistance. However, if you fail I will skin you alive while simultaneously crushing every bone in your body. I say this to help motivate you to succeed. I have found that humans perform better with proper motivation.''

Pirouetting on his heel, Mr. Gordons marched in a

direct line back for the building. Beemer, Graham and the group of armed men had to jump out of his way.

Still standing in the parking lot, Colonel Codwin sniffled proudly as he considered Gordons's threat.

"Danged if you ain't a man after this old flyboy's heart," he choked out softly.

Blowing his nose loudly once more, Zipp and his entourage followed Mr. Gordons inside the building.

28

Remo knew something was amiss when the first guard they encountered on their way into the Kennedy Space Center jumped into a golf cart and sped down the empty road before them.

"Codwin's great at setting a trap," he said blandly as they followed the racing cart along NASA Parkway onto the grounds of the space center. "I'm surprised he didn't balance a box on a stick over the whole damn place."

The driver of the cart was dressed in the same white jumpsuit and domed helmet as the men from Maine. As they drove, Chiun was peering at the back of the cart.

"It's not Gordons, Little Father," Remo said. "He didn't move funny enough when he ran."

"Have you forgotten the lesson of Master Shiko so soon?" Chiun asked dully. He continued to stare ahead. "Do not be certain of everything you are told to see. I was not looking at the driver."

Remo nodded understanding. That was the problem with Mr. Gordons. He could literally be anything. A lamp, a desk, a chair. Even a golf cart.

They lost sight of the cart as it whipped around the side of a huge hangar off Kennedy Parkway. When they drove around the corner a moment later they found that the cart had been abandoned in the center of a vast stretch of asphalt near the orbiter processing facility.

Remo parked their rental car behind it.

"Be careful," he warned as he popped the door.

Chiun's curt nod held the same warning.

They climbed out of car. Circling to the front, they closed around to either side of the cart.

Remo watched the sides for any small irregularities. A sudden tiny eruption could warn of another spear-tipped spider leg being launched their way. But as they circled the small vehicle, they saw nothing out of the ordinary.

"I don't think it's him," Remo whispered.

On the other side of the cart, Chiun carefully explored a side panel with the toe of one sandal.

"It is not," he stated firmly.

Remo put his hands on his hips. "Looks like they've got us standing under the box," he said, glancing around the wide stretch of vacant tarmac. The wind blew his short brown hair. "Isn't it time to yank the string?"

As if in response, a high-pitched electronic whine sounded above the breeze. When Remo and Chiun honed in on the source, they saw something long and black swooping down toward them from out the sky.

"What the hell?" Remo asked, squinting.

If the thing was supposed to be an airplane, whoever had designed it had obviously gotten it wrong.
The main body was far too small to fit a man inside.
It would have looked like a toy model if the wings
hadn't been so long.

The massive wings stretched to comical lengths
from the menacing black fuselage. As the thing
soared toward them out of the heavens, both Remo
and Chiun remained fixed to the asphalt. They
watched the small plane fly in.

"Gordons?" Remo questioned Chiun.

"He has never attacked us from the air before,"
the Master of Sinanju replied.

Remo nodded. "Anyway, I doubt it's him. Too creative. Besides, that thing doesn't have too much heft.
He'd have to shuck too much of that probe he swallowed to turn into that."

The whining aircraft was nearly upon them, zoom-
ing along roughly five feet off the ground.

Not perceiving a threat, the two men split apart and
waited for it to buzz up to them. When it did, they
would simply snap off both wings and let the detached fuselage slide to a stop on the long empty lot.

A thrust of displaced air from the fore of the craft
reached Remo seconds before the plane was upon
them. He was reaching out with one hand when he
caught a glint of too sharp sunlight off the leading
edge of the right wing.

His breath caught in his chest.

"Watch the wings, Chiun!" Remo yelled. The instant he shouted, he dropped to his belly on the hot tar.

The Master of Sinanju's hand had been streaking out to snap off the left wing. At the last second he sensed what his pupil had seen. The entire length of the wing from fuselage to wing tip was honed to a deadly sharp edge. The wings were nothing more than massive knife blades.

The instant before his palm touched steel, Chiun snapped his hand away, flattening himself on the ground.

The small plane flew over both their prone forms, soaring back up into the pale blue Florida sky. It banked hard to one side and with a growing whine from its small engine swooped back around. It screamed down between the big hangars. With fatal purpose the plane flew in for another pass.

FROM THE SAFETY of the orbiter processing facility, Colonel Zipp Codwin watched on security cameras as the aircraft flew down toward Remo and Chiun. The plane was supposed to be a simple data-gathering drone for military reconnaissance. Codwin had had it converted to his own private use.

At first he assumed this was overkill. Gordons had to have overthought the abilities of the two men who were after him. After all, they didn't look like anything special.

But when they'd both ducked out of the path of the decapitating wings with impossible speed, Zipp realized there might be something more to them than could be seen with the naked eye. Still, they weren't astronauts or androids. They were mere men. And mere men could be killed.

Besides, even if the wing blades of his drone didn't get them, there was another little surprise on board.

A knowing smile split wide across his granite jaw. Steely eyes trained on the monitor, Colonel Codwin watched as the drone swept down for another run.

REMO AND CHIUN SCURRIED to their feet. They spun to face the incoming drone.

Remo's face was hard. "I've got this one," he growled.

The Master of Sinanju nodded sharply before bounding out of the path of the small plane.

This time when it reached him, Remo was ready.

The plane was eight yards away and coming fast. Two yards, a foot. At an inch away the aircraft obliterated the sun. Remo dropped below the menacing shadow, this time at a crouch. When it passed overhead, he shot his hand up, cracking the right wing hard from underneath.

The ten-foot-long appendage sheered away from the main fuselage and skipped away across the ground.

Still airborne, the fatally injured plane plowed ahead.

With a shriek from its engines, the drone whipped around in a wide, wobbling circle. It bounced across the roof of Remo's parked car and came to a final, fatal stop against the side of the nearest hangar.

There was no crash. Instead, the sharpened edge of the remaining wing bit deep into the wall of the building and the drone stopped dead. Its engine spluttered and fell silent.

The aircraft was wobbling to a stop as Chiun came back up to Remo. The old man was sniffing the air.

Remo, too, had detected something faint on the wind.

Like twin bloodhounds, their heads swiveled slowly, tracing the scent back to the stalled drone.

All at once their heads snapped back toward each other. Each man wore a look of alarm.

And at the precise moment that Remo and Chiun recognized the scent, the explosives that were packed on board the drone detonated with a deafening blast.

THE EXPLOSION WAS a burst of orange fire. It ripped a massive hole in the side of the hangar. The abandoned golf cart was flung up in the air by the force of the blast. It flipped end over end across the asphalt.

As he watched the explosion on his monitor, Zipp Codwin flashed a row of sharp white teeth.

Remo and Chiun were gone. Vanished in a burst of flame and a choking cloud of dust.

Zipp glanced over his shoulder. Standing behind him was Pete Graham. As he watched the action, the scientist was chewing nervously on the end of his thumb.

"Now *that's* how NASA used to work," Codwin enthused. "None of this namby-pamby pantywaist bullshit about weather delays and putting off launches 'cause a goddamn bird's built a nest in your launch tower. This is how we did it in the old days. See a problem, deal with the problem. In fact, we should include that in a press release." He glanced around the room. "Hey, where's that idiot Beemer? I want him to write that one down."

Graham shook his head. "He was here a minute ago," the young man volunteered. When he looked back, he found that the only men in the room were the space cadets Codwin had kept to protect them from Mr. Gordons's enemies.

"Worthless PR hack," Codwin muttered. "Probably in the can. I should have filleted him when he let Gordons get away in the first place. Speaking of which, we'd better tell that bucket of bolts we solved his little problem for him."

He slapped his hands to his knees. He was just pushing himself to his feet when he spied something moving on his monitor. When he saw what it was, Codwin's face blanched.

The dust cloud from the explosion was settling back to the hot ground. From the very edge of the collapsing cloud, two figures had just emerged.

When he saw Remo and Chiun walking, unharmed, across the tarmac, Zipp dropped back to his seat, shocked.

"Dang," the colonel breathed.

They were walking away from the buildings. The Banana River separated the main portion of Merritt Island, on which the space center was built, from the twin launching pads used for the space shuttles. Remo and Chiun were heading toward the shore. Pads A and B rose across the water.

For Zipp Codwin, the minor momentary relief at the fact that they were at least heading in the opposite direction was eclipsed by fresh concern. Something else was moving on the monitor.

It was a person. Whoever it was was in the process of dragging a boat across the rough shore toward the river.

"Who's that?" Pete Graham asked worriedly.

Zipp squinted at the monitor. When he recognized the face of the distant figure, his sharp eyes grew wide.

"Beemer, you weasel!" he boomed.

As soon as Codwin said the name, Graham recognized NASA's top PR man. The boat bounced off rocks as Clark Beemer yanked it desperately toward the waves.

Colonel Codwin leaped to his feet, pounding a balled fist against the console. "Damn you, you cowardly bastard!" the administrator roared. Ropy knots bulged in his purple neck. He wheeled on Graham. "That man is a traitor to space and every man who's ever set foot in it! He has now officially become bait. Man your station and aim for the yellow stripe up his back. We'll take those other two out in the blast."

As Graham scurried on weak legs over to a console, Zipp Codwin dropped back in his chair. Furious eyes flashed back to the screen.

"No one leaves NASA in the lurch," the colonel growled.

REMO AND CHIUN WEATHERED the blast beneath their rental car. They had spotted the man dragging the boat as soon as they'd climbed out from under the charred car.

"I hate it when they blow us up," Remo complained. He brushed stone dust from his hair as they walked.

"If you had disposed of that flying contraption the correct way, we would not have been anywhere near it when it boomed," Chiun sniffed. With delicate hands he brushed puffs of dust from his sleeves.

Remo gave him a baleful look. "And what's the right way, Mr. Know-It-All?"

"Did it blow up?" Chiun asked blandly.

"Yeah," Remo replied.

"Then the right way would be the opposite of whatever it was you did."

At the shore they stepped down the black rocks to the oily little man with slicked-back hair. Clark Beemer was straining hard to lug his motorboat into the water. He had nearly succeeded when he heard Remo's voice behind him.

"Where's Mr. Gordons?"

Beemer whipped around. When he saw the young

white man and the old Asian standing on the rocks before him, his jaw dropped wide.

"It wasn't me!" Beemer begged. "It's Zipp Codwin. He's gone *nuts*. NASA used to stand for something, like dipping rocks in glitter paint and saying they were filled with Martian bugs or selling space-shuttle posters to grammar schools. But now Zipp's got it in his crazy head that he can start exploring space again. All because of that bank-robbing psycho robot of his."

Remo apparently wasn't happy with Beemer's non-answer. Remo convinced him to be more forthcoming in his replies. He did this by shattering the PR man's right kneecap.

"Aahhhrrgg!" Beemer screamed as he tipped sideways onto the rocks of the shore.

As the PR man grabbed his broken knee in both hands, Remo crouched beside him.

"Okay, let's try this again," he said coldly. "Where is Mr. Gordons?"

"I don't know!" Beemer gasped. "I think he said he didn't want to stay on the base while Zipp went after you guys. He didn't think it was safe. But I don't know where he is now." His eyes were watering from the pain in his leg.

Remo stood. "He didn't want to stay here, huh?" he said flatly. His eyes strayed across the stretch of water.

A space shuttle sat on the nearest launching pad. It

was nestled back on its thrusters, its black nose aimed skyward.

Remo's eyes narrowed as he looked over at the shuttle.

"That time Gordons was launched into space, he got back home on board one of those things," Remo said, nodding toward the silent space shuttle.

"That thing-that-is-not-a-man has in the past equated safety with survival," Chiun agreed. His hazel eyes were trained on the distant shape of the shuttle.

Remo glanced down at Beemer. "You're driving."

Hefting Beemer up, he tossed the NASA PR agent into the back of the motorboat. With Beemer aboard he lifted the boat up and dumped it into the water.

Chiun scampered up to the prow, leaving the center seat for Remo. Clark Beemer didn't dare refuse. Wincing at the pain in his knee, he started the outboard motor.

Leaving a wake of frothy white, the boat sped away from shore. It bounced across the rolling waves toward Pad 39A and the looming shape of the space shuttle.

They had gotten barely halfway across the wide stretch of water when Remo heard a high-pitched whistling noise. It registered as an abrupt itchiness on his eardrums.

It was not so much a sound as something that was felt.

A noise beyond ordinary sound, beyond the normal

human capacity to hear. It was as if in a bright-flashing instant, something had attacked the very nature of the physical world as Remo had been trained to perceive it.

Nothing traveled as fast as the sound that struck his ears. Nothing, save the object that at that moment came screaming from the mainland toward their spluttering boat.

And, Remo realized in an instant of slow-motion shock, it wasn't a noise he had heard, but the sensation of something flying toward them at an impossible speed.

The object was fat, small and moved faster than anything Remo had ever encountered.

Faster than any bullet could travel, faster than any man could react, the projectile roared into the rear of the boat.

From start to finish it had taken less than one-hundredth of a slivered second. Remo didn't know if Chiun had felt the strange sensation. So fast did it come, he didn't even have time to speak a word of warning.

Wood splintered at the vicious impact. The outboard motor was ripped into twisted scrap.

When the trailing sound finally cracked like a sonic boom over the desolate wastes of the Kennedy Space Center—catching up with the deadly projectile—it thundered over the churning river on which floated pathetic scraps of pulped wood.

And as the sound waves echoed off into the distance, the first mangled slabs of raw human flesh splattered in wet red gobs on the distant, moss-covered rocks of Merritt Island.

IN THE SHADOW of the space shuttle *Discovery,* Mr. Gordons clung to the side of the metal service structure. He had once more assumed his spider shape. From the safety of the crisscrossing network of steel girders, he scanned the water with cold mechanical eyes.

There were but a few fragments of wood visible bobbing on the surface. A widening dark stain was dissipating on the surface of the clear blue water. Mr. Gordons calculated a one hundred percent probability that this was human blood. However, since there was another human being on board the boat at the time of impact, he could only further compute a ninety-two percent probability that some of this blood was that of his enemies.

An eight percent margin of error was unacceptable. And since a visual inspection from this distance could not produce definitive results, he concluded that closer inspection would be necessary.

The data was processed and the conclusion was made in less than the blink of an eye.

Decision made, Mr. Gordons began crawling down the side of the tower on eight furry legs.

29

No one noticed the tall, thin man as he limped across the dock at the busy Cocoa Beach marina. His shaggy hair was tucked up under his hat, his upper lip pulled down tight over his long incisors. The rest of his face was hidden behind a pair of dark sunglasses.

He had rented the motorboat with a phony credit card. He had several of them—one for each of his pen names. They worked great whenever he desired anonymity.

He had regretted his actions since fleeing in terror the previous day. The greatest jolt of inspiration he'd been given in the past two years and he'd run away from it.

But he knew where his inspiration would go. After all, even as he had set up his trap, the soulless automaton had kept going on about his family. And the outfits on the men who had come to collect him were a dead giveaway.

He'd be at NASA. Waiting to inspire nightmares in the midnight hearts of timid souls the world over.

The boat engine chugged with spluttering determination. His jaw firmly set, Stewart McQueen putted out into the choppy waves of the Atlantic.

30

When he saw the speeding boat smash to smithereens on his monitor, Colonel Zipp Codwin allowed himself yet another unaccustomed smile.

The two groundlubbers hadn't even had a chance to see the weapon that had been fired at them.

The electromagnetic launcher was part of a proto-type space-based defense system that his boys had been tinkering with for the past ten years. Capable of firing a projectile at hypervelocity, three of the high-tech guns were at Zipp's disposal. To aid Gordons, the NASA head had loaded each of the launchers on a swivel base and pointed the business end out their respective hangar doors. He figured that the two fellas were bound to wander into the range of one of the guns, and sure as shootin', they hadn't disappointed old Zipp.

The boat was there one instant—skimming the waves of the Banana River—and the next it was pulp. Along with Gordons's two pals. That the traitorous Clark Beemer had also been blasted into a zillion scraps of fish food was a bonus that the NASA head savored as he climbed to his feet.

"Good shooting, Graham," Codwin remarked. He nodded approval to the scientist.

At the launcher controls, Pete Graham's face was ashen. He nodded nervously as he swallowed.

"Now that that nonsense is out of the way, we can finally get back to doing what NASA does best," Zipp said.

And for the first time since taking command of the space agency, Colonel Zipp Codwin wasn't thinking of the endless cycle of raising enough funds in order to sponsor nothing but another round of even bigger fund-raising. That was what he had been forced to do all these years. Whore himself out along with the space agency he loved so dearly. Now, thanks to Mr. Gordons, NASA was about to enter a new golden age.

The money would come. And not the nickels and dimes of the past week. With Gordons on his side he could have every member of Congress quaking in their boots. Hell, with the skills the android possessed, the White House was his for the taking. And not just for so simple a thing as shaking down the President. After all, the real benefits would come to NASA only with a true sympathizer to the cause of space exploration living at 1600 Pennsylvania Avenue.

President Zipp Codwin. And the gross national product of an entire nation turned over to the single goal of colonizing and exploring the final frontier.

With starry-eyed images of moon colonies and space stations dancing in his head, Zipp exited the control room.

Pete Graham and a group of space cadets followed him downstairs.

In the empty parking lot next to the command center was a waiting helicopter. While Graham and the rest of the men ducked from the powerful downdraft of the whirling rotor blades, Zipp Codwin kept his head held high. The NASA administrator strode to the front of the waiting craft.

As Zipp climbed in beside the pilot, the rest of the men scurried up into the back. Graham was still scampering aboard as the wheels pulled off the ground.

Nose dipping, the chopper flew across the river to the shuttle launch pads.

By now the remnants of the broken boat were barely visible. Zipp nodded deep approval as the helicopter swept over the tiny chunks of floating debris.

The chopper landed near one of the low concrete shuttle control bunkers. Sand swirled angrily around a wide area as Zipp and his team climbed down to the ground.

From the shadow of the launch tower a figure was scampering toward them.

The thing that had been the Virgil probe looked like the featured performer in some 1950s B movie on the folly of atomic testing. Codwin watched without reaction as the eight-legged creature sped across the asphalt.

Several of the space cadets who were seeing Mr. Gordons for the first time took a frightened step back. In a panic a few started to raise weapons.

"At ease, men," Colonel Codwin barked, nudging down the barrels of two of the nearest guns.

As he spoke, the legs of the approaching creature began to shorten visibly. The spider still came at them, but it slowed its pace. At twenty yards four of its legs had been absorbed into the body. At ten it was rearing upright. By five the remaining spider legs had re-formed into human appendages. By the time it reached Zipp's entourage, the spider had bled completely away, replaced by the familiar human form of Mr. Gordons.

The stiff, emotionless android stopped before Codwin.

Before Gordons had a chance to speak, Zipp grinned widely. "Success, sonny boy," he enthused.

Gordons shook his head evenly.

"That statement cannot be made with one hundred percent accuracy," Mr. Gordons disagreed.

"Are you kidding me?" Codwin scoffed. "They're *dead*, Gordo, old pal. Right now your friends are combing silt from the sea floor alongside Gus Grissom's faulty escape hatch. Now, what say the two of us sit down and have a long father-to-son talk about NASA's future."

But Mr. Gordons didn't seem interested in the space agency or Zipp Codwin. His eyes were scanning the shore.

With mechanical precision Gordons turned his head from west to east, covering the entire visible shoreline. When he came to the road that led over from

Complex 39 and the orbiter processing facility, his head locked in place. For the first time the almost smile that was fixed to his lips in perpetuity disappeared.

Mr. Gordons took a step back.

"Negative, negative," Gordons said. "Maximum failure level. Threat to survival imminent."

Standing before him, Zipp Codwin frowned. If the NASA administrator didn't know better, he would have sworn there was a hint of true fear on the android's face.

Zipp followed Gordons's line of sight. When his eyes locked on what the android had seen, Colonel Codwin felt his own steel heart quail.

There were two men strolling up the wide road from the main base.

"It can't be," Codwin muttered.

It was the two men Mr. Gordons wanted dead. They were walking along, as free as you please. Completely unharmed.

No, not walking. It only looked as if they were going slowly. In fact, they were running. Fast.

And in that moment Colonel Zipp Codwin understood how two mere mortal groundlubbers could spark fear in the soul of an android.

Zipp didn't know how he managed to find his voice. The words were out almost without his even knowing it was he who had shouted them. They rose high up the towering form of the massive, dormant space shuttle and echoed away across the vast stretch of barren land.

"Execute Plan C!" Codwin screamed.

When the colonel whirled and ran back for the control bunker, the space cadets clamored to take up defensive positions around building and helicopter. Codwin and Graham ducked inside, slamming the steel door behind them.

As the soldiers opened fire on the pair of running men, no one saw Mr. Gordons slip around the side of the bunker, the first hint of his reappearing spider legs springing like questing buds from the sides of his suit jacket.

REMO AND CHIUN HAD glimpsed the cluster of men as soon as they'd climbed up from the shore.

They stood away from the shuttle near a squat building. A helicopter blocked the view of some of the men, but the white boots of the space cadets were still visible. Of those they could see clearly, Remo instantly recognized Zipp Codwin, as well as the young scientist he and Chiun had met while at NASA. Most important of all was the man standing with them.

It was Gordons. The android wore the same face he had made for himself years ago. His flat eyes were scanning the horizon. The instant he spied Remo and Chiun coming toward him, he took a step back.

"Looks like he's pissing 10-40 weight," Remo commented, nodding in satisfaction.

As they ran, each man raised his skin temperature. Their rapidly drying clothes left thin puffs of steam in the air behind them.

"Just remain alert this time," Chiun warned. His pipe-stem legs matched his pupil's sprinting gait. "I am finding it harder and harder to come up with creative ways to explain your failures to stop this machine in the sacred scrolls."

Remo's head whipped around. "You've been blaming *me* for Gordons always getting away?" he demanded.

The old man's eyes remained fixed on the group of men. "For your sake I have left some ambiguity." He shrugged. "It is either you or some other pale-skinned Apprentice Reigning Master who was trained by the last Master of the pure bloodline. I will allow future generations to decide who exactly this might be."

"Are you gonna tell them that it was *me* who saved you from that whatever-it-was back there?"

At the moment before the projectile from Codwin's electromagnetic launcher had struck the rear of their boat, Remo's instinct had tripped him into action. A blindingly fast jerk to one side had sent him and the Master of Sinanju into the water. Unfortunately for Clark Beemer, the incredible speed of Remo's maneuver had affected only those whose senses were in tune with the harmonic forces of the universe. Like water kept in an upended bucket by centrifugal force, the NASA public-relations man had remained glued to his seat when the projectile hit.

"To give you credit for your one success, I would have to mention you by name," Chiun replied reasonably. "Were I to do that in this instance, future historians would have no difficulty linking you to your many and varied failures. By omitting your name, I am actually doing you a favor."

Remo turned back ahead. "I can't wait until I get a crack at those scrolls," he muttered.

Far ahead Zipp Codwin had just bellowed something about executing Plan C. After that all hell broke loose.

Gordons, Codwin and Graham ran toward the bunker, disappearing behind the helicopter. At the same moment the half-dozen space cadets opened fire. Bullets whizzed around Remo's and Chiun's heads like angry insects.

The route along which they ran was the one used to transport the space shuttle to the launch towers. The wide road fed toward the bunker and Colonel Codwin's idle helicopter. Though they appeared to run in a straight line up the road, not a single bullet had kissed their skin by the time they reached the first of the space cadets.

Remo fed the first two men he came upon up through the helicopter's swirling rotor blades. By the time the twin splats of red were decorating the tarmac like carnival swirl art, he'd already moved on to the next man. Remo took out this one with a heel to the chest that sent the man flying through one open side door of the helicopter and out the other. The man was still soaring through the air when Remo turned back to the Master of Sinanju.

Chiun had torn into the remaining three men with the ferocity of a living paper shredder. Silver space suits surrendered a harvest of limbs as raw stumps pumped spurts of blood onto the dry ground. When Remo reached the Master of Sinanju, the final space cadet had just relinquished both helmet and head. The upended dome and its grisly contents were rolling to a fatal stop at the old Korean's feet.

"They went thataway," Remo said.

Chiun nodded sharply. Spinning from the bodies, the two Masters of Sinanju raced to the concrete bunker. Chiun planted a foot against the steel door and it screamed off its frame, crashing into the shadowy interior. In a twirl of kimono skirts the old man followed the door inside.

Remo was about to duck inside when he noticed a flash of movement with his peripheral vision.

His head snapped around.

At the edge of the shore beyond the bunker, what appeared to be a long red dock extended out into the Atlantic. And at the far end of the dock scurried a massive spider shape. With barely a splash the creature slid off the dock's edge. It slipped under the waves and vanished from sight.

"Chiun, Gordons is getting away!" Remo yelled into the building.

He didn't know if the Master of Sinanju had even heard him. Without waiting for the Korean to reappear, Remo flew around the side of the building. He made it to the shore in two dozen massive strides, kicking off his shoes as he ran.

The sides of the strange dock angled down into the water. Staying in the middle, Remo bounded down its length, diving into the water after the fleeing android.

He hit without making a single splash. Knifing below the surface, Remo instantly extended his senses.

With a normal foe he'd be able to focus on life signs, but Gordons wasn't so easy to track.

His eyes wide and his body alert, he scanned the immediate area.

The red surface of the dock from which he'd just jumped continued in a massive arc underwater, forming a huge tube. Extending from the nearest end of that tube were what looked like two conical tunnels. After jumping in, Remo had to slip down between them.

The mouth of each of the tunnels formed a dark minicavern. And Gordons could be hiding in one of them.

Toes flexing against the water, Remo swam a few cautious yards away, trying to see inside both caves at once.

He didn't see Gordons in either of them.

He was about to turn away when he heard a faint click. It carried to his hypersensitive ears through the water.

The click was followed by a rumble. And in the next horrifying instant, the world turned a blinding yellow.

And the massive burst of flame that disgorged from the two dark caverns around the stunned form of Remo Williams seemed to burst out from the very gates of Hell itself.

DEEP IN THE BOWELS of the bunker, Zipp Codwin watched Remo disappear below the waves.

"He's in!" Codwin snapped.

"What about the other one?" Peter Graham asked worriedly. Seated behind his console, the young man's eyes were locked on his monitor screen.

The long red finger that was the arced dock extended far into the water.

"One at a time," Zipp growled. "Get this one while we've got the chance. Gordons can handle the geyser."

Graham didn't seem certain. "But—"

"Dammit, man," Zipp interrupted angrily, "do I have to do *everything* around here?"

A single red button sat in the middle of Graham's console. Jumping around the seated scientist, the NASA head dropped a flat, furious palm onto the switch.

The instant he depressed the button, the ground began to rumble. On the monitor the weirdly shaped red dock shook visibly.

Of course, it wasn't a dock. When Zipp ordered that the external shuttle tank with its solid rocket boosters be put in the water, he never thought they'd need it. The thing that propelled the shuttle into space would certainly be overkill in the extreme.

Now he was glad he'd done it.

As he watched the rocket boosters rumble to life, Zipp Codwin frowned deeply. As much for Mr. Gordons, this had now become a matter of life and death for the old astronaut, as well as for the agency he led.

This *had* to work. With that much fuel burning off, there was no way anyone would be able to survive.

Ocean water turned to steam. A white haze enveloped the shore like beckoning fog. The rumbling continued unabated. And as the very walls around them shook, the reverberations seemed to suddenly increase.

Fearing that the rockets were somehow misfiring, Zipp leaned down over the monitor. As he did, the rumble found focus at the control room's locked steel door.

In a spray of concrete dust, the thick door buckled and flew into the room. And coming in behind it, like some nightmare-inspired wraith, swirled the Master of Sinanju.

"Where is the evil machine-man?" Chiun boomed, his accusing tone more fearsome and low than the continuing rumble from the rocket boosters.

Zipp gasped, falling back against the monitor.

"That's—that's impossible," he stammered. "That was a NASA door. It was built to withstand the punishment of a thousand shuttle launches."

Chiun's hands appeared from the folds of his voluminous kimono sleeves. Zipp Codwin was surprised to see that the tiny Korean held a familiar object.

"Sinanju reserves punishment for men, not doors," the old man intoned.

And raising one leathery hand, he let the object fly.

The toy rocket Chiun had taken from Zipp's desk hopped from slender fingers. It became a blinding plastic blur, eating up the space between Chiun and the colonel. Before the former astronaut even knew what had happened, the blunt nose cone had tracked a course straight through his protruding Adam's apple.

Although the impulse to grab at his throat was there, the NASA leader's arms could not respond. The burrowing nose of the rocket had bored straight through Zipp's neck, severing his spinal cord.

His eyes bulged wide.

His hands locked in a final, fatal clench, the old astronaut toppled to the floor.

Zipp was in the last stages of slipping the surly bonds of Earth when Chiun wheeled on Pete Graham.

"*Where?*" the old man barked.

Shaking visibly, Graham pointed a weak finger at the monitor. "There," he offered. "He tricked your friend into following him into the water."

Chiun saw nothing on the monitor but a great swirl of impenetrable steam. So thick was the cloud that even his keen vision couldn't pierce its depths.

"Remo," the Master of Sinanju breathed. He wheeled on Graham. "Shut it off!" he commanded.

"I can't," Graham pleaded. "The abort's been disabled. It'll burn until it runs out of fuel."

Chiun didn't hesitate.

There was not time to make Pete Graham suffer for his sins. With a backward slap the Master of Sinanju sent the scientist's head deep inside his computer monitor. As sparks and smoke erupted from the shattered screen, the wizened Asian was already bolting for the door.

And all around, the unearthly rumble of the still firing rockets shook the Earth to its molten core.

THE INSTANT the flames were released from the pair of giant nozzles, every muscle in Remo's body tensed.

Before the onrush of flame from the firing boosters had a chance to char him to ash, he snapped his back hard and thrust his feet downward. He shot to the surface, breaking up through the waves like a vaulting porpoise. He was running before the soles of his feet had even brushed the swirling surface of the churning water.

Fire roiled hot below, turning the placid blue sea into a savage orange. Clouds of steam burst upward, blotting his vision and flooding the air like some superheated outdoor sauna.

His feet slapping against the boiling water's swirling surface, Remo raced to where the shore had been. Blisters erupted on the soles of his feet.

The long sleek shape of the fuel tank appeared through the dense fog to his left. Though all around was boiling, there was no heat from the insulated tank.

Banking left, Remo ran for the metal casing. By

now he had run past the firing boosters. With a leap he bounded from the surface of the bubbling water, plastering himself against the rounded side.

The huge tank bucked like a rodeo bull, yet Remo's fingers remained plastered to the side. It couldn't last much longer. He'd hold on until it was over.

He was riding out the bone-rattling vibrations when he suddenly felt something at his bare ankle.

Twisting around, he caught a glimpse of a furry black appendage sticking up from below the surface of the water.

One of Mr. Gordons's spider legs. Like a coiling snake it wrapped tight around his ankle.

Remo couldn't fight without loosening his grip.

A million thoughts flooded through his mind at the same time, none good.

The fuel continued to burn. The tank beneath him shook madly. At the far end flames still tore wildly at the sea.

And in a single moment of bursting clarity, Remo realized that there was a chance.

In the instant when he felt the yank on his ankle that he knew would come, Remo released his grip, allowing himself to be pulled below the ocean's bubbling surface.

31

The water burned his skin. His clothes stuck against his blistering flesh like a hot shroud.

Although Remo was at the side of the tank, away from the belching flames, the water all around was superheated beyond even Sinanju tolerance.

The grip on his ankle never weakened.

Although his entire body screamed in pain, Remo endured. He shut down the nerve endings in his skin, canceling out warnings that were redundant.

Another minute in that boiling inferno and he'd be dead. But for what he had planned, Remo wouldn't need a minute.

Gordons seemed content to hold him in place, allowing the boiling water to finally do for him the task he had for years failed to accomplish on his own.

Remo refused to satisfy the android's blood lust.

Twisting, Remo swam downward. Gordons unreeled his leg to its full length, allowing Remo to taste freedom.

The water cooled slightly the lower he went. Ever mindful of the grip around his ankle, he raked the sea floor with his hand.

His fingers had just clutched on to something when he felt himself being yanked back up.

Gordons was toying with him.

But Remo was no toy. He was a man. More than that. He was a Master of Sinanju, a being trained to the full potential of both mind and body. And compared to this the machine that was attempting to extinguish the flame that was his life was little more than a child's plaything.

Shooting up from the sea bottom, Remo opened his lids to a slivered squint. A protective film of thick mucus instantly formed on the surface of his eyes. Through the haze and the pain and the boiling water—surrounded by a backdrop of raging flame—Remo saw close-up the form of Mr. Gordons.

The android had altered his shape once more. Half man, half spider, Gordons's human head was studying its victim with clinical dispassion.

Remo's grip tightened around the object in his hand.

It was one of the basalt rocks that littered the shore around Merritt Island. He kept the small, sharp rock hidden behind his body as he floated in toward the android.

Gordons failed to notice the weapon.

Remo kept his body limp, as if the life had all but drained from it. When he came within arm's reach of his attacker, Remo thrust the rock out, hard.

The makeshift knife stuck deep in the android's chest cavity. When Remo jerked upward, the human veneer and the protective heat panels beneath it yawned wide.

Sparks erupted from the cavity.

The blow had to have severed some of Gordons's motor controls, for the android's spider legs went limp. The tightness at Remo's ankle lessened.

Slashing down with his hand, Remo severed the leg. Despite the fact that he'd largely shut down his nerves, the pain was horrific. Yet he endured.

Pushing close, Remo grabbed on to either side of the sparking chest hole. Wrenching hard, he tore the incision into a two-foot-wide gash.

As the flashing fireworks of sparks increased, Gordons seemed to recover. Backup systems booted up in remote locations, compensating for the damage Remo had caused. With renewed vigor all eight of the spider legs lashed out.

Too late.

Remo had already twisted around, propping his feet against the android's chest, soles pressed to either side of the sparking gash. Bracing one hand against the side of the rumbling tank, he gave a mighty shove.

Out of his element and caught by surprise, Mr. Gordons spiraled down the length of the tank, catching the surge of flame from the boosters.

The fire instantly flooded into the breach in his heat-resistant panels. Wires melted and circuitry turned to slag. His body stiffened, then went limp.

Like an undersea comet and trailing eight legs, the burning android disappeared in the fiery slipstream.

Remo didn't stay to watch him vanish. Kicking sharply, he launched himself back up the side of the tank. The instant his hands broke the surface, bony hands clutched on to both his wrists. He felt himself being lifted from the water with delicate urgency.

The coolness of the eighty-degree air shocked him. As careful hands laid him down on the bucking surface of the tank, Remo shivered uncontrollably.

Tender fingers wiped his eyes clear.

He found himself staring up into the deeply concerned face of the Master of Sinanju. His mouth forming a grim frown, the old man inspected the mass of burned and blistered flesh that covered his pupil's body.

With a splutter the boosters stopped firing. The tank below them shuddered, then stopped dead.

Remo tried to push himself to his elbows. The struggle proved too much. "We have to—" he said weakly as he fell back to the tank's curved surface. "Check, Chiun. We have to make sure this time."

"The machine matters not, my son," the old man said softly. "We must tend to your injuries."

"I'm fine," Remo insisted. But he knew it was not true.

His body was one big burn. A prickly rash of confusion swam through his brain. As the delirium grew, his vision blurred. Behind the kaleidoscopic swirl that was his teacher, he saw a shadow loom up out of the water.

Chiun sensed the motion behind him. Standing sharply, the old man whirled.

The fog had largely burned away, replaced by pockets of wispy steam that swirled across the surface of the water. And from that calming sea, the Virgil probe was clambering up the arced surface of the external shuttle tank.

The machine was badly damaged. Droplets of hissing slag dripped from its ruptured belly. The legs were largely burned away. It crawled on stumps of melted metal.

Chiun saw the thin wire trailing into the steaming water. It was the same technique Gordons had used to animate the various creatures in Maine.

"You are not Mr. Gordons," the old Korean pronounced.

The voice that answered was that of Gordons, filtered through the battered speaker of the probe.

"No," replied the voice that spoke through the Virgil probe. "I have been damaged. But I will repair myself."

Lying on his back behind the Master of Sinanju, Remo had been squinting at the probe. As he watched, he realized that his eyes had been injured more than he thought, for a black haze suddenly began to swirl before him.

He tried to blink the illusion away, but it only intensified. And as he watched in stunned silence, the swirl of black brightened and congealed. Remo found himself staring up into a pair of disturbingly familiar eyes.

The otherworldly figure who had appeared above him was only four feet tall with shiny black hair.

Remo recognized the moon face of the Korean child. It was Song, the ghost of Chiun's dead son. The same boy who had appeared to Remo more than a year before to warn him of the hardships he would face. But there had been more than just that to his prophesying.

At first Remo wasn't sure if the ghost he was looking at was real or if it was just a vision caused by his delirium.

But then the boy nodded.

And in that moment, Remo understood. *Truly* understood. The knowledge flooded his mind and heart, and he knew with all his being that it was right.

Song offered a childlike smile and was gone. With calm acceptance Remo dropped his head back to the dock.

Unmindful of the importance of what had just occurred behind him, the Master of Sinanju continued to face down Mr. Gordons's emissary.

"I am a survival machine," the probe was saying. "I will do whatever is necessary to maximize my survival."

"And we will do whatever is necessary to minimize it," the Master of Sinanju replied.

If Gordons wanted to say more, Chiun didn't give him a chance. Bending, he snipped the wire with a single nail. A nudge from his sandal sent the Virgil probe back into the water. It hit with a mighty splash, sinking from sight.

The instant he did so, the distant sound of an outboard motor carried to his shell-like ears.

Far off on the bobbing waves of the Atlantic, a small motorboat raced away. Chiun noted that the boat moved at speeds far greater than it should have been able to achieve. In a matter of seconds it had disappeared from sight.

His face tight, the old man spun back around.

When he returned to Remo's side, the Master of Sinanju was surprised to find a smile on his pupil's burned and chapped lips. Chiun's frown deepened.

"We must tend your wounds," the old Korean said, gently tucking his hands beneath his pupil.

As he lifted Remo into the air, the smile never left the younger man's lips.

The hint of sadness that might have flicked across Remo's eyes as he looked up at the old man's face, was supplanted by a sense of honor, pride and tradition.

"It's time, Chiun," Remo said. And the words felt right.

The Master of Sinanju didn't have time to ask what his pupil meant. Fatigue and injury took firm hold, and Remo faded into the soothing oblivion of peaceful slumber.

32

When the ambulance passed through the gates of Folcroft Sanitarium three days later, Harold W. Smith and Mark Howard were waiting on the broad front steps.

On opening the rear door, the ambulance attendants were surprised to see their patient not strapped to his gurney.

Remo stepped down to the gravel drive. The Master of Sinanju flounced down after him.

Thanks to Chiun's ministrations, the younger Master of Sinanju had made great progress on the road to recovery. His skin was still a bright crimson, but the blisters were drying and beginning to scab over. He looked exhausted.

Smith's face was grave. Howard's expression mirrored that of his employer.

"Stop looking like this is a wake," Remo groused at them. "I'm fine."

"No, he is not," Chiun chimed in. "He is better, thanks to my expert care, but he still needs time to recuperate."

Smith turned to Howard. "Mark, summon two orderlies and a gurney."

"Do it and they're the ones who'll need a stretcher," Remo warned. "I just wanna go lie down."

His lips thinning, Smith nodded tightly.

Dismissing the ambulance attendants, the four men made their way into the building. Only when they were in the common room of Remo and Chiun's quarters, the door closed tightly behind them, did Smith feel free to speak.

"What of Gordons?" the CURE director asked.

Remo had sunk into a living-room chair. Smith and Howard were on the sofa while Chiun sat on the floor.

"Didn't Chiun tell you?" Remo asked.

Smith glanced at the old man. "Given his concern for you and your injuries, Master Chiun was, er, vague on the details," he said tactfully.

"Only detail you need to know is that he got away," Remo said. "Good news is it looks like he shed that cockamamie probe thing, so we might not be seeing spider-Gordons again. But he's still out there somewhere."

Smith clearly wasn't happy with this news. "Very well," he said with a troubled frown. "I suppose we shall have to satisfy ourselves with the fact that you survived your encounter with him."

"Don't sound so disappointed," Remo droned.

Smith forged ahead. "In case you did not hear while you were recovering, the truth of what Zipp

Codwin was up to at NASA has come to light. It turns out that he spent the bulk of the agency's budget on everything but scientific research. It is mismanagement on a grand scale. Given his reputation and all that has come to light in the last thirty-six hours, it has been accepted by all that Codwin and his soldiers were to blame for everything odd that has happened there these past few days. So that is that." He stood to go.

"Wait, what about that crackpot writer?" Remo asked. "You want me and Chiun to punch his ticket?"

The Master of Sinanju was quick to chime in. "Remo needs to remain here while he recovers. But I will gladly travel to the Potato Province, Emperor."

Remo noted the cunning in his tone. "You're not going house shopping without me, Little Father," he warned.

The aged Korean raised an eyebrow. "Who said anything about shopping?" he sniffed. "If it is Emperor Smith's wish, that scribbler's home will soon be vacant."

"I am absolutely not living in Stewart McQueen's house of horrors," Remo said firmly.

"No, you are not," echoed Smith. "While his involvement in this is bothersome, we have decided to leave him alone."

"*We?*" Remo asked. He turned a dull eye on Howard.

For the first time the young man didn't squirm under Remo's glare. A calm certainty seemed to have descended on the assistant CURE director. He was looking beyond Remo, past the kitchenette to the two bedroom doors.

"It would be too high profile," Smith insisted. "Especially so soon after Barrabas Anson."

"Plus Stewart McQueen's become his old prolific self again," Mark Howard interjected. "I read this morning he's got three books coming out in the next three weeks. As a hot property again, it's too risky to connect him to CURE."

Remo only shook his head. "Whatever," he sighed.

"You should rest," Smith said. "I will be in my office. Remo, Master Chiun."

"I'll catch up, Dr. Smith," Mark said as the older man stepped out into the hallway.

Howard waited on the sofa as Remo climbed to his feet. Remo said not a word to the assistant CURE director as he walked over to his bedroom door.

Given all that had happened these past few days, Remo had forgotten all about the articles he had stuck to his wall. He remembered the instant he switched on the light.

Every last newspaper and magazine article was gone. The wallboard was riddled with tiny pinholes. The multicolored thumbtacks had been left in a big glass jar on his bureau.

"What the hell did you do in here?" Remo demanded.

Howard's face was flushed as he screwed up his courage. Rising to his feet, he crossed over to Remo's door. He glanced around the empty bedroom walls.

"I burned everything in the furnace," Howard said. He still seemed somewhat intimidated by Remo, yet he held his ground. "I know what you were trying to do," he quickly added. "You wanted to spook me into thinking you're some kind of serial killer. But I'm not stupid, Remo, no matter what you think. You said it yourself. You're an assassin, not a killer. I know now there's a difference. And I'd really appreciate it if in the future you'd refrain from pulling this kind of childish crap again."

There was relief on his face for having spoken the rehearsed words. With a tight nod to the Master of Sinanju, the red-faced young man left the room.

"Well, what do you know," Remo said after the door clicked shut. "I actually hate him even more."

He went into the bedroom. Kicking off his shoes, he sank to his sleeping mat. He was reaching up for the light on the nightstand when he noted a silent presence across the room. When he glanced over, he found the Master of Sinanju framed in the doorway. The old man wore a somber expression.

"I have been meaning to ask you something," Chiun said quietly. "After I dealt with the machine-man's surrogate, you said something before you lost consciousness."

"Oh, yeah," Remo said. "That." He fell silent.

Chiun waited for his pupil to fill the pause. When Remo didn't, the old man persisted.

"You said that it was time."

Remo felt his shoulders slump. It had to be said. And yet it would change everything.

"It is," he began. "It's just that...well...it's hard, that's all." He closed his eyes. Maybe if he didn't look at Chiun it would be easier. "It's time...for me to be more than just Apprentice Reigning Master." The words were too important to blurt out. Yet speaking them quickly would make it so much easier. "You are the Master who trained me and made me more than anything I deserve to be, and you're also my father and I love you more than anything else on the planet, but the feeling is there and I know that it's right. It hit me back in Florida and I've been afraid to say it these past three days, and it doesn't mean that I don't respect you or want you around anymore, because I think I'll need you more than ever before, but it's time that I take the last step—" he took a deep breath "—and assumed the title of Reigning Master." His eyes still squeezed tightly shut, he winced, waiting for the shoe to drop.

There was a moment of silence during which he expected something to happen. He figured it would mostly involve yelling. But there was no yelling. Just a thoughtful exhale of air. When Chiun spoke, his voice was calm.

"Well, it is about time," the Master of Sinanju said.

Stunned, Remo opened one careful eye.

Chiun still stood in the doorway. There was a knowing look on the old man's face. His hazel eyes twinkled.

Remo thought he'd been ready for any reaction. But this one came as a surprise. "Huh?" he said.

"I did not know how long you were going to take to utter those words," Chiun said, padding into the room. "Honestly, Remo, I had visions of my spirit being forced to forego the Void in order to lead you around by the hand in the Old Assassins' Home, never having made the final step to full Masterhood."

"I don't understand," Remo said. "I figured you'd be upset."

"Upset?" Chiun asked. "Upset that you have achieved what no white ever has? Upset that you have surpassed most Masters who have come before? Upset that you have made every moment of your existence a hymn glorifying the House of Sinanju? How could I be upset with you, Remo Williams?"

"I don't know." Remo shrugged. "Years of practice?"

"When the time finally comes to ascend, a Master knows it. Therefore, if you say you are ready, you are." His narrow chest puffed out with pride. "What's more, *I*, the Master who trained you, say you are."

"That's it?" Remo asked. "I just have to say I'm the Master of Sinanju and I become the Master of Sinanju? Zip, bang, boom, end of story?"

At this the old man cackled. Shaking his head, he turned from Remo's bedside. There were tears of mirth in his eyes.

"End of story," the tiny Korean said, laughing.

He was still laughing when he left the room.

Finally alone, Remo sank back into his reed mat. "I don't like the sounds of that," he muttered to himself.

"Believe me, you shouldn't," came the disembodied reply.

Epilogue

He Keeps Going and Going
By Richard L. Hertz

MAINE—It's not easy to keep up with Stewart McQueen these days. After a near fatal accident two years ago, it was rumored that the famed horror novelist had been haunted by the real-life specter of writer's block.

"That was never true, obviously," says Shirley Ederman, a spokesperson for Scrimshaw Publishing. "Stewart had simply taken some time off to recuperate and reflect."

He has obviously emerged from his seclusion well-rested. The novelist—long famous for his tireless work ethic and prolific output—has been burning up the bestseller lists with no less than three number-one books in as many weeks. The release of a fourth is planned for next week.

Retailers are already swamped with preorders for *The Devil Dolphins of the Town in Which I Live*.

McQueen surprised many in the press when

he showed up at the book party for *Dolphins* without the limp that has plagued him since his accident. In a statement after the event, the author said, "I was damaged, but I have initiated repairs."

Take
2 explosive books
plus a
mystery bonus
FREE